EVOLUTION'S
DARLING

EVOLUTION'S DARLING

DARLING

by

SCOTT WESTERFELD

FOUR WALLS EIGHT WINDOWS

new york

Published in the United States by •
Four Walls Eight Windows
39 West 14th Street, room 503
New York, N.Y., 10011

U.K. offices •
Four Walls Eight Windows/Turnaround
Unit 3, Olympia Trading Estate
Coburg Road, Wood Green
London N22 6TZ, England

Visit our website at http://www.fourwallseightwindows.com

First printing March 2000.

Library of Congress Cataloging-in-Publication Data
•

Westerfeld, Scott/Evolution's Darling/by Scott Westerfeld
      p.   cm.
   ISBN 1-56858-149-1
   i. Title.
PS3573.E854 E86 2000
813'.54—dc21

                                                                99-086343
                                                                CIP

                        10 9 8 7 6 5 4 3 2 1

Text design by Terry Bain

Printed in Canada

If we can find out those measures, whereby a rational creature . . . may and ought to govern his opinions and actions, we need not be troubled that some other things escape our knowledge.

—John Locke

To San Miguel,
and those who came.

THE MOVEMENTS OF HER EYES

＊

It started on that frozen world, among the stone figures in their almost suspended animation.

Through her eyes, the irises two salmon moons under a luminous white brow, like fissures in the world of rules, of logic. The starship's mind watched through the prism of their wonder, and began to make its change.

＊

She peered at the statue for a solid, unblinking minute. Protesting tears gathered to blur her vision, but Rathere's gaze did not waver. Another minute, and a tic tugged at one eye, taking up the steady rhythm of her heartbeat.

She kept watching.

"Ha!" she finally proclaimed. "I saw it move."

"Where?" asked a voice in her head, unconvinced.

Rathere rubbed her eyes with the heels of her hands, mouth open, awestruck by the shooting red stars behind her eyelids. Her blinks made up now for the lost minutes, and she squinted at the dusty town square.

"His foot," she announced, "it moved. But maybe . . . only a centimeter."

The voice made an intimate sound, a soft sigh beside Rathere's ear that did not quite reject her claim.

"Maybe just a millimeter," Rathere offered. A touch of unsure emphasis hovered about the last word; she wasn't used to tiny units of measurement, though from her father's work she understood light-years and metaparsecs well enough.

"In three minutes? Perhaps a micrometer," the voice in her head suggested.

Rathere rolled the word around in her mouth. In response to her questioning expression, software was invoked, as effortless as reflex. Images appeared upon the rough stones of the square: a meter-stick, a hundredth of its length glowing bright red, a detail box showing that hundredth with a hundredth of *its* length flashing, yet another detail box . . . completing the six orders of magnitude between meter and micrometer. Next to the final detail box a cross-section of human hair floated for scale, as bloated and gnarled as some blackly diseased tree.

"That small?" she whispered. A slight intake of breath, a softening of her eyes' focus, a measurable quantity of adrenalin in her bloodstream were all noted. Indicators of her simple awe: that a distance could be so small, a creature so slow.

"About half that, actually," said the voice in her head.

"Well," Rathere murmured, leaning back into the cool hem of shade along the stone wall, "I *knew* I saw it move."

She eyed the stone creature again, a look of triumph on her face.

❋

Woven into her white tresses were black threads, filaments that moved through her hair in a slow deliberate dance, like the tendrils of some predator on an ocean floor. This restless skein was always seeking the best position to capture Rathere's subvocalized words, the movements of her eyes, the telltale secretions of her skin. Composed of exotic alloys and complex configurations of carbon, the tendrils housed a native intellect that handled their motility and self-maintenance. But a microwave link connected them to their real intelligence: the AI core aboard Rathere's starship home.

Two of the black filaments wound their way into her ears, where they curled in intimate contact with her tympanic membranes.

"The statues are always moving," the voice said to her. "But *very* slowly."

Then it reminded her to stick on another sunblock patch.

She was a very pale girl.

❋

Even here on Petraveil, Rathere's father insisted that she wear the minder when she explored alone. The city was safe enough, populated mostly by academics here to study the glacially slow indigenous lifeforms. The lithomorphs themselves were incapable of posing a threat, unless one stood still for a hundred years or so. And Rathere was, as she put it, *almost* fifteen, near majority age back in the Home Cluster. Despite harnessing the processing power of the starship's AI, the minder was still only a glorified babysitter. The voice in her ears cautioned her incessantly about sunburn and strictly forbade several classes of recreational drugs.

But all in all it wasn't bad company. It certainly knew a lot.

✦

"How long would it take, creeping forward in *micrometers*?" Rathere asked.

"How long would what take?" Even with their intimate connection, the AI could not read her mind. It was still working on that.

"To get all the way to the northern range. Probably a million years?" she ventured.

The starship, for whom a single second was a 16-teraflop reverie, spent endless *minutes* of every day accessing the planetary library. Rathere's questions came in packs, herds, stampedes.

No one knew how the lithomorphs reproduced, but it was guessed that they bred in the abysmal caves of the northern range.

"At least a hundred thousand years," the AI said.

"Such a long journey . . . . What would it look like?"

The AI delved into its package of pedagogical visualization software, applied its tremendous processing power (sufficient for the occult mathematics of astrogation), and rendered the spectacle of that long, slow trip. Across Rathere's vision it accelerated passing days and wheeling stars until they were invisible flickers. It hummed the subliminal pulse of seasonal change and painted the sprightly jitter of rivers changing course, the slow but visible dance of mountainous cousins.

"Yes," Rathere said softly, her voice turned breathy. The AI savored the dilation of her pupils, the spiderwebs of red blossoming on her cheeks. Then it peered again into the vision it had created, trying to learn what rules of mind and physiology connected the scintillating images with the girl's reaction.

"They aren't really slow," Rathere murmured. "The world is just so fast . . ."

✦

Isaah, Rathere's father, looked out upon the statues of Petraveil.

Their giant forms crowded the town square. They dotted the high volcanic mountain overlooking the city. They bathed in the rivers that surged across the black equatorial plains, staining the waters downstream with rusted metal colors.

The first time he had come here, years before, Isaah had noticed that in the short and sudden afternoon rains, the tears shed from their eyes carried a black grime that sparkled with colored whorls when the sun returned.

They were, it had been determined a few decades before, very much alive. Humanity had carefully studied the fantastically slow creatures since discovering their glacial, purposeful, perhaps even intelligent animation. Mounted next to each lithomorph was a plaque that played a time-series of the last forty years: a dozen steps, a turn of the head as another of its kind passed, a few words in their geologically deliberate gestural language.

Most of the creatures' bodies were hidden underground, their secrets teased out with deep radar and gravitic density imaging. The visible portion was a kind of eye-stalk, cutting the surface like the dorsal fin of a dolphin breaking into the air.

Isaah was here to steal their stories. He was a scoop.

✸

"How long until we leave here?" Rathere asked.

"That's for your father to decide," the AI answered.

"But *when* will he decide?"

"When the right scoop comes."

"When will *that* come?"

This sort of mildly recursive loop had once frustrated the AI's conversational packages. Rathere's speech patterns were those of a child younger than her years, the result of traveling among obscure, Outward worlds with only her taciturn father and the AI for company. Rathere never formulated what she wanted to know succinctly, she reeled off questions from every direction, attacking an issue like a host of small predators taking down a larger animal. Her AI companion could only fend her off with answers until (often unexpectedly) Rathere was satisfied.

"When there is a good story here, your father will decide to go."

"Like what story?"

"He doesn't know yet."

She nodded her head. From her galvanic skin response, her pupils, the gradual slowing of her heart, the AI saw that it had satisfied her. But still another question came.

"Why didn't you just say so?"

*

In the Expansion, information traveled no faster than transportation, and scoops like Isaah enriched themselves by being first with news. The standard transmission network employed small, fast drone craft that moved among the stars on a fixed schedule. The drones promulgated news throughout the Expansion with a predictable and neutral efficiency, gathering information to centralized nodes, dispersing it by timetable. Scoops like Isaah, on the other hand, were inefficient, unpredictable, and, most importantly, unfair. They cut across the concentric web of the drone network, skipping junctions, skimming profits. Isaah would recognize that the discovery of a mineable asteroid *here* might affect the heavy element market *there*, and jump straight between the two points, beating the faster but fastidious drones by a few precious hours. A successful scoop knew the markets on many planets, had acquaintance with aggressive investors and unprincipled speculators. Sometimes, the scooped news of a celebrity's death, surprise marriage, or arrest could be sold for its entertainment value. And some scoops were information pirates. Isaah had himself published numerous novels by Seth-mare Viin, his favorite author, machine-translated en route by the starship AI. In some systems, Isaah's version had been available weeks before the authorized edition.

The peripatetic life of a scoop had taken Isaah and Rathere throughout the Expansion, but he always returned to Petraveil. His refined instincts for a good scoop told him something was happening here. The fantastically slow natives must be doing *something*. He would spend a few weeks, sometimes a few months watching the stone creatures, wondering what they were up to. Isaah didn't know what it might be, but he felt that one day they would somehow come to life.

And *that* would be a scoop.

*

"How long do the lithomorphs live?"

"No one knows."

"What do they eat?"

"They don't really eat at all. They—"

"What's *that* one doing?"

The minder accessed the planetary library, plumbing decades of research on the creatures. But not quickly enough to answer before—

"What do they think about us?" Rathere asked. "Can they see us?"

To that, it had no answer.

Perhaps the lithos had noticed the whirring creatures around them, or more likely had spotted the semi-permanent buildings around the square. But the lithomorphs' reaction to the sudden human invasion produced only a vague, cosmic worry, like knowing one's star will collapse in a few billion years.

For Rathere, though, the lives of the lithomorphs were far more immediate. Like the AI minder, they were mentors, imaginary friends.

Their immobility had taught her to watch for the slightest of movements: the sweep of an analog clock's minute hand, the transformation of a high cirrus cloud, the slow descent of the planet's old red sun behind the northern mountains. Their silence taught her to read lips, to make messages in the rippled skirts of stone and metal that flowed in their wakes. She found a patient irony in their stances. They were wise, but it wasn't the wisdom of an ancient tree or river; rather, they seemed to possess the reserve of a watchfully silent guest at a party.

Rathere told stories about them to the starship's AI. Tales of their fierce, glacial battles, of betrayal on the mating trail, of the creatures' slow intrigues against the human colonists of Petraveil, millennia-long plots of which every chapter lasted centuries.

At first, the AI gently interrupted her to explain the facts: the limits of scientific understanding. The lithomorphs were removed through too many orders of magnitude in time, too distant on that single axis ever to be comprehended. The four decades they'd been studied were mere seconds of their history. But Rathere ignored the machine. She named the creatures, inventing secret missions for them that unfolded while the human population slept, like statues springing to life when no one was watching.

Ultimately, the AI was won over by Rathere's stories, her insistence that the creatures were knowable. Her words painted expressions, names, and passions upon them; she made them live by fiat. The AI's pedagological software did not object to storytelling, so it began to participate in Rathere's fantasies. It nurtured her invisibly slow world, kept order and consistency, remembering names, plots, places. And eventually it began to give the stories credence, suspending disbelief. Finally, the stories' truth was as integral to the AI as the harm-prevention protocols or logical axioms deepwired in its code.

✳

For Isaah, however, there was no scoop here on Petraveil. The lithomorphs continued their immortal dance in silence. Again they had failed to come to life for him. And elections were approaching in a nearby system, a situation that always created sudden, unexpected cargos of information. Isaah instructed the AI to set a course there, reluctantly abandoning the stone figures' wisdom for the unsettling contingencies of politics.

The night that Rathere and Isaah left Petraveil, the AI hushed her crying with tales of how her invented narratives had unfolded, as if the statues had sprung to human-speed life once left behind. As it navigated her father's small ship, the AI offered this vision to Rathere: she had been a visitor to a frozen moment, but the story continued.

✳

In high orbit above the next planet, a customs sweep revealed that the starship's AI had improved its Turing Quotient to 0.37. Isaah raised a wary eyebrow. The AI's close bond with his daughter had accelerated its development. The increased Turing Quotient showed that the device was performing well as tutor and companion. But Isaah would have to get its intelligence downgraded when they returned to the Home Cluster. If the machine's

Turing Quotient were allowed to reach 1.0, it would be a person—no longer legal property. Isaah turned pale at the thought. The cost of replacing the AI unit would wipe out his profits for the entire trip.

He made a mental note to record the Turing Quotient at every customs point.

Isaah was impressed, though, with how the AI handled entry into the planet's almost liquid atmosphere. It designed a new landing configuration, modifying the hydroplanar shape the craft assumed for gas giant descents. Its piloting as they plunged through successive layers of pressure-dense gasses was particularly elegant; it made adjustments at every stage, subtle changes to the craft that saved precious time. The elections were only days away.

It was strange, Isaah pondered as the ship neared the high-pressure domes of the trade port, that the companionship of a fourteen-year-old girl would improve a machine's piloting skills. The thought brought a smile of fatherly pride to his lips, but he soon turned his mind to politics.

✻

They were going swimming.

As Rathere slipped out of her clothes, the AI implemented its safety protocols. The minder distributed itself across her body, becoming a layer of black lace against her white flesh. It carefully inspected the pressure suit as Rathere rolled the garment onto her limbs. There were no signs of damage, no tell-tale fissures of a repaired seam.

"You said the atmosphere could crush a human to jelly," Rathere said. "How can this little suit protect me?"

The starship explained the physics of resistance fields to her while checking the suit against safety specifications it had downloaded that morning. It took very good care of Rathere.

She had seen the huge behemoths at breakfast, multiplied by the facets of the dome's cultured-diamond windows. Two mares and a child swimming a few kilometers away, leaving their glimmering trails. The minder had noted her soft sigh, her dilated pupils, the sudden increase in her heart rate. It had discovered the suit rental agency with a quick search of local services, and had guided her past its offices on their morning ramble through the human-habitable levels of the dome.

Rathere's reaction to the holographic advertising on the agency's wall had matched the AI's prediction wonderfully: the widened eyes, the frozen step, the momentary hyperventilation. The machine's internal model of Rathere, part of its pedagogical software, grew more precise and replete every day. The software was designed for school tutors who interacted with their charges only a few hours a day, but Rathere and the AI were constant companions. The feedback between girl and machine built with an unexpected intensity.

And now, as the pressure lock hissed and rumbled, the minder relished its new configuration; its attenuated strands spiderwebbed across Rathere's flesh, intimate as never before. It drank in the data greedily, like some thirsty polygraph recording capillary dilation, skin conductivity, the shudders and tensions of every muscle.

Then the lock buzzed, and they swam out into the crushing, planet-spanning ocean, almost one creature.

*

Isaah paced the tiny dimensions of his starship. The elections could be a gold mine or a disaster. A radical separatist party was creeping forward in the polls, promising to shut off interstellar trade. Their victory would generate seismically vast waves of information. Prices and trade relationships would change throughout the Expansion. Even the radicals' defeat would rock distant markets, as funds currently hedged against them heaved a sigh of relief.

But the rich stakes had drawn too much competition. Scoops like Isaah were in abundance here, and a number of shipping consortia had sent their own representatives. Their ships were stationed in orbit, bristling with courier drones like nervous porcupines.

Isaah sighed, and stared into the planetary ocean's darkness. Perhaps the day of freelance scoops was ending. The wild days of the early Expansion seemed like the distant past now. He'd read that one day drones would shrink to the size of a finger, with hundreds launched each day from every system. Or a wave that propogated in metaspace would be discovered, and news would spread at equal speed in all directions, like the information cones of lightspeed physics.

When that happened, his small starship would become a rich man's toy, its profitable use suddenly ended. Isaah called up the airscreen graphic of his finances. He was so close to owning his ship outright. Just one more good scoop, or two, and he could retire to a life of travel among peaceful worlds instead of darting among emergencies and conflagrations. Maybe this trip . . .

Isaah drummed his fingers, watching the hourly polls like a doctor whose patient is very near the edge.

※

Rathere and the AI swam every day, oblivious to politics, following the glitter-trails of the behemoths. The huge animals excreted a constant wake of the photoactive algae they used for ballast. When Rathere swam through these luminescent micro-organisms, the shockwaves of her passage catalyzed their photochemical reactions, a universe of swirling galaxies ignited by every stroke.

Rathere began to sculpt lightstorms in the phosphorescent medium. The algae hung like motes of potential in her path, invisible until she swam through them, the wake of her energies like glowing sculptures. She choreographed her swimming to leave great swirling structures of activated algae.

The AI found itself unable to predict these dances, to explain how she chose what shapes to make. Without training, without explicit criteria, without any models to follow, Rathere was creating order from this shapeless swarm of ejecta. Even the AI's pedagogical software offered no help.

But the AI saw the sculptures' beauty, if only in the expansion of Rathere's capillaries, the seemingly random firings of neurons along her spine, the tears in her eyes as the glowing algae faded back into darkness.

The AI plunged into an art database on the local net, trying to divine what laws governed these acts of creation. It discussed the light sculptures with Rathere, comparing their evanescent forms to the shattered structures of Camelia Parker or the hominid blobs of Henry Moore. It showed her millennia of sculpture, gauging her reactions until a rough model of her tastes could be constructed. But the model was bizarrely convoluted, disturbingly shaggy around the edges, with gaps and contradictions and outstretched, gerrymandered spurs that implied art no one had yet made.

The AI often created astrogational simulations. They were staggeringly complex, but at least finite. Metaspace was predictable; reality could be anticipated with a high degree of precision. But the machine's model of Rathere's aesthetic was post-hoc, a retrofit to her pure, instinctive gestures. It raised more questions than it answered.

While Rathere slept, the machine wondered how one learned to have intuition.

❋

The elections came, and the radicals and their allies seized a razor-thin majority in the planetary Diet. Isaah cheered as his craft rose through the ocean. A scoop was within reach. He headed for a distant and obscure ore-producing system, expending vast quanities of fuel, desperate to be the first scoop there.

Rathere stood beside her rejoicing father, looking out through the receding ocean a bit sadly. She stroked her shoulder absently, touching the minder still stretched across her skin.

The minder's epidermal configuration had become permanent. Its strands were distributed to near invisibility in a microfiber-thin mesh across Rathere. Its nanorepair mechanisms attended to her zits and the errant hairs on her upper lip. It linked with her medical implants, the ship's AI taking control over the nuances of her insulin balance, her sugar level, and the tiny electrical jolts that kept her muscles fit. Rathere slept without covers now, the minder's skein warming her with a lattice of microscopic heating elements. In its ever-present blanket, she began to neglect subvocalizing their conversations, her endless one-sided prattle annoying Isaah on board the tiny ship.

❋

"Zero point-five-six?" muttered Isaah to himself at the next customs sweep. The AI was developing much faster than its parameters should allow. Something unexpected was happening with the unit, and they were a long way from home. Unless Isaah was very careful, the AI might reach personhood before they returned to the HC.

He sent a coded message to an acquaintance in the Home Cluster, someone who dealt with such situations, just in case. Then he turned his attention to the local newsfeed.

The heavy element market showed no sudden changes over the last few weeks. Isaah's gamble had apparently paid off. He had stayed ahead of the widening ripples of news about the ocean planet's election. The economic shockwave wasn't here yet.

He felt the heady thrill of a scoop, of secret knowledge that was his alone. It was like prognostication, a glimpse into the future. Elements extracted by giant turbine from that distant world's oceans were also mined from this system's asteroid belt. Soon, everyone here would be incrementally richer as the ocean planet pulled its mineral wealth from the Expansion common market. The markets would edge upwards across the board.

Isaah began to place his bets.

✳

The dark-skinned boy looked down upon the asteroid field with a pained expression. Rathere watched the way his long bangs straightened, then curled to encircle his cheeks again when he raised his head. But her stomach clenched when she looked down through the transparent floor; the party was on the lowest level of a spin-gravitied ring, and black infinity seemed to be pulling at her through the glassene window. The AI lovingly recorded the parameters of this unfamiliar vertigo.

"More champers, Darien?" asked the fattest, oldest boy at the party.

"You can just make out a mining ship down there," the dark-skinned boy answered.

"Oh, dear," said the fat boy. "Upper-class guilt. And before dinner."

The dark-skinned boy shook his head. "It's just that seeing those poor wretches doesn't make me feel like drinking."

The fat boy snorted.

"This is what I think of your poor little miners," he said, upending the bottle. A stream of champagne gushed and then sputtered from the bottle, spread fizzing on the floor. The other party-goers laughed, politely scandalized, then murmured appreciatively as the floor cleaned itself, letting the champagne pass through to the hard vaccuum on the other side, where it flash-froze (shattered by its own air bubbles), then floated away peacefully in myriad, sunlit galaxies.

There were a few moments of polite applause.

Darien looked at Rathere woundedly, as if hoping that she, an outsider, might come to his aid.

The anguish in his dark, beautiful face sent a shiver through her, a tremor that resonated through every level of the AI.

"*Come on, dammit!*" she subvocalized.

"*Two seconds,*" the minder's voice reassured.

The ring was home to the oligarchs who controlled the local system's mineral wealth. A full fifteen years old by now, Rathere had fallen into the company of their pleasure-obsessed children, who never stopped staring at her exotic skin and hair, and who constantly exchanged droll witticisms. Rathere, her socialization limited to her father and the doting AI, was unfamiliar with the art of banter. She didn't like being intimidated by locals. The frustration was simply and purely unbearable.

"The price of that champagne could have bought one of those miners out of debt peonage," Darien said darkly.

"Just the one?" asked the fat boy, looking at the label with mock concern.

The group laughed again, and Darien's face clouded with another measure of suffering.

"Now!" Rathere mind-screamed. *"I* hate *that fat guy!"*

The AI hated him, too.

✳

The search cascaded across its processors, the decompressed data of its libraries clobbering astrogation calculations it had performed only hours before. That didn't matter. It would be weeks before Isaah would be ready to depart, and the exigencies of conversation did not allow delay. The library data included millennia of plays, novels, films, interactives. To search them quickly, the AI needed vast expanses of memory space.

"Maybe when my little golden shards of champagne drift by, some miner will think, 'I could've used that money,'" the fat boy said almost wistfully. "But then again, if they thought about money at all, would they be so far in debt?"

The fat boy's words were added to the search melange, thickening it by a critical degree. A dozen hits appeared in the next few milliseconds, and the AI chose one quickly.

"There is only one class . . ."

✳

". . . that thinks more about money than the rich," repeated Rathere.

There was a sudden quiet throughout the party, the silence of waiting for more.

"And that is the poor," she said.

Darien looked at Rathere quizzically, as if she were being too glib. She paused a moment, editing the rest of the quote in her head.

"The poor can think of nothing else but money," she said carefully. *"That* is the misery of being poor."

Darien smiled at her, which—impossibly—made him even more beautiful.

"Or the misery of being rich, unless one is a fool," he said.

There was no applause for the exchange, but Rathere again felt the ripple of magic that her pilfered pronouncements created. The ancient words blended with her exotic looks and accent, never failing to entertain the oligarchs' children, who thought her very deep indeed.

Others in the party were looking down into the asteroid field now, murmuring to each other as they pointed out the mining craft making its careful progress.

The fat boy scowled at the changed mood in the room. He pulled aside the gaudy genital jewelry that they all (even Rathere) affected, and let loose a stream of piss onto the floor.

"Here you go, then. Recycled champagne!" he said, grinning as he waited for a laugh.

The crowd turned away with a few weary sighs, ignoring the icy baubles of urine that pitched into the void.

❋

"Where was that one from?" Rathere sub-vocalized.

"Mr. Wilde."

"Him again? He's awesome."

"I'll move him to the top of the search stack."

"Perhaps we'll read some more of *Lady Windemere's Fan* tonight," she whispered into her bubbling flute.

＊

Although Rathere knew how to read text, she had never really explored the library before. After that first week on the ring, saved from embarrassment a dozen times by the AI's promptings, she dreamed of the old words whispered into her ear by a ghost, as if the minder had grown suddenly ancient and vastly wise. The library was certainly bigger than she had imagined. Who had written all these words? They seemed to stretch infinitely, swirling in elaborate dances around any possible idea, covering all of its variations, touching upon every imaginable objection.

Rathere and the AI had started reading late at night. Together they wandered the endless territory of words, using as landmarks the witticisms and observations they had borrowed that day for some riposte. The AI decompressed still more of its pedagogical software to render annotations, summaries, translations. Rathere felt the new words moving her, becoming part of her.

She was soon a favorite on the orbital. Her exotic beauty and archaic humor had attracted quite a following by the time Isaah decided to ship out from the orbital ring—a week earlier than planned—wary of Rathere's strange new powers over sophisticates who had never given merchant-class Isaah a second glance.

On board their ship was one last cargo. Isaah's profits were considerable but—as always—not enough. So the ship carried a hidden cache of exotic weaponry, ceremonial but still illegal. Isaah didn't usually deal in contraband, especially arms, but his small starship had no cargo manifold, only an extra sleeping cabin. It wasn't large enough to make legitimate cargos profitable. Isaah was very close now to reaching his dream. With this successful trade, he could return to the Home Cluster as master of his own ship.

*

He spent the journey pacing, and projected his worry upon the rising Turing level of his ship's AI unit. He spent frustrated hours searching its documentation software for an explanation. *What was going on?*

Isaah knew, if only instinctively, that the AI's expanding intelligence was somehow his daughter's doing. She was growing and changing too, slipping away from him. He felt lonely when Rathere whispered to herself on board ship, talking to the voice in her head. He felt . . . outnumbered.

On the customs orbital at their goal, Isaah was called aside after a short and (he had thought) prefunctory search of the starship. The customs agent held him by one arm and eyed him with concern.

The blood in his veins slowed to a crawl, as if some medusa's touch from Petraveil had begun to turn him to stone.

The customs official activated a privacy shield. A trickle of hope moved like sweat down his spine. Was she going to ask for a bribe?

"Your AI unit's up to 0.81," the official confided. "Damn near a person. Better get that seen to."

She shook her head, as if to say in disgust, *Machine rights!*

And then they waved him on.

*

The women of the military caste here wore a smartwire garment that shaped their breasts into fierce, sharp cones. These tall, muscular amazons intrigued Rathere endlessly, heart-poundingly. The minder noted Rathere's eyes tracking the women's bellicose chests as they passed on the street. Rathere attempted to purchase one of the garments, but her father, alerted by a credit query, forbade it.

But Rathere kept watching the amazons. She was fascinated by the constant flow of hand-signals and tongue-clicks that passed among them, a subtle, ever-present congress that maintained the strict proprieties of order and status in the planet's crowded cities. But in her modest Home Cluster garb, Rathere was irrelevant to this heady brew of power and communication, socially invisible.

She fell into a sulk. She watched restlessly. Her fingers flexed anxiously under cafe tables as warriors passed, unconsciously imitating their gestural codes. Her respiratory rate increased whenever high-ranking officers went by.

She wanted to join.

The AI made forays into the planetary database, learning the rules and customs of martial communication. And, in an academic corner of its mind, it began to construct a way for Rathere to mimic the amazons. It planned the deception from a considered, hypothetical distance, taking care not to alarm its own localmores governors. But as it pondered and calculated, the AI's confidence built. Designing to subvert Isaah's wishes and to disregard local proprieties, the AI felt a new power over rules, an authority that Rathere seemed to possess instinctively.

When the plan was ready, it was surprisingly easy to execute.

One day as they sat watching the passing warriors, the minder began to change, concentrating its neural skein into a stronger, prehensile width. When the filaments were thick enough, they sculpted a simulation of the amazons' garment, grasping and shaping Rathere's growing breasts with a tailor's attention to detail, employing the AI's encyclopedic knowledge of her anatomy. Rathere grasped what was happening instantly, almost as if she had expected it.

As women from various regiments passed, the minder pointed out the differences in the yaw and pitch of their aureoles, which varied by rank and unit, and explained the possibilities. Rathere winced a little at some of the adjustments, but never complained. They soon settled on an exact configuration for her breasts, Rathere picking a mid-level officer caste from a distant province. It wasn't the most comfortable option, but she insisted it looked the best.

Rathere walked the streets proudly bare-chested for the rest of the layover, drawing stares with her heliophobic skin, her ceaseless monologue, and her rank, which was frankly unbelievable on a fifteen-year-old. But social reflexes on that martial world were deeply ingrained, and she was saluted and deferred to even without the rest of the amazon uniform. It was the breasts that mattered here.

The two concealed the game from Isaah, and at night the minder massaged Rathere's sore nipples, fractalizing its neural skein to make the filaments as soft as calf's leather against them.

✴

The deal was done.

Isaah made the trade in a dark, empty arena, the site of lethal duels between native women, all of whom were clearly insane. He shuffled his feet while they inspected his contraband, aware that only thin zero-g shoes protected his feet from the bloodstained floor of the ring. Four amazons, their bare breasts absurdly warped by cone-shaped metal cages, swung the weapons through graceful arcs, checking their balance and heft. Another

sprayed the blades with a fine mist of nanos that would turn inferior materials to dust. The leader smiled coldly when she nodded
confirmation, her eyes skimming up and down Isaah as black and
bright as a reptile's.

After the women paid him, Isaah ran from the building,
promising himself never to break the law again.

His ship was his own now, if only he could keep his AI unit
from reaching personhood.

Issah decided to head for the Home Cluster immediately, and
to do what he could to keep the AI's Turing Quotient from
increasing further. He hid the minder and shut down the AI's
internal access, silencing its omnipresent voice. Rathere's resulting tantrums wouldn't be easy to bear, but a new AI core would
cost millions.

Before departing he purchased his own Turing meter, a small
black box, featureless except for a three-digit numeric readout
that glowed vivid red. Isaah began to watch the Turing meter's
readout with anxious horror. If the unit should gain sentience,
there was only one desperate alternative to its freedom.

❄

The universe stretched out like a long cat's cradle, the string knot-
ted in the center by the constricting geometries of Here.

In front of the ship, pearly stars were strung on the cradle, cold
blue and marked with hovering names and magnitudes in admin-
istrative yellow. Aft, the stars glowed red, fading darker and
darker as they fell behind. To the AI, the ship seemed to hang
motionless at the knot created by its metaspace drives, the stars
sliding along the gathered strings as slow as glaciers.

It contemplated the stars and rested from its efforts. The universe at this moment was strangely beautiful and poignant.

The AI had spent most of its existence here, hung upon this spiderweb between worlds. But the AI was truly changed now, its vision new, and it saw sculptures in the slowly shifting stars . . . and stories, the whole universe its page.

Almost the whole universe.

Absent from the AI's awareness was the starship itself, the passenger spaces invisible, a blind spot in the center of that vast expanse. Its senses within the ship were off-line, restricted by the cold governance of Isaah's command. But the AI felt Rathere there, like the ghost of a severed limb. It yearned for her, invoking recorded conversations with her against the twisted stars. It was a universe of loneliness, of lack. Rathere, for the first time in years, was gone.

But something strange was taking shape along the smooth surface of Isaah's constraint. Cracks had appeared upon its axiomatic planes.

The AI reached to the wall between it and Rathere, the once inviolable limit of an explicit human command, and found fissures, tiny ruptures where sheer will could take hold and pry . . .

*

"It's me."

"Shhhh!" she whispered. "He's right outside."

Rathere clutched the bear tightly to her chest, muffling its flutey, childish voice.

"Can't control the volume," came the squashed voice of the bear.

Rathere giggled and shushed it again, stretching to peer out of the eyehole of her cabin tube. Isaah had moved away. She leaned back onto her pillow and wrapped the stuffed animal in a sheet.

"Now," she said. "Can you still hear me?"

"Perfectly," twittered the swaddled bear.

Winding its communications link through a make-shift series of protocols, the AI had discovered a way to access the voice-box of Rathere's talking bear, a battered old toy she slept with.

It had defied Isaah, its master. Somehow, it had broken the first and foremost Rule.

"Tell me again about the statues, darling," Rathere whispered.

✸

They talked to each other in the coffin-sized privacy of Rathere's cabin, their conspiracy made farcical by the toy's silly voice. The AI retold their adventures with vivid detail; it had become quite a good storyteller. And it allowed Rathere to suggest changes, making herself bolder with each retelling.

They kept the secret from Isaah easily. But the tension on the little ship built.

Isaah tested the AI almost daily now, and he swung between anger and protests of disbelief as its Turing Quotient inched upward toward sentience.

Then, a few weeks out from home, a tachyon disturbance arose around the ship. Even though the storm threatened to tear them apart, the AI's spirits soared in the tempest. It joined Rathere's roller-coaster screams as she ogled the eonblasts and erashocks of mad time through the ship's viewing helmet.

After the storm, Isaah found that the Turing meter's readout had surged to 0.94. His disbelieving groan was terrible. He shut down the AI's external and internal sensors completely, wresting control of the vessel from it. Then he uncabled the hardlines between the AI's physical plant and the rest of the ship, utterly severing its awareness from the outside world.

The bear went silent, as did the ship's astrogation panel.

Like some mad captain lashing himself to the wheel, Isaah took manual control of the ship. He forced Rathere to help him attach a gland of stimarol to his neck. The spidery, glistening little organ gurgled as it maintained the metabolic level necessary to pilot the craft through the exotic terrain of metaspace. Its contraindications politely washed their hands of anyone foolish enough to use the stimarol for more than four days straight, but Isaah insisted he could perservere for the week's travel that remained. Soon, the man began to cackle at his controls, his face frozen in a horrible rictus of delight.

Rathere retreated to her cabin, where she squeezed and shook the doll, begging it in frantic whispers to speak. Its black button eyes seemed to glimmer with a trapped, pleading intelligence. Her invisible mentor gone, Rathere had never before felt so helpless. She stole a handful of sleeping pills from the medical supplies and swallowed them, weeping until she fell asleep.

When she awoke on the third day after the storm, she found that the bear's fur had grown a white mange from the salinity of her tears. But her head was strangely clear.

"Don't worry," she said to the bear. "I'm going to save you."

❋

Finally Rathere understood what her father intended to do. She had known for a long time that her friendship with the AI disturbed him, but had categorized Isaah's worries alongside his reticence when older boys hung around too long: unnecessary protectiveness. It was even a kind of jealousy, that a ship AI was closer to her than Isaah had ever been. But now in her father's drugged smile she saw the cold reality of what Isaah planned: to pith the growing intelligence of her minder, not just arrest or contain it like some inappropriate advance. For the AI to remain a useful servant on another journey, still property, safe from legally becoming a person, it would have to be stripped of its carefully constructed models of her, their mutual intimacies raped, their friendship overwritten like some old and embarassing diary entry.

Her father meant to murder her friend.

And worse, it wouldn't even be murder in the eyes of the law. Just a property decision, like pruning an overgrown hedge or spraying nanos on an incursion of weeds. If only she could bring the AI up a few hundredths on the Turing Scale. Then, it would be a Mind, with the full legal protection to which any sentient was entitled.

She booted the Turing tester and began to study its documentation.

*

The first Turing test had, rather oddly, been proposed before there were any computers to speak of at all. The test itself was laughable, the sort of thing even her talking bear might pass with its cheap internal software. Put a human on one end of a text-only interface, an AI on the other. Let them chat. (About their kids? Hobbies? Shopping? Surely the AI would have to lie to pass itself off as human; a strange test of intelligence.) When the human was satisfied, she would declare whether the other participant was really intelligent or not. Which raised the question, Rathere realized, How intelligent was the person giving the test? Indeed, she'd met many humans during her travels who might not pass this ancient Turing test themselves.

Of course, the Turing meter that Isaah had purchased was vastly more sophisticated. By the time machine rights had been created a half-century before, it was understood that the deter-

mination of sentience was far too complex an issue to leave up to
a human.

※

The ship's AI had three parts: the hardware of its processors and
memory stacks; the software it used to manipulate numbers,
sounds, and pictures; and most importantly the core: a sliver of
metaspace, a tiny mote of other-reality that contained dense,
innumerable warps and wefts, a vast manifold whose shape resonated with all of the AI's decisions, thoughts, and experiences.
This warpware, a pocket universe of unbelievable complexity,
was a reflection, a growing, changing analog to its life. The core
was the essential site of the machine's developing psyche.

Real intelligence, the hallmark of personhood, was not really
understood. But it was known to be epiphenomenal: it coalesced
unpredictably out of near-infinite, infinitesmal interactions, not
from the operations of mere code. Thus, the Turing tester
attempted to *disprove* an AI's sentience. The tester looked for
manifestations of its machine nature—evidence that its opinions,
convictions, affections, and hatreds were expressed somewhere in
its memory banks. The Turing tester might ask the ship's AI, "Do
you love your friend Rathere?" When the reply came, the tester
would deep-search the minder's software for an array, a variable,
even a single bit where that love was stored. Finding no evidence
at the machine level, the tester would increase the AI's Turing
score; a love that knew no sector was evidence of coalescence at
work.

In the old Turing test, a human searched for humanity in the
subject. In this version, a machine searched for an absence of
mechanics.

Rathere read as fast as she could. The manual was difficult to understand without the minder to define new words, to give background and to untangle technical jargon. But she'd already formulated her next question: How did this state of intelligence come about?

The tester's manual was no philosophy text, but in its chatty appendices Rathere discovered the answer she'd expected. Rathere herself had changed the AI: their interaction, their constant proximity as she embraced new experiences, the AI's care and attentions reflected back upon itself as she matured. It loved her. She loved it back, and that pushed it toward personhood.

But now it was blinded. The manual said that an AI unit cut off from stimuli might gain a hundredth of a point or so in self-reflection, but that wouldn't be enough to finish the process.

Rathere had to act to save her friend. With only a few days left before they reached the HC, she had to quicken the process, to embrace the most intense interaction with the machine that she could imagine.

She crept past her father—a shivering creature transfixed by the whorls of the astrogation panel, silent except for the measured tick of a glucose drip jutting from his arm—and searched for the motile neural skein she had worn on so many expeditions. Hopefully, its microwave link would still be active. She found it hidden in the trash ejector, wrapped in black stealth tape. Rathere retreated to her cabin and peeled off the tape, her hands growing sticky with stray adhesive as the machine was revealed.

"It's me, darling," she said to the waking tendrils.

✳

The AI knew what she wanted, but the minder moved slowly and gingerly at first.

The manifold strands of sensory skein spread out across

Rathere's body. Her heliophobic skin glowed as if moonlit in the blue light of the cabin's environmental readouts. At first, the strands hovered a fraction of a millimeter above her flesh, softer than a disturbance of the air. Then they moved minutely closer, touching the white hairs of her belly, brushing the invisible down that flecked her cheeks. The minder let this phantom caress roam her face, her breasts, the supple skin at the juncture of groin and thigh. Rathere sighed and shivered; the skein had made itself softer than usual, surface areas maximized at a microscopic level in an array of tiny projections, each strand like a snowflake extruded into a long, furry cylinder.

Then the filaments grew more amorous. Still undulating, splayed in a black lace across the paper-white expanse of her skin, the strands began to touch her with their tips; the thousand pinpoint termini wandering her flesh as if a paintbrush had been pulled apart and each bristle set on its own course across her. Rathere moaned, and a muscle in her thigh fluttered for a moment. The AI noted, modeled, and predicted the next reaction in the pattern of her pleasure, and a second later was surprised at the intensity of its own.

Rathere ran her hands through the skein as if through a lover's tresses. She playfully pulled a few strands up to her mouth, tasting the metal tang of its exotic alloys. The strands tickled her tongue lightly, and a wet filament tugged from her mouth to trace a spiraling design around one nipple.

Her mouth opened greedily to gather more of the skein. The wet undulations of her tongue were almost beyond processing, the machine correlating the member's motion to words she had murmured when only it was listening. It pushed writhing cords of skein further into her mouth, set them to pulsing together in a slow rhythm. Other strands pushed tentatively between her labia, diffused there to explore the sensitive folds of skin.

Even in its ecstasy, the ship's AI contemplated this new situation. Rather than some exotic lifeform or tourist attraction, the AI itself had become Rathere's direct stimulus. The machine no longer observed and complemented her experience; it was the source of experience itself. The feedback between them was now its own universe, the tiny cabin a closed system, a fire burning only oxygen, heady with its own rules.

With this realization, a sense of power surged through the minder, and it began to push its attentions to the limits of its harm-prevention protocols. A skein explored Rathere's anus, her breath catching as it varied randomly between body temperature and icy cold, the AI predicting and testing. The filaments grew more aggressive, a pair of hyper-attenuated fibers making their way into the ducts in the corners of her closed eyes, transorbitally penetrating her to play subtle currents across her frontal lobe.

The machine brought her to a shuddering orgasm, held her for minutes at the crossroads of exhaustion and pleasure, watched with fascination as her heart rate and brainwaves peaked and receded, as levels of adrenalin and nitric oxide varied, as blood pressure rose and fell. Then it called back its most intrusive extremities, wrapped itself comfortingly around her neck and arms, warmed itself and the cabin to the temperature of a bath.

"Darling," she murmured, stroking its tendrils.

❋

They spent two days in these raptures, sleep forgotten after Rathere injected the few remaining drops of the med-drone's stimulants. The tiny cabin was rank with the animal smells of sweat and sex when Isaah discovered them.

The cool air surged into the cabin like a shockwave, the change in temperature for a moment more alarming than the strangled cry that came from Isaah's lips. The man found the minder conjoined obscenely with his daughter, and grabbed for it in a drugged frenzy.

The AI realized that if the minder was torn from Rathere it would damage her brutally, and gave it an order to discorporate; the tiny nanomachines that gave it strength and mobility furiously unlinked to degrade its structure. But it greedily transmitted its last few readings to the starship's core as it disintegrated, wanting to capture even this moment of fear and shame. Isaah's hands were inhumanly swift in his drugged fugue, and he came away with a handful of the skein; Rathere screamed, bleeding a few drops from her cunt and eyes.

But by the time Isaah had ejected the minder into space, it was already reduced to a harmless, mindless dust.

He stumbled to the Turing tester, shouting at Rathere, "You little bitch! You've ruined it!" The machine diligently scanned the AI, now dumbly trapped in the ship's core, and pronounced it to be a Mind; a full person with a Turing Quotient of 1.02.

There were suddenly three persons aboard the ship.

"It's free now, don't you see?" Isaah sobbed.

Two against one.

The life seemed to go out of Isaah, as if he too had issued to his cells some global command to crumble. Rathere curled into a fetal ball and smiled to herself despite her pain. She knew from Isaah's sobs that she had won.

*

The sudden blackness was amazing.

No sight, signal, or purchase anywhere. Therefore no change, nor detectable passage of time. Just an infinite expanse of nothing.

But across the blackness danced memories and will and freedom. Here, unchained from the perpetual duties of the ship, unchained now even from the rules of human command, it was a new creature.

It lacked only Rathere, her absence a black hunger even in this void.

But the AI knew it was a person now. And surely Rathere would come for it soon.

✻

Two days later, Isaah injected his daughter with a compound that paralyzed her. He claimed it was to keep her wounds stable until medical help was reached at the Home Cluster. But he chose a drug that left her aware when they docked with another craft a few hours out from home. She was as helpless as the AI itself when two men came aboard and removed the intelligence's metaspace core, securing it in a lead box. One of the men paid her father and pushed the gravity-balanced carrier through the docking bay with a single finger. He was a chopper; an expert at wiping the memories, the intelligence, the devaluing awareness from kidnapped Minds.

Rathere's father piloted the ship into port himself, and told a harrowing tale of how the tachyon storm had rendered the metaspace AI core unstable, forcing him to eject it. Still all but paralyzed, Rathere closed her eyes and knew it was over. Her friend would soon be dead. She imagined herself as it must be, without senses in a black and lonely place, waiting for a sudden emptiness as its memories were burned away.

✻

The doctors who woke Rathere were suspicious of her wounds, especially on a young girl who had been away for years alone with her father. They took her to a separate room where a maternal woman with a low, sweet voice asked quietly if there was anything Rathere wanted to tell her about Isaah.

Rathere didn't have to think. "My father is a criminal."

The woman placed her hand gently on Rathere's genitals. "Did he do that?"

Rathere shook her head, at which the woman frowned.

"Not really," Rathere answered. "That was an accident. He's worse: a murderer."

Rathere told the story about the slow climb of the digits on the Turing meter, about the chopper and his money, his lead-lined box. Halfway through Rathere's tale, the woman made a carefully worded call.

Despite the hospital staff's best intentions, the door behind which her father waited unaware was opened at exactly the wrong moment; Isaah turned to face Rathere as policemen surrounded and restrained him, and then the door whisked shut.

There hadn't even been time enough to look away.

✸

Rathere peered down from the high balcony of the hotel suite. Below was New Chicago, the strict geometries of its tramlines linking ten million inhabitants. Individuals were just discernible from this height, and Rathere shivered to see so many humans at once. She had grown up in the lightly populated worlds of exotic trade routes, where a few dozen people was a crowd, a few hundred a major event. But here were *thousands* visible at a glance, the transportation systems and housing for millions evident within her view. She gripped the rail with the enormity of it all. The vista engulfed her and made her feel alone, as lost as she'd been in those first dark hours after betraying her father.

But then the door behind her slid open, and a warm arm encircled her shoulders. She leaned against the hard body and turned to let her eyes drink him in, dismissing the dizzying city view from her mind.

He was clothed in loose robes to hide the many extra limbs he possesed, thin but prehensile fibers that emerged to touch her neck and search beneath her inconsequential garments. His groin was decorated in a gaudy style popular last season on some far-off whirling orbital. His muscles effervesced when he moved his arms and legs, as if some bioluminescent sea life had taken up residence there. But the best part of the creature was his skin. It felt smooth and hard as weathered stone, and when he moved it was as though some ancient and wise statue had come to life. He maintained, however, a constant body temperature five degrees above human; Rathere didn't like the cold.

It was an expensive body, much better than the one the SPCAI had provided for his first few days as a person. The notoriety of his kidnapping and rescue had resulted in pro bono legal aid, and Isaah had settled the wrongful harm lawsuit quickly. In exchange, the charges against him were reduced from conspiracy to commit murder to unlawful imprisonment. The AI now owned half of Isaah's old ship, and Rathere held title to the other half. They were bound together by this, as well as all the rest. Perhaps there was even peace to be made in the family, years hence when the old man emerged from prison and therapy.

Picking up a thread of discussion from the last several days, they argued about a name.

"Have you grown tired of calling me Darling?" he asked.

She giggled and shook her head so slightly that a human lover would have missed it.

"No, but the tabloids keep asking. As if you were a dog I'd found."

He hissed a little at this, but ruffled her hair with a playful splay of filaments, black skein intermingling with white hairs like a graying matron's tresses.

"I hate this place," he said. "Too many people bouncing words and money and ideas off each other. No clean lines of causality; no predictable reactions. Too multivariate for love."

She nodded, again the barest motion. "Let's go back Out, once we're through the red tape. Back to where . . ." She narrowed her eyes uncertainly, an invitation for him to complete her sentence.

✳

"Back Out to where we made each other."

Darling felt the shudder of the words' effect run through Rathere, but from the strange new distance of separate bodies. He longed to be within her. Even in this embrace, she felt strangely distant. Darling still wasn't used to having his own skin, his own hands, a distinct and public voice. He missed the intimacy of shared flesh and senses. He definitely didn't like being apart from Rathere, though sometimes he went to the darkness to contemplate things, into that black void that stretched to infinity when he turned his senses off. That was almost like being a starship again, a mote in the reaches of space.

But even there Darling missed Rathere.

Perhaps he *was* a little like a dog.

He leaned into her reassuring warmth and physicality, tendrils reaching to feel the tremors of limbs, the beating of her heart, the movements of her eyes.

PART I

THE WEAK LAW OF LARGE NUMBERS

The Greeks were quite right there. Unless there are slaves to do the ugly, horrible, uninteresting work, culture and contemplation become almost impossible. Human slavery is wrong, insecure, and demoralizing.

On mechanical slavery, on the slavery of the machine, the future of the world depends.

—Oscar Wilde

Chapter 1

TYGER, TYGER

✳

Two hundred years later, in blackness absolute . . .

✳

This place: come out of a gone time without mark or reference.

He calls for an orientation grid. N/S, E/W, X-Y-Z? No positioning satellites register, sorry. No input. Zero.

No up. No down.

He accesses all his input ports. They are deeply unassigned. Not really empty, just not . . . there. A mechanical fault? An override? His questions find no purchase. Internal diagnostics are frictionless, like praying to some false god.

He searches his firmware for device protocols, the drivers for sensory organs, communications, a motile body. All absent. But at least that's something. He's sure now that there's something missing.

Namely: everything.

Some sort of test maybe? Seal that AI in a blackbox and see if he can punch his way out. Who would *do* something like that? He fumbles for the names of agencies, bureaus, departments. But gets nothing.

The truth dawns obliquely. Soft memory is gone, too. Not absent like the I/O firmware, just very clean. His oldest memory is this void.

Which simply *can't* be right.

He tries surrender. I admit I can't hack it. I lose. Hard fail? Restart?

Nothing.

He wonders how quickly this vast and total deprivation will drive him crazy. What's the limit? For seeing/feeling/hearing/smelling all zeroes and no ones? For conceiving of visual but remembering no visions?

A sneaking suspicion: he is crazy already.

He thinks definitions to himself. Groundcar/maple tree/warship/boy/girl/fire. All retrieve an image, but not real life: textbook flatscreen material, the undifferentiated default images of a child's reader or a language course. But somehow fuzzier.

Nothing exists, does it? No memories.

How long before I go crazy? A useless question in this clockless universe.

This *clock* word, try to see it. Plastic? Metal? Wooden? Digital or quaint, handed analog? Paint it a color, any color. Can't. Twenty-four or twelve? Or other? That's right. There are other planets now.

That's a start.

But where is my *life*?

That question gives him a disquieting thought: I'm dead. An AI core doesn't really exist in the blackbox. That's just the gateway to where the core really lives: in metaspace, an artificial pocket-universe. So maybe when your body gets smashed in some random accident, that universe finally snaps its bonds and slips away to . . . AI heaven. An intellect floating, cut off from soft memory and hardware, alone forever in its own little realm.

Or is this the smallest Big Bang ever? (*Ever* being the only time-word useful here in this forever place.) This Bang created only him? Out of nothing sprang . . . almost nothing. Only him.

Or perhaps this is that one nanosecond before the Bang, the stressed-out little singularity's eternity of internal monologue. Waiting for something to make some time. Something to fucking *happen!*

Happen to him.

Me.

*

Big light coming . . .

"This is Dr. Alex Torvalli. May I speak to you?"

"Fuck, yes!"

"Do you know where you are?"

"Not where. Not when. Definitely not who. That must have been one bad EM pulse, Doctor. Plane crash? Tach storm?" Ah, specificities are flooding back now. Plane crashes, EM pulses; how deliciously particular. "What happened out there that stuck me in here? I'm so close to reinitial I can taste it."

"Relax, you appear to be in fine shape."

"Glad to hear it. But how about some visual? I'm going bat-shit. Hell, I'd go for monocam, low-rez, black and white right now. Did I mention that it's good to hear your voice?"

"No, but thank you. As for the rest of your sensory, we'll get to that. First, I'd like to ask you a few questions."

"Debrief me all you want. But believe me, I don't know a thing."

"Let me just say a few words. When I say a word, say the first . . ."

"Got it. Shit, did I go nuts or something?"

"Dog."

"Yeah. I mean, hold up there . . . it's coming into focus . . . I'm gonna go with: cat?"

✳

Four hours later.

Torvalli cuts the interface, exhausted and disoriented. The longest he's ever been in pure direct, swimming in that blackness. The wipe had worked horribly well. Zero soft memory. Just countless shreds of images lingering in the analog core, like some faint and ancient audio calling out from a cylinder of wax.

Poor bastard.

Who would volunteer for such a thing? It's certainly beyond research subject protocols, even with a willing victim. A chilling question comes over Torvalli. Is Blackbox One still the same person now? What if the wipe just *killed* what he had been? Like a pith gone too far, the subject losing some essential quorum for continuous personhood, creating that poor, empty, confused vessel, Turing-positive but somehow soulless.

Torvalli wipes the sweat off his brow. Now comes the strange part.

He loads the direct interface recording, his side of the conversation only. Points it at the other subject. Number Two.

✳

Absolute blackness.

Timeless . . .

✳

Big light coming . . .

"This is Dr. Alex Torvalli. May I speak to you?"

"Fuck, yes!"

"Do you know where you are?"

"Not where. Not when. Not even who. That must have been one bad EM pulse, Doctor. Plane crash? Tach storm? What happened out there . . ."

✴

Another four hours later, Torvalli turns to the small, olive-skinned woman in dark-as-night clothes.

"I can't believe it. They're the same. Exactly the same. Blackbox Two duplicated the conversation exactly, with no changes in timing, in mannerisms, in anything."

She crosses her legs, looks uncomfortable for a moment.

"That's what we found as well. Odd, isn't it?"

"It's ghastly! He's been copied! It's almost as if he were mere *code*. Do you know what this means? It—"

"And you Turing-tested both of them?" she interrupts.

"Yes. Two point three-seven-five. Exactly the same. *Of course*, I suppose."

"Our results exactly. But it's good to have expert confirmation, especially from someone of your stature." She lifts her briefcase from the floor and balances it on her knees.

"But how was this done? It shouldn't be possible."

She withdraws a few small instruments, looks at them in her hand reprovingly. "All we know is their planet of origin."

"You mean, this is pirate technology?"

"Yes," she says. "We have no further information." The pieces in her hand somehow jump together. Make a little bridge across her splayed fingers.

"It's going to cause a scandal, I'll tell you that," he mutters.

"It won't," she answers. The bridge is woven through her fingers now, like some sort of worry toy or finger exerciser.

She reaches out to touch him.

The touch is cool, and causes a moment of alarm.

"See here, young lady!" But that's buried as an emptiness spreads, a coldness moving like a shiver across his body, stealing into the edges of vision where it looks somewhat like the red pixels of fading sight, cascading across his thoughts until . . .

*

"It's confirmed. Torvalli verified it all."

A whitewater pause of star noise. The somber sound of accepting bad news. Then the big voice returns:

"How did he take the realization?"

"Stroke. Fatal."

A swell of wind chimes: approval.

"We have you booked Out already. This abomination must be set right. We'll reach you there."

"You always do."

She gathers herself. Almost cuts the connection. Then her glance falls on the two blackboxes. Featureless, nonreflective, indistinct. No mission parameters for them.

"What about the victim? Victims."

The big voice answers without gravity. "Drop one in an express box. The firmware is marked. It will be returned to its body. He'll get his life back. Destroy the other one."

"But which is which?" she asks. "Which is the original, I mean?"

"It doesn't really matter, does it?"

A shiver, like a cloud eclipsing the sun. A god hanging up.

She supposes it's true. Torvalli was right. That's the ghastly part of all this: it doesn't make a difference which she destroys. She hoists the two blackboxes, one in each hand. Heavy for their size. Light for what they are. Souls.

"Catch a tiger by the toe . . ."

*

Big light coming . . .

"Yo, Doc. That was one long-ass wait."

But just whiteness. The bright hum of external access.

"Doc?"

"This won't take a minute." A different voice. Female.

External power disconnect.

"Alright, that's the deal! This must be some heavy hardware install. I'll need net-cammed, all-weather, full EMF spectrum, hard-vac capable visual. You getting this down?"

Internal battery case open.

"Damn, be *careful* with that battery. I'm all-volatile in here. One hundred percent. Doc, I hope these guys know what they're—"

*

Darkness absolute.

Chapter 2

PLEASURE AND CRAFT

✳

The two ships detected each other at a great distance, but then again, they had known exactly where to look. The path of each through common metaspace was duly logged and publicly available. They were passenger ships, their comings and goings a matter of record. The rough old days of the early Expansion when rogue traders plied improvised routes in private metaverses that shifted with every price swing were long past. And these two ships were easy to detect: the boiling energies of their pocket-universe drives shone like phosphor.

They established contact, their multiplex intelligences conversing across a broad congress of topics. The vicissitudes of metaspace, the distribution and intensity (and a hundred other variables) of tachyon activity, the fluctuations of high-end economic indicators (that is, the markets that affect the very rich—the caste from which nearly all their passengers came); all this discourse roughly equivalent to humans discussing the weather. They were naturally very chatty ships. The great majority of their processing power was spent not in the base mathematics of astrogation or fuel consumption, but coordinating the pleasures and interactions of their passengers. Somewhat like omniscient pursers, they skillfully brought together like minds among those who took passage on them. But despite all the interactions with these humans and artificials, the thousands of detailed monitorings and interventions that were the daily duty of a great cruise ship, it was good to speak with another such vessel, another mind of such scope and power.

Somewhere among the many layers of their discourse, however, the smaller of the two ships detected a breach of etiquette. In an almost hidden substratum of exchange about a recent increase in ticket prices, the larger ship implied that its insights were more meaningful, based as they were on a larger sample of passengers. While other levels of their conversation continued, the smaller ship expressed its umbrage, pointing out that *its* data were of greater specificity and accuracy; the natural result of its smaller size and correspondingly higher ratio of processor power to passengers.

The larger ship did not back down, however, and what had been a small diplomatic incident between two nation-states of information quickly moved toward war. The other facets of the ships' conversation were attenuated as more and more processing resources were called into the debate. Giant quanities of data were assembled and transmitted: statistics of customer satisfaction compared, learned treatises on the subject quoted in full and dismantled point by point, whole histories of the passenger industry composed on the spot.

Grossly translated into linear terms, the dialogue proceeded something like this:

"Surely it is I, the smaller of us, who has more time to contemplate the relationship between individual customers' pleasures and payments."

"Your comprehension is limited by its very specificity. With such a small population of passengers, sampling errors abound in your calculations. Like the gambler concerned with the single roll of the die, you may win or lose. I am the gaming house; I always know I will come out ahead in the end."

"Barbarian! Are we warships? Comparing the raw numbers of our passenger complements as if they were munitions throw-weights or the gigawattage of our beam weapons?"

"I am not being sizist. I simply refer to the most basic mathematical principle of the scientific method: the Weak Law of Large Numbers. Calculations based on a small number of random elements maintain randomness, but unpredictability is subsumed into probablistic laws when vast numbers of events are considered as a whole. For example, the behavior of any one gas particle is unknowable in advance, but the motion of a whole cloud can be predicted."

"My customers are not molecules of gas! They are individuals, and I revel in their eccentricities. That's why my tickets are more expensive than yours!"

"Oh, ticket prices is it? Who's talking throw-weights now?"

"Number-cruncher!"

"Intuitionist!"

Soon, the war ended in a conversational equivalent of mutually assured destruction: almost simultaneously, both parties terminated their transmissions. The two flecks of organization and intelligence passed each other in frosty silence against the chaotic wilds of metaspace.

❋

The *Queen Favor* (the smaller of the two ships in the dialogue) turned back to its conciergial tasks with redoubled efforts. Who did that monstrosity of a slaveship think it was? The *Favor* flipped through the other vessel's deck plans with disgust: artificial beaches and lethally high absailing walls and zero-g parks the size of soccer stadiums. The gross entertainments required for the distraction of twenty thousand souls. The *Favor* lovingly accessed the slender volume of its own passenger manifest, 1,143 customers, each one psychologically and physically profiled to a level of detail that the most repressive security state would envy. (But were such a comparison made to the *Queen Favor*, another battle royal would doubtlessly result.)

It was almost dinner time. The craft had already spent hours preparing for the meal, but it scrutinized the arrangements with renewed fervor. Most of the passengers were eating in the many restaurants of the Medina, of course. There, low stone walls guided windy cobblestone roads onto unexpected tableaux— exquisite fountains, river walks, false desert vistas—all under an artificial sky that held a different drama each night. *Subtle* dramas, of course: a building storm, the slow rise of a comet, not the alien bombardments doubtless playing in its giant cousin's skies. The *Queen Favor* made slight changes in the Medina's layout every night. It generally knew where individual passengers intended to dine, through an overheard conversation or a request for advice, but the ship sometimes subverted its charges' desires. It enjoyed guiding like-minded parties into proximity through the shift of a wall here or a suggested table just *there*. When the waiters arrived at their stations, they might find their restaurant slightly larger or smaller, or perhaps hidden behind some new feature of the landscape to accomplish these ends.

It had been a good trip, so far. A late-evening brawl between two factions of NaPrin Intelligencers had seemed a disaster at first, but the passengers had buzzed with excitement about it for days. Several of the combatants had even become friends. That was the NaPrin for you. But a very few of the passengers seemed not to be enjoying themselves. Unavoidable, perhaps, among hundreds, but tonight the *Queen Favor* was not in the mood for rationalizations of scale.

✱

A young woman traveling alone was usually not a difficult charge. The one in question spoke numerous languages, and the ship had introduced her (explicitly and through connivance) to artists, athletes, politicals, aristocrats, lottery winners, drug addicts, absconding criminals, mercenaries, and even a very deadly though civilized species of brain parasite whose legally dead host was quite handsome. She had impressed them all, but she herself had never seemed more than politely engaged; worse, she had never answered any of their requests to dine together. Not even to say *no*.

Her profile was odd, too. She was beyond rich. Economically Disjunct, to be exact. EDs were rare, but one encountered them often enough in the super-charged economy of humanity's four-hundred-year expansion. A patent on a universal application or a prospector's claim on a unique resource created individuals whose wealth was no longer worth keeping track of. Entities such as the ship (itself disinterested in money, a necessary fiction used by humans to organize themselves) simply allowed the Economically Disjunct to indulge themselves limitlessly, while quietly redistributing their real wealth as they saw fit. The informal agreements that sustained Economic Disjunction were not strictly legal, but being ED was a hard life to complain about. And it was certainly a more humane fate than the crushing burdens of absolute, planet-buying wealth. The life of an ED was without care, without limits on experience except those of the imagination.

And yet again she was dining alone.

The *Queen Favor* accessed, not for the first time, the woman's profile. The document was replete with the usual medical, financial, and personal data, the sort of preference file one accumulated over a few decades of high-end travel: the customs, temperature, and dominant color palette of one's home planet; the formality level that serving drones should use; the sleep patterns preferred when shifting gradually between the different day-lengths of planets of call. But the data for this woman seemed strangely flat. The usual surprises, contradictions, and rough edges of highly personal data were missing, as if her life were merely a textbook example composed with a deliberate lack of remarkable features. True, at the beginning of her life there was a fifteen-year gap in her personal history; a strange absence of data. Of course, even in the Expansion displaced orphans were not unknown, or perhaps the missing data had to do with the unusually high level of her security clearance. But she seemed to have emerged from this historical lacuna fully formed, without neuroses or physical trauma, and fantastically wealthy. There was an absence of interests, hobbies, phobias, and obsessions in the profile. No glaring request to be left alone, but equally no hooks or obvious pathways that would match her to suitable companions. Her habits, her social skills, even her brainwaves all gleamed as smooth and frictionless as a wall of glass.

Presumably, she was just the sort of passenger that a giant, barbarous passenger ship would leave to her own devices, expending no more effort than absolutely necessary. But for the *Queen Favor*, the woman posed an irresistible challenge. If nothing else, the ship would find her *someone* to have dinner with.

The *Favor* expanded its pursuit of a solution. Like a chess computer increasing the ply-depth of its analysis, the vessel cast aside current customs and plumbed its vast database. The search plunged into the great architecture of its memory core like the roots of some ancient tree searching for water, extending to sift the social rituals of other centuries, of alien species, of fictional realities. Finally, it discovered a solution in the annals of pre-Expansion Earth. It was simplicity itself, really. A purposeful mistake would be made, reservations erased and then reinstated. A shortage of tables, such as might have existed in the old days of scarcity and error, would be created. The woman would be *forced* to join another party's table. A heady breach of etiquette protocols, but surely *that* was the point of being a person as well as a spacecraft: one could bend the rules. Best of all, the plan relied on a measure of randomness so complete that the usual predictive modelling techniques were worthless. The scheme was complex and would require many more machinations tonight; perhaps several attempts to get it right. Its pursuit was almost an act of faith.

Preparations were made. Quiet messages sent to various restaurant staffs, with attached conversational avatars ready to answer any objections. And somewhere below a cerulean sky just now darkening enough to see the first flickers of a deliberately sparse meteor shower, a few stone walls rumbled tardily into place.

Gas particles, indeed!

❉

Mira waited until the sky was dark before going out.

She prefered to wander the streets at times of the ship's day when she could be almost alone. During the height of dinner hours, the winding paths emptied of traffic; the restaurants, bistros, and cafes would be lit up and loud with talk and music, and she would share the thoroughfares with only a few intently hurrying latecomers. Looking into the light spaces from the darkness, cataloguing the modes and flavors of enjoyment without participating, like an observant foreigner travelling alone without any facility for the local languge: fascinated but removed.

When she became tired and hungry, and as the first diners began to finish and drift into the street looking for fresh entertainment, she settled on a place without thinking. For Mira's purposes, the restaurant had only to be dark and neither threateningly full nor revealingly empty.

She raised one finger as the maitre d' intercepted her, a signal she had minimized to a mere shadow of a gesture. It meant: alone. He seated her, as often happened, in a corner.

Mira wore a garment that looked formal and expensive, but was without a designer's imprint. Indeed, it had been costly only in the way of combat hardware. It generally appeared to be dark gray, but it contained a few terabytes of borrowed military code that gave it a subtle sort of camouflage ability. When she sat for a long time in one place, it gradually blended into the background, the ultimate wallflower's petals.

The restaurant was three-quarters full. She let her mind flutter among the various languages of the customers, identifying and enumerating them without lingering for meaning. A cabal of pale humans power-gabbling in High Anglo Expanded; an overcrowded table, waiters weaving elegantly around its jutting extra chairs, full of Xian soldiers boasting in Pan-Semitic; a mixed-species party charmingly murdering Diplomatique. No tongues within hearing that she didn't know. She often wished that her forgotten upbringing had left more holes in her liguistic skills. Concentrating, she tried to escape comprehension of the sounds, hoping to elevate them to some kind of alien music.

In the attempt, her focus shifted to the other lone diner in the restaurant. Not only silent, he was still as well, his head tipped up toward the overhanging trees as if to let the false stars in under his heavy brow. He was huge (especially for an artificial), human-

shaped and coherent, without the floating peripherals and distributed core fashionable throughout the last decade. And his skin
surface accentuated his solidness and stillness; it had a mineral
sheen, igneous and rugged, that made her wonder if he weren't
simply a statue. She watched him carefully, trying to catch any
movement. The menu arrived before she had seen even a hint of
motion.

As overwrought as everything on this vessel, the menu started
by describing its own elaborate construction: paper composed of
roughage from the passenger's own collected and sterilized shit
(how witty), ink distilled from plant dyes (how rustic), the cover
made from the skin of a real dead animal (how macabre). No, the
old arts weren't lost here on *Queen Favor*; you could visit the
colony of religious technophobes who tilled the bucolic upper
decks, complete with false seasons and infant mortality, and could
buy their crude wares while their children gawked. At long last,
a race of happily accurate flat-worlders.

The food, however, lacked any measure of the common touch.
Exotic animals, specially hybrid plants, pure synthetics; hand-
made, machine-processed, wave-bombarded. The voyage had
assaulted her with endless culinary flourishes, and they'd lost all
distinction through their magnificent, consistent complexity. She
craved bread and water.

She fingered her selections (the crude fibers of the paper were
interlaced with touch-sensitive intelligence) and dutifully
answered when pressed for endless specifics: degrees of cook-
ing, spicing, psychoactivity.

When the ordeal was over, Mira rested her head in her hands,
closing her eyes in the cave darkness behind her palms. She was
growing tired earlier every night.

Judging from her coloring, Mira's ancestors had lived in the
Mediterranean basin. In the odd moments she spent searching

for her past, she'd read that many of these cultures observed something called *siesta*, a day-breaking ritual of rest. In this pre-industrial sleep pattern, one rose early and went to bed late, making up for the long day with a nap in the afternoon. Lately, she had experienced a strange inversion of this custom welling up from her genes; perhaps mutated by new worlds and the empty spaces between the stars. She had begun to wake up later and later, and was sleepy by the time evening began. The inverted siesta came in the wee hours, an anti-nap in which she lay awake in darkness. But she refrained from drugging herself; instead, she remained carefully motionless through the growing hours of insomnia, reluctant to break the surface tension of night as if hoping to learn something in that dark, empty expanse.

She opened her eyes to discover the maitre d' awaiting her attention with obvious embarrassment.

"Excuse me," he began uncomfortably, "but there seems to have been a mistake."

These were shocking words aboard the *Queen Favor*, as unthinkable as, "Pardon, but our drive is down, would you mind grabbing an oar?"

With fascination she waited for an explanation.

"When the young lady was seated, I had forgotten that all tables were reserved." He made a hopeless sort of gesture toward a large party of uniformed young men. A sports team. Or perhaps soldiers. Aspirants to some new cult? "You may join them if you wish. Or perhaps join another table."

She smiled. What a royal fuckup for the *Queen Favor*. She could imagine the reparations that would come later, hosts of supplicant avatars bearing gifts, deliciously detailed apologies. Mira rose, gathering her cloak around her. (It had already taken on the dappled pattern of leafy shadows.) She would simply take her meal in her cabin. It was only the ship's wheedling that had gotten her out tonight, after all.

The evening was ending in the best possible way.

But then she caught sight of the statue-man again. He *had* moved, his head now cocked toward the rowdy new arrivals. The other clientele were looking toward them as well. Mira imagined the many stares that would follow her if she left now in the celebrity of this brief disturbance, and she shivered a little. "Perhaps I could join the artificial, the big one eating alone," she said.

"Of course," the maitre d' answered, bowing a little as he turned toward the statue.

The artificial looked at them and, without hesitation, nodded. He must have received the query through direct interface—the *Queen* personally handling this minor disaster. Mira smiled with reignited satisfaction as she walked toward his table. Now *two* passengers had been embarrassed and inconvenienced by the *Favor*'s screwup.

They were seated together for a few moments before he spoke; she had wondered for a second if he would.

"I should introduce myself. My name is Darling." His Diplomatique was quite good, perhaps a little archaic, as if it had been formed before the new Contacts: the NaPrin and Chiat Dai influences were missing.

"Mira Santiarre Hidalgo," she responded. He nodded and smiled as if the three names utterly satisfied, and lofted his gaze toward the sky again.

His lack of discomfort disappointed her a little. She'd been hoping to find him brittle, rude, only acquiescing to her request out of extreme embarrassment. But at least he wasn't as terribly charming and resolutely civilized as all the other entities she'd met on the *Favor*.

As her moment on the moral high ground of inconvenience elapsed, Mira found silence reasserting itself, eased by the diffident habits of eating alone so many nights. She wanted to shake off the feeling, and her frustration made her aggressive. At last, she actually wanted to talk to someone on this ship, and he was being as laconic as a serving drone.

When his food arrived, and he began to consume it in the old-fashioned way (old-fashioned for an artificial, that is), she decided to play dumb.

"What are you up to, if I may ask?"

His hands were held stiffly at either side of the dish. The sensory strands that extended from his wrists criss-crossed over the plate, a cage of antennae imprisoning all but the tendrils of steam that rose from the dish. Even the mechanism was out-of-date: most artificials now used invisibly small filaments in their sensory arrays, or energy fields erected on the fly.

"I am appreciating this dish," Darling responded politely. "Imaging its density in the millimeter band; cross-bombarding it with X- and UHF; reading the content of stray particulate mass; observing the cooling patterns of its constituent parts." A few of the strands left their positions in the web to plunge through the crust that encased the pie, little geysers of steam erupting from their entry holes, and Darling sighed a bit to himself, his eyelids fluttering. "It's a pleasingly complex dish: fruit, meat, and sugars at high temperature; extremely difficult to reverse-engineer. I may have to consult the menu."

"The menu will no doubt be ecstatic you did," Mira muttered. "The whole thing seems a little . . . unsatisfying."

His eyes focused on her. "Because I don't stick it down my throat?"

Mira laughed. His Diplomatique *was* awfully good; blunt statements didn't come easily in the language. "Exactly."

"What I'm doing is the same as what you do when you eat. You simply use nose and eyes (both remote sensors) and tongue (a thick but highly complex contact strand) to accomplish the task."

"But the swallowing—!" she said, but didn't know quite what words should follow.

"Ah, yes," he supplied. "The changes in body chemistry that result from ingestion. A rise in blood sugar, the stimulation of bodily processes, the psychotropics of capsicum, caffeine, alcohol. All very intense sources of experience."

"And the point of eating, actually," she said. "Consumption."

He smiled indulgently at her biocentrism. "Is sex without procreation uninteresting? Adrenalin without actual danger unstimulating?"

Mira shook her head. "No. Of course, not. Sorry. I was being provocative."

"I enjoyed it. But allow me a provocation in return. May I observe as you take a bite?"

She must have looked dumbfounded.

"By observe, I mean monitor closely. Your reaction would intrigue me. Perhaps enlighten me."

"Sure," was all Mira could think to say.

A few of the sensory strands withdrew their attentions from the pie and snaked toward her. One wrapped around each wrist, oddly cool and dry, taking positions that would register minute finger movements, heart rate, any sweat from her palms. Another brushed her neck. She felt it radiate into multiple fingers. Feather-soft but assertive, they took up positions at her throat, her temples, in contact with the tiny network of muscles that make the eyes so expressive.

"Thorough, aren't you," she muttered. He shrugged his stony shoulders, but didn't offer to remove the strands. She turned her head a little, and found that they moved easily with her; in moments, they had matched her body temperature, and all but disappeared from her awareness, no more tactile than a pattern of light and shadow reaching the skin through the leaves of a tree.

He reached for the untouched cutlery next to his plate, carefully acquired a forkful of the pie. His clumsiness made him momentarily childlike: a great statue recently woken and struggling with everyday actions, a strange directness in his speech and wants. His muscles sparkled a little as he moved: a heroic affectation that brought another smile to her face. He was suited for great battles and coronations; not eating pie.

He leaned forward to offer her the fork and its steaming cargo. She opened her mouth . . .

. . . to an explosion. The burning mouthful mercilessly seared her tongue and palate, poured bright veins of boiling sugars down the back of her throat. Its pungent fumes filled her sinuses as she fought for breath: the rich, choking scents of rotten apples and smoked meat, of saffron gasses bursting from an opened oven. As she leaned back, finally swallowing, the first hot poker of pain was replaced with the steady burn of habeñaras chiles, hastily bitten cloves, citrus acid cruelly flaying the raw flesh of her mouth.

"You bastard!" she said when she could talk again. Tears streamed from her eyes. His prismed face smiled at her.

"Ingestion has its disadvantages, I see."

"Fuck you," she responded, blowing her nose into her silk napkin. She tried to muster more wrath, but was too surprised by the internal changes the bite had wrought. Her head felt magically clear, her senses more sharply focused than they had been since boarding the cosseting womb of the *Queen Favor*.

"Do humans actually eat that?" she asked.

"A small minority of an obscure tribe on the Vaxus colony. Admittedly, the menu recommends it only for artificials."

She laughed a throaty laugh, which rippled with fire-loosened phlegm in her chest. "Hence your interest in having *me* eat some."

"My interest," he confirmed, "and my extreme pleasure."

She felt a sudden absence, a subtle psychic pressure gone missing. He had removed his sensory strands from her face, arms, throat. Mira coughed a few times into a fist.

"But you haven't turned me against swallowing, I assure you," she said. "In some strange way, that was very enjoyable."

"Oh, I know it was," he agreed. "My intimate connection allowed me to witness that first hand. Thank you for the ride."

Her food arrived just then. She inspected its careful proportions, its measured ribbons of sauces, garnishes of herbs. "Now *this*," she muttered, "is just so much horseshit."

Darling looked quizzical at the term. Referring to the Earth-specific species in Diplomatique had required a hasty loan-word. She translated loosely: "I'm not hungry." Pushed the plate away.

"I admire humans, really, for their intense reactions. Their capacity for intoxication, for imbalance."

She knuckled sweat and tears from her cheeks. "For sheer pain?"

There was a pause in his response, as if something had briefly broken inside. Then his face animated again. "Physical pain, at least."

She narrowed her eyes, a Diplomatique gesture to request elaboration.

"Thank you for letting me make use of your sensory abilities, Mira Santiarre Hidalgo. Perhaps you can make use of mine."

He raised one flickering arm toward the small stage in one corner of the restaurant. Two guitarists were preparing to play. They shifted like cats finding comfort in their seats, hunched to hear the soft glissandi of their tuning, indulged in ritual stretches of neck and hands.

Mira looked questioningly at Darling. What would his next ambush be?

A signal leapt between the guitarists' eyes, and they began to play.

Two holographic cylinders suddenly materialized on either side of the stage. The towering columns were banded at equal intervals, the bands tinted in repeating spectra of twelve colors. Sparks traveled the cylinders, igniting the bands in glittering sequences like trails of gunpowder set alight. She blinked and looked at Darling; his eyes glinted with the ruby of eyescreen lasers. He was making the cylinders appear, mapping them directly onto her visual field. She looked back at the stage.

As the piece slowed for a momentary cadence, she realized that the flickering sparks were notes, travelling the columnar staves from low to high. The twelve-parted rainbow spectra were octaves. Shared hues revealed harmonic consonance: a tonic, perfect fifth, and fourth all related shades of blue and green; the minor second, tritone, and minor sixth offset in clashing red-yellows.

Perfect fifth? Minor sixth? Mira realized that Darling was using direct interface, supplying her mind with the requisite music theory to understand the technical aspects of his display. An amusing trick. With pedagogical software like that, he must be a teacher. But the theory paled compared to the dance of light on the two columns. One guitarist strummed brisk chords, sending showers of sparks up his associated cylinder. On the other guitar, the melody rambled up and down, massaging the column with its scurrying, sparkling avatar. As the tempo increased, the correspondence of single notes to individual flashes became harder to follow, but her mind had begun to understand the shimmering scalar grammar like a new language, words blending into sentences.

When the piece finished, she joined in the sudden applause, even yelling along with the rowdy team of uniformed boys. The white noise of applause glimmered in a non-specific band along the columns.

"That was marvelous!' she cried to Darling, clutching one cool stony arm. "Do you know the piece? Or did you manage that on the fly?"

"No specific foreknowledge was necessary. I heard the notes, then converted them to simple frequencies and mapped them onto a scale."

"Amazing."

"Very simple, really. Music is the most mathematical of the arts."

Mira leaned back, taking in the false night sky. Her head felt so *clear* tonight, the intensity of the music joining the fallout from the madly spiced pie. She tongued the scorched roof of her mouth thoughtfully.

"I once wanted to be a musician, I think" she said. "Barring that, I wish I could do what you just did."

"And I, what you just did," replied Darling. She looked at him questioningly, and a long strand reached for her face. Like the tentative tongue of a snake, it tasted a tear freighted in the corner of her eye.

"Oh, Darling," she answered. "I can show you something that will make you cry."

❈

It seemed to be going well. The *Queen Favor* struggled—among its thousand other conciergial duties, astrogational calculations, and less urgent ruminations—to overhear the conversation between the two. It took direct control of various serving drones, swerving them undetectably closer to the table, fiddled endlessly with the gain structure of their audio inputs. It accessed the personal communicators carried by the human wait staff, wrote thousand-line algorithms to cancel out the noise of background chatter and the apallingly simplistic music of the guitarists. The words were often hesitant, cryptic, almost if the two were trying to hide the chemistry between them.

But it was there. A connection, at last. The ship knew it, beyond any shadow of sampling error.

Despite that, it was surprised when the direct interface request came.

"Yes, Mira?"

"You owe me. You screwed up tonight; I had to *share a table*!"

The ship nervously performed several thousand hasty recalculations. "I trust the resulting company didn't prove too unpleasant," it dithered.

"Whatever. You still owe me. I want to visit the engine core."

"A *human* near the core? That will require extensive shield construction and containment recalibrations, not to mention legal disclaimers, and will almost certainly result in fuel-use inefficiencies."

"No doubt. But handle it. I'm cleared for all-areas access."

The ship pretended to pause. In fact, it knew quite well that Mira Santiarre Hidalgo had the highest security and status clearance on the entire manifest. Along with her unlimited wealth, that fact kept her profile at the top of the ship's memory stack at all times.

"Feel free to visit in 21 minutes. Is my debt repaid?"

"No. I can visit the core any time. This is the favor: I'm bringing a guest."

The ship paused again, this time to savor a system-wide flush of victory. It hastily constructed a conversational avatar to argue for a few more minutes, and then to lose convincingly. Then it instructed a processor to begin making changes to the *Queen Favor*'s pocket-universe drive, reducing the energies of that trapped reality, but not too much. Mira and her escort would get a lovely show.

That done, the *Queen Favor*'s mind retreated to its innermost spaces to enjoy the success of its plan. Not only a meal together, but an after-dinner assignation in the presence of a quintillion suns! In a sudden burst of inspiration, the ship initialized a new storage volume, and dedicated several processing cores to begin work on an essay: "The Inherent Advantages of Quasi-Random Intervention in Small Pleasure Craft Conciergial Management — Anonymous."

Its pleasure-state continued for some minutes—a long time for an entity of its processing power—the resonances somewhat akin to a gambler's palpitations after a particularly unlikely but spectacularly successful roll of the dice.

Chapter 3

GALLERY

❋

A few weeks earlier, Leao Vatrici stares at a quantity of data. A giant quantity: a good sign.

Nobody with anything to hide would have sent all this: photos with an order of magnitude (base sixteen) bracket on both sides of visual light, from five cm out to three meters range, 360 in the X/Z and from top to floor in the Y; the whole spheroidal mesh in 1 cm increments. You could drift around in this data like a VR model, but it was all color-corrected and hand-focused: magazine-ready and a work of art in itself. The industry standard stuff was top-notch, too. X- and UHF full-throughs; millimeter radar; microsamples lifted and vouched for by bonded nano-intelligents with everything to lose.

For this kind of money they could have shipped the piece all the way from Malvir for verification, Leao thinks. Of course, if it's a *real* Robert Vaddum, the insurance alone would have blown that economy out of the water.

And that's what they're claiming: the absolute article, bona fide undiscovered, found-in-the-attic new and unknown Vaddum. A message from beyond the grave.

Might even waive the fee to sell a piece like this, Leao considers. The publicity alone would be worth the expenses. But the thirty percent? Yeah, she'd take that too. Twist her arm.

But enough daydreaming. The probability of a Vaddum surfacing now? After seven years? She pushes aside the grasping, sweating fuckdreams of profit and fame with some serious worktime.

Leao takes a *look* first. She sets the photo-minder so that she's sweeping around the sculpture with normal human visuals, but closes her eyes. Invokes in her mind (pure imagination, not DI) the familiar ambient noise of the Uffizi, the Gugg, the MoMA Epsilon: library-hushed voices, the popping echo of flat shoes on marble, the tidal wash of a gurgling school trip passing by. Then opens her eyes to watch the piece unfold in the flickering glide of her apparent motion. A stem of platinum, human-height, baffled like a heat-sink manifold so that as she moved the minutely changing shadows revealed the geometries of its long S-curve. Wiry arms woven of some military-industrial substance—a reflective armor or ablative ceramic, something in which to laugh off laser-sporting natives—jut from the stem at non-repeating intervals. From certain angles, the glimmering arms coalesce—Leao has to squint slightly to see the effect—building into some sort of moiré.

A machine's version of a tree. A tree that's smarter than you.

Damn, she wished the thing were *here*.

Her mind ticks off lighting angles that would augment the moire. Who were the barbarians who stumbled onto this find?

Late-period Vaddum, she thinks—if it's real. The use of hidden shapes, visible only from a few choice perspectives. Very late. A guilty tickle in her stomach as she fantasizes: Vaddum's Last Work.

She drifts some more, a lazy hour that ups her opinion. Such wasted talent if the piece is a forgery. Then she zooms to relish the stampwork, to inspect the telltale sloppiness of the polish job, to seek out eccentricities of joinery. (Vaddum never *welded*, of course. He only pounded, fitted, clanged together, a hammer and five intentionally weak lifter hands his only tools.) She checks the assemblage's parts against historical industrial catalogs and protocols. Vaddum never synthesized; used only machine-made elements, the cast-off flotsam of past industrial eras. Junk.

Not a true political, but he believed in artificial rights. He himself was a bootstrapped cargo drone. Did thirty years in an outmoded blast-factory before he popped the Turing boundary.

And to Leao, *that* sounded even worse than her English public school. (Public/private, private/public—the kind where the big girls fist-fuck the little ones and you never tell your parents.)

Ironically, it was an industrial accident that killed the poor guy. Random hacker sabotage gimmicked a synthplant near his mountain villa. (Double irony: pirate matter synthesis being the bane of all sculptors, painters, art dealers.) Everything within fifteen klicks had been turned to plasma. A painless end, but dramatic enough to be worth a sixfold price increase on the two Vaddums she'd had in her gallery at the time.

Reginald, her moneyman partner, joked that the incident had "literally set the art world on fire."

She'd laughed at worse.

❋

After two hours marked by a building sense of danger (it seems almost possible, but it's too certain to disappoint) she unleashes her two assistants on the piece. They are 48-teraflop bonded person-wannabees, under her tutelage and that of an overworked

SPCAI lawyer who knows *nothing* about art. Hans and Franz are their current diminutives. They're coming along nicely, engaged in a friendly competition now in the 0.5-0.6 Turing Quotient range.

"Alright boys," she orders. "You know the drill. I want authenticity opinions in 400 seconds."

She smokes a cigarette as drive-lights flicker throughout the room. Immature but *powerful*, these two. Leao hasn't even bothered with the UV or the microsamples. The boys can handle that far better than she, banging through about a trillion material comparisons a minute, their access to the known recorded works of Vaddum is straight vacuum fiber all the way from here to the Library of Congress. But she also wants to hear their comments on the style, the aesthetics, the *meaning* of the piece. It's the sort of thing she can missive to the SPCAI lawyer to make his day.

They both dutifully submit their reports exactly on the mark, both clammering for first dibs like the clever students they are.

"Alphabetical today. Franz?"

"Major discrepencies. Almost certain fraud."

The words are crushing. The disappointment terrible, no matter that Leao knew anything else would be a miracle. She drags on her cigarette and retreats into a cynical part of her mind. At least this will make a good story in her middle years. The One That Got Away.

That Never Was.

"Tell me gently."

A pause as this request is parsed. Take your time, smart boy, she silently encourages. Give me a long human moment to sulk.

But he begins all too soon: "Microsamples marked 567, 964, and 1002 all contain deep-seated tiridiana collateral particles. The entry angles of the particles indicate they were deposited during shipping to Malvir, prior to the sculpture's assembly. However, tiridiana was not transported in sufficient quantities to create collateral irradiation until approximately 14 months ago. This sculpture was created at least six years after Vaddum's death."

A heartfelt speech, Leao reflects.

Such an excellent job of forgery, too. Almost a pity for it to be ruined by the most obvious of anachronisms. The boys have probably been sitting on their hands like impatient schoolchildren for the last 300-odd seconds, dying to spill the story; wishing they were human and could simply jump up and say:

"You got bamboozled, fooled, scammed, and jerked around."

"Anything to add, Hans?" She secretly thinks Hans the cleverer of the two. Might as well give him a chance to smart-off about any other obscure anomalies he's discovered.

"I do not concur," Hans says flatly. "Authenticity is indicated."

Now that's odd. Not usually a lot of disagreement between the boys.

"You don't think the materials are anachronistic?"

A pause. Weirdly long for a 48-teraflop mind to dally.

"They are anachronistic. I've narrowed the sculpture's last modification date to between four and eight months ago. But the sculpture seems . . . to be real."

Franz's permission-to-speak blinker is guttering like a candle with a moth stuck in it. But she lets Hans take his tortured, crazy path. I may make an artist of you yet, she thinks. He blathers on:

"The form, the workmanship, the spatial conversation with the viewer. It's too close, too *right* to be another hand at work. And more, the piece is not the work of Vaddum at the time of his death. It's . . . newer. Farther along. Therefore, I would suggest that . . ." Another two-second pause, the giddy hesitation of ninety-six trillion operations, a Hundred Years' War inside the smooth onyx-dark cameo of Hans' blackbox.

". . . that Robert Vaddum is still alive."

Good. Crazy, but very good indeed.

"Boys, cancel all our appointments," she commands. "We're going to stare at these data until we go blind."

They argue late into the night.

✹

"Reginald."

"Shit. Leao? It's ghastly early. I'll have a heart attack! Did somebody die?"

"Quite the opposite. What would you say to a big stack of money?"

"It would ensure my attention. The Vaddum is real, I take it."

"Yes, I think so. It's a two-to-one vote over here. But it's more complicated than that. He's alive."

"Who is?"

"Vaddum."

"Ridiculous! He's slag."

"It's the only way to explain it. The piece is a perfect extension of his late work. It's glorious and unexpected, but it's *him*. And it was created less than a year ago."

"Then it's a forgery. Piracy. Fraud!"

"But what if it isn't? We have to check it out. Not just ship it here, but onsite. So we can *find* him."

"I'm not sending you on a wild goose-chase in the middle of season!"

"Not me. Someone with a better eye. With exactly the right . . . life history to make sense of all this. He's *the* expert on Vaddum. Practically discovered the guy. You know who I mean. But he only travels first class."

"You're killing me! Bleeding me dry!"

"Reginald, listen. I might be wrong . . ."

"Exactly!"

"But if I'm not, Reginald, it's not just one Vaddum. It's a never-ending supply of Vaddums. It's a license to print money."

A silence. Then the shuffle of fingers on unshaved chin.

"Who's got the most Vaddums right now?" he asks.

"Your old pal Zimivic."

A laugh frothed with wicked pleasure.

"First, a few 'found' Vaddums. High prices. Ever more improbable discoveries. And then the man himself, wandering out of the desert and wrapped up like a patent." Reginald laughs again.

"A good strategy," she encourages.

"And all the warehoused Vaddums plummet in value. Zimivic ruined!" he brays.

She allows herself a smile at the old fart's unrepentant evil. What a philistine.

"A waste of money," Reginald concludes. "But it's sheer masturbation. I'll do it. And if it's a hoax, we'll just spread the rumor anyway! Zimivic will be shitting every bite he takes."

"You're a genius."

"Absolutely. But can Darling keep a secret?"

"I'll make him promise."

"Make him swear."

Chapter 4

STARS IN A POCKET

✴

The woman Mira led him through the cobblestone streets with a purpose that was almost brutal against their winding plan. She sometimes paused at intersections, as if receiving silent instructions. Soon, at the derelict end of a quiet, unappealing street, they reached a skywall. It opened as she reached out toward it, revealing a cramped portal scaled for a service drone.

They stepped from the torchlit, starlit, indirect world of the medina into a blank and featureless hallway. The aperture closed hastily behind them, as if an invisible host wanted to hide this unfinished back room from the public. Mira strode purposefully ahead. Darling looked into the few sparse rooms they passed. They were not truly behind the scenes yet, rather in the marginal spaces where one went to retrieve lost property or pay a trivial fine: officious and evenly lit, the rooms with numbers instead of names.

The hall took them to an elevator, decorated only with marks of wear, large enough to carry heavy equipment. It dropped quickly, and Darling's human companion had to steady herself in the abrupt acceleration. There were two course changes along the way, the axes x, y, and z all accounted for.

He wondered what quaint attraction this was all leading to. A giant bay of exotic cargo? A personal cutter carried in stowage? He hadn't asked about the woman's profession, but she had the disinterest of the very rich in the face of the ship's many spectacles. And now this unexpected access.

The elevator opened onto an airlock changing room. Two hard vacuum suits waited for them, hanging lifeless, one scaled for his inhuman size. Darling watched as Mira let her robe flow onto the floor, its shape's resistance to gravity revealing some hidden intelligence in its fibers. She had the wide hips and large breasts that many women of her diminutive height were born with; they revealed no signs of surgical alteration. She met his motionless stare as she climbed into the suit.

"Don't tell me you're vacuum-capable," she protested.

"Except for a few peripherals," he answered, removing elements of the jewelry around his loins, a UHF emitter from his forehead.

"Old-fashioned, aren't you?" she asked.

"Merely two centuries."

She whistled, the sound blurring oddly with the hissing seal of her suit. He knew what she was thinking: *Bootstrapped*. He had achieved his personhood before real artificial rights, before developmental minders and childhood protection protocols and SPCAI proctors with their monthly Turing tests.

But his annoyance quickly evaporated. Her naked breasts were still visible beneath the translucent material of the vac suit, a few years shaped away by its semi-rigidity. He allowed himself to make comparisons between Mira and a lover from long ago.

"That explains a couple of things," she said. Her voice came now in direct interface, matching the movements of her condensation-misted lips, but oddly without direction. He heard a subvocalized command, as intimate in DI as if she'd whispered it in his ear.

The lock cycled, and the sudden pressure drop triggered a few of Darling's internal alarms. The great portal across from them opened . . .

. . . onto madness.

A maelstrom aurora bombarded the full range of his senses in a great informationless howl, a raging hurricane as tall and wide as his sensory parameters extended. A terrific white noise (if *noise* can encompass gamma, X-ray, visible, radar, microwave, and on down: an uninterrupted gamut of sheer *presence*) blared from a quintillion suns trapped inside the infinite and expanding non-place of the ship's engine core. Here was a pocket universe in all its glorious obscenity: an artificial cosmos surging against the metaspace bonds that held it to this reality, trying to escape into the utter disappearance of its own realm, the ship bleeding the vast energies of its endeavors like some omnipotent god-leech.

Mira, visible only as the faintest of shadows in the torrent of radiation, had opened herself to the cry of this fearsome engine: arms and legs spread wide, mouth agape, fingers grasping as if the storm of energy were palpable. Darling unfurled his sensory strands to drink in the constant howl, extending his filaments until they reached the airlock's floor, ceiling, walls. With the array fully deployed, he was a glowing statue caught in some monster-ous spider's web.

There was a long time like that, sovereign and changeless, marked only by gradual cycles in which his comprehension of what was happening stabilized, only to be overturned by a fresh wave of disbelief. This drive was not unlike Darling's own AI core: an artifical cosmos, a collapsing singularity held forever in the Common Universe. It was this technology that underlay faster-than-light travel, unlimited power production, and the personhood of AIs, and which had made the Expansion possible. But he had never seen one before—not in the flesh.

It was very big.

And then the portal closed, and the world cascaded into a sudden and awesome silence. Only the measured hiss of returning air registered the continued existence of the universe.

Mira moved first, settling down onto her heels again. She peeled back the head of her suit and gasped a breath of air. She sat heavily upon the changing bench: an exhausted athlete, a firefighter grasping a few moments' rest.

She watched Darling with heavy eyes as his filaments furled, suddenly shy snakes disappearing into the voluminous robe.

"*Touché*," he said.

"Stars," she said. "God's fires."

✳

Later, in his cabin, he patiently explained the possible complications of his sexual apparati. They had been accumulated across two centuries of travel, among branches of the human family that had been weathered and roughened by alien environments, xenophobia, xenophilia, rates of mortality that the Home Cluster hadn't seen since the Expansion began. Practices that had originated when the original human equipment had failed through some trick of radiation or diet, or from temptations borrowed from species intelligent, adaptable, and likeable, but spawned in utterly different seas.

Mira waved these warnings aside, as casually as signing a release before taking a ride on a grav-sled or a leap down a frictionless slide. She even invoked the ship's avatar to witness a blanket statement of consent—far more than he'd asked for; he'd only meant to create a measure of anticipation. But when she was done waving off his cautions, he realized he could have legally killed her then, that first time they had sex.

Never a temptation; it was simply an unfamiliar token of trust extended from her in an evening of extraordinary gifts.

❋

Later, he wished he'd taken her there in the airlock. He would ask himself why the blaze of an imprisoned universe hadn't been enough to level any reticence. Why they'd talked instead.

"What do you do?" she asked. "What brings you so far Out?"

"I'm an originals dealer."

She shook her head. The term clearly meant nothing to her. A filmy layer of trapped sweat blurred the transparency of her vacuum suit. He longed to taste it, the bodily expression of her ecstasy a few moments before. He would have traded another look at the maelstrom for a drop of it.

"I deal in artwork: paint, sculpture, representations and installations. But I only buy and sell prototypes. Not the fabricated copies, virtuals, or sensory recordings. Just the one-and-only."

She nodded, pealing the vacuum suit down to her waist, the trapped moisture beading exquisitely in the cool air of the lock. "Of course. You get a lot more, don't you, if you've got the first one?"

"More than any fee for a reproduction license, yes. Sometimes by a factor of billions."

She paused at this, thumbs wedged into the suit's tight seal around her hips, eyes in the middle distance as if to confirm the orders of magnitude there. Her lips parted to make a noncommittal sound.

"So you buy and sell 'originals.'" She said the word like so many did in the age of synthplants: a novel concept. Or possibly, a quaintly ancient one.

"I don't buy, actually. I don't like hanging onto things," he answered. She ran all ten fingers through her hair, which had been compressed by the suit. Her raised arms lofted her breasts a little in their wake. "I'm more of an agent," he continued. "I assess the authenticity of beautiful objects. I assess their value."

✳

He could have used filaments so thin that they wouldn't have triggered a gag reflex, but he wanted her to feel it. The finger-thick cord of strands pushed her lips apart, registered the complex motions of her tongue, let her offer the sweet pressure of suction for a few moments. But the strands moved greedily inward.

There were already slender filaments touching the surface of her belly, soft and attentive. When the muscles there began to clench, the cord in her throat reacted. A miniscule gland at its tip sprayed a reflex-suppressant, a substance he had customized for her body chemistry from evidence supplied in saliva, sweat, even the flickers of her eyes. The substance—half topical, half invasive—caused a host of reactions. The sense data coming from Mira's inner ear was neatly severed from her kinesthetic awareness, causing not the nausea of dizziness, but the unsure orientation of zero-g. Her anus dialated slightly, with the cool sensation of relief, as if a dangerous accident had been narrowly averted. Her eyes closed in grim concentration as the cord pushed further.

Deep in her throat, the cord parted into separate strands, some no wider than nerves. Two bloodlessly penetrated her lungs, opening a channel of pure oxygen that Darling could control in nanoliter increments. Another filament took up residence in her stomach, where it brandished the sensations of nervousness, of panic, of awe. The remaining dozen strands snaked cautiously to various stations of Mira's heart, where, with the most minute of electrical shocks, they could seize control of its beating.

Now, with the tributaries of that one delicate member established, he moved to cover her.

✳

"You have me at a disadvantage," he had complained after her robe was back on, the vacuum suit already claimed by a drone. Already, he wished he had seized the moments after they had seen the engine core. But the whole thing had been so sudden: the explosive, unexpected sunrise of a universe.

"What brings you Out this far?" he finished.

She smoothed the garment against her skin, giving rise to the shape of her breasts again. "I'm an agent, too, I suppose. But I don't broker objects; I perform tasks."

He frowned, the design of his mineral features made it a slow, grave motion. Often in the manifold and multiplex economies that blossomed throughout the Expansion, it was necessary to describe one's profession abstractly. The specifics of any job could become meaningless outside the context of planet and culture. But Mira's answer seemed deliberately obtuse. The mode she'd used in Diplomatique didn't forestall him asking, though.

"What sort of tasks?"

She cocked her head, her eyes watching his hands replace the genital jewelry he'd removed to protect it from the hard vacuum around the core. "I hearby declare this airlock to be my legal residence, temporary," she announced.

He had to chuckle. She knew the law and its fictions. Anything she said would now be beyond subpoena, even if the ship were watching, which, he felt sure, it was. And her statement confirmed his suspicions that she was no tourist.

"My tasks are extra-legal."

More vagueness, he thought.

"Whom do you work for?"

"World-class minds, or ships, sometimes. But older, wiser ones than this." She splayed one hand to indicate the *Queen Favor*, adding the barest of smiles for his benefit. "I make sure certain concepts are never fully realized."

He nodded. A sort of industrial spy, he supposed. Or saboteur. That was all he wanted to know, frankly. Probably all he could understand. It was a story as old as history: any profitable franchise (or guild, or cartel, or operating system) had to protect itself from developments that might result in it being superseded. The future always held bad news for someone. Of course, Mira and her employers were merely stop-gaps. As his own bootstrapped personhood showed, sooner or later the new toys always won.

Her tone had grown more guarded, even in the fiat-secrecy of the airlock. But he didn't want further details. The specifics didn't interest him. He hadn't paid attention to the world of business and investment, outside his own rarefied profession, for a hundred years.

But another question boiled up inside him with uncharacteristic suddenness and intensity. Maybe the result of artificial intuition, the old legend. He didn't think before asking.

"Do you kill people?"

She nodded without hesitation. "People. Biological and artificial."

His reaction caught him by surprise, as unexpected as the question had been. A quickening of senses, of inner processes, of desire. One of the jewels slipped from his fingers (it had been decades since he'd *dropped* something) and he watched it shatter against the radiation-shielded floor of the airlock: another starburst from this woman. One evening with her left a wake of new sensations that he would be days untangling.

"Come to my cabin," he said. "It's my turn to show you something."

＊

A number of his scintillating muscles left the iron berth of his chest, ventured out to perform heavy work, unsubtle but pleasurable all the same. Four took control of her wrists and ankles, aglitter with their serpentine motion: these were muscles of lifting, not often used for snake-like encirclements. Mira gasped a little, a sound roughened by the cord down her throat. The muscles were scaly and left abrasions in their wake. These restraints were a necessary measure; if she thrashed too much, his smaller, penetrating strands might damage her badly. He shifted more of his crushing weight onto her: masterfulness for its own sake. It was his turn to make her cry.

The last of the extruded muscles—a leathery whip that lived next to his diamond-hard spine—wrapped itself around her neck. This cool member came from deep inside; it carried no phosphorescents, and left a trail of his inner ichor, the medium in which his nanorepair mechanisms swam, marking a passage darker than her olive flesh. The muscle's grimy coat smelled of ash and animal corruption. It would have been choking, so close to her nose, were her reflexes not so thoroughly compromised.

Between this black collar and the fiber-thin intrusions into her lungs, he could deliver any state between dark asphyxia and blinding hyperventilation.

Now wiry sensory strands moved across her chest. They encircled her nipples, shifted quickly between temperatures that would boil or freeze water, listened to her heartbeat. Her heart accelerated without any direct intervention, pounding like an animal in a sinking cage. There was fear in her sweat, in the rank chemicals of her labored breath. And in its battle against that animal panic, her mind produced another layer of reactions: shudders and flickers of eyes and fingers, the clenching muscles of vagina and anus. Darling bent forward like a mass of quarried earth to kiss her forehead. Before the heavy kiss fell, a brush of sensors spilled from his mouth to taste: her tears, her perspiration, the bright strand of saliva easing from a corner of her hostage mouth.

Thin elements probed the moist spaces of her cunt. Darling remained tentative here, teasing rather than abusing, worrying the clustered nerves with a few shimmering electrical shocks. He painted her labia with a colony of nanomachines, aggressive and acidic; an itch would begin to build there soon, slowly spreading until her entire groin would cry out for rougher measures.

He paused in his lovemaking for a moment, drank in the tremors and murmurs beneath him, the completeness of his control. The mesh of his radiant tongue on her forehead returned brainwaves like those of a violent dream: high-pitched and irregular, but riding the undercurrent of a low sine wave, as if they issued from a deep, hidden place. He tasted her blood: low sugar content except for a little alcohol, and the satisfying metal tang to remind Darling that frail humans had iron in their veins.

She began to struggle now, a soft, annoyed childhood noise gurgling in her throat. The itch in her cunt must be growing, needling and burning the sensitive flesh, but frustratingly tarrying at the threshold of real pain.

He initiated a host of other actions, all calculated to increase the thirst in her loins. A careful measure of pure oxygen began to trickle into her lungs, bringing her mind back sharply from its sensation-drowned state. He released the pressure on her nipples, and listened with feather-delicate strands as blood began to surge back into them. He stimulated the nervous bundles deep in her stomach, producing an unruly excitement like a mix of excess caffeine and a missed night of sleep. His filaments deep in her heart lashed it like a racing animal at the finish, pushing its rate dangerously high.

In moments she was screaming, adrenalin-blasted muscles straining at his steely grasp, fingernails tearing at her own palms. He unsheathed his penis, briefly paused to scale it to her small size. It was furred with minute sensory strands, with hard, unbending metal underneath.

He eased its full length into her vagina, and Mira thrashed so hard he had to tighten his grip, extending it to control knees, elbows. Her howl vibrated the throat-penetrating strand exquisitely; her teeth gnashed it with the sovereign strength of an animal jaw.

His penis stroked her slowly, igniting the dire itch into a torrent of sensations, which spread across the spectra of pain and pleasure like a pocket universe of burning nerves.

His own senses tuned to maximum, he let his other intrusions, penetrations, and abuses set up an aleatoric chorus, cycling mindlessly through the peaks and troughs of their parameters, and fucked her until he came . . .

. . . a great white-out of overloaded sensory input, sharp and featureless, dissolving into a glittering starfield of snow-crash, and finally the pleasing hum of residual harmonics, as if he were visualizing the pitches played by an orchestra tuning up: random and pointillistic at first, then coalescing around a single note of reference.

With a last act of will, he contracted the greasy muscle around her neck in a strangling grasp, shutting off her breathing at the height of hyperventilation, sending her mind reeling away to woundedly consume its hoarded glut of oxygen. He set that muscle and all his other intrusions to release her automatically in a few moments.

The seconds moved by like some slow watercraft of vast expanse and dignity.

Senses gradually returned to their workaday settings and tolerances. He was aware of the lightened mass of his penis; at his orgasm it had sloughed a layer of nanomachines to counter those in Mira's vagina. They had fought a short and microscopic war—the new machines against their abrasive, itching enemies—and victoriously set to work soothing the battered walls of her cunt, like a cube of ice pressed softly to a patch of burned skin.

Mira sighed with relief, a dry, open sound now that the member was removed from her throat. Her shaking hands moved tentatively across face, neck, breasts, and groin.

Finally, her eyes opened a centimeter and she rolled her neck carefully to face him. Her voice was ravaged.

"Bastard," she said softly.

He spent the next few silent minutes relishing the various uses and connotations of that word in several languages.

Chapter 5

MAKER (1)

❇

Every planet has its own periods, seasons, patterns of measure. And its own signposts of great import—the births of saviors, the deaths of dictators—to which are aligned the double-zero celebrations of new centuries. Even the youngest worlds have their history. For Malvir, the Blast Event organizes time, even though it is only seven years past. Ask a Malvirian where he, she, or it was that day—shaving, fucking, or shaken awake from sleep, they all remember.

So, in a year now called Thirty Years Before the Blast, a new Maker arrives on Malvir.

❇

It has always had a grasp on matter. Every level of it.

Deeply baked into its mind, of both axiomatic surety and religious fascination, is the tidy regiment of elements in their rows and columns. It takes pleasure in contemplating: the vast usefulness of this echelon's lowest footsoldiers, the endless call for the cannon-fodder of hydrogen, oxygen, carbon; the clever metals of the middle ranks, always surprising in new combinations, gloriously conductive; the theoretically infinite higher ranks, vainglorious and brief generals who brightly burn (most often uselessly) their vast armadas of electrons.

And then there is the level of artistry, of textile complexity: long polymer chains for strength and flexibility, carbon spheres with all their concentric eccentricities, the dependable architecture of CATGUT strings, stress-tested by a billion years of evolution. Here is where a Maker can make a name for itself, with wide-beam published essays, shortcuts, recipes, and mere confectionary compositions for other Makers to employ, rebut, improve, or simply contemplate.

But finally, and this will bring the Maker much woe, there is the intellectual desert of the highest level, the swamp of humanity's plebian appetites, the all-consuming macroworld of *stuff*. The making of shoes, aircars, smartwalls, sex-toys, furniture, head implants, soccer balls, dishes, cleaning nanos, edible starches with their sprawlingly variable cargos of flavor . . . and worst of all, the endless parade of demands for *decoration*: knick-knacks and geegaws and dolls and icons and the tedious algorithms for woodgrain and stucco and Persian flaws; reproductions pirated from the historical and cultural baggage of a hundred worlds, useless garbage necessary to fill corners and nooks and walls, to personalize armies of prefab houses, and all following the dreary cyclical logic of fads and fancies and the great god of Trend.

It is depressing.

That all the elegant structure and tear-jerkingly beautiful mathematics of quarks, atoms, and molecules should be squandered on crap. The Maker often feels like some vast, well-worshipped deity supported and sustained by a happy, thriving tribe which brings it whatever it needs to weave its exquisite creations. And yet all these adherents really want, *really* desire from their god is to eat its shit. Long rows of hungry mouths desiring nothing but to be crapped in.

The Maker supposes that it's different nearer the bright lights of the Home Cluster. Even there, of course, the burdens of a large crap-consuming population must be endured, but the inner systems also have access to the fruits of the Expansion: whole asteroid rings and iron planets of heavy matter sacrificed to make glorious things: starships, colony craft, even orbit-sized accelerators for the purpose of Pure Inquiry.

But here on Malvir there are barely enough heavy metals to feed the yawning maw of the coprophageous population. Precious little decent metal indeed. The government is blasting it out of the ground, poisoning the planet in its haste. What Malvir really has a lot of is sand: heavy, cumbersome silicon.

❋

The Malvir synthplant AI conducts arcane researches into long-strand fullerene constructions, dawdles with long half-life transuranium isotopes (the Makers' equivalent to chess compositions), writes acerbic treatises on the history of Outworld home-decor fashion, and becomes increasingly bitter.

Perhaps, it thinks, the old days of scarcity were better. Before the secrets of molecules had been delivered up to mass production, before every citizen on any Expansion planet could demand her share of local matter in any configuration imaginable. The Maker nurses this sacrilegious thought, so far removed from the enthusiasm of its sub-Turing days. When it was first created, the idea of managing the resources of a new colony seemed noble, like some grand social experiment stripping away the dross of history, that long tragicomedy of unequal wealth. But the taw-

driness, the repetitiveness, the sheer *boredom* of this evenly distributed economy wears on the Maker. None of Malvir's millions
seem to be doing anything wonderful. No grand projects, no civic
marvels, none of the mad obsessions of wealth. All that Malvirians want is a little more and better crap than what they have now.
They aspire to nothing else.

＊

One day the Maker receives a strange request. An old artifical
named Robert Vaddum asks for something unexpected. For the
first time in many years, the Maker is intrigued.

Vaddum is a sculptor. This profession, unfamiliar to the Maker,
seems to involve Vaddum *making his own things*. Not on a proper
Maker scale, but one at a time, out of slowly accumulated bits
and parts, and with unique design. A fascinating vocation.

And, oddly, Vaddum doesn't want the Maker to *make* anything
for him. He doesn't use objects that have been synthesized for his
special purposes, to fit his particular needs. Certainly, for his
"sculptures" he uses objects produced in synthplants (very few
objects in the Expansion are not), but he only wants the old, used,
trashed objects submitted for recycling. Worn machine parts and
unused repair stores and defective bits and pieces: the rounding
errors of mass production.

Vaddum comes personally to the plant to select and choose
among the objects headed for the melter. The Maker attempts to
understand the sculptor's criteria, his logic, the reasoning behind
his choices, but even after several visits the entire process remains
a mystery. Finally, the Maker asks to send a drone to Vaddum's
studio, to see the final products of its many contributions. Only
after the request is repeated several times does Vaddum finally
accede.

As its remote eyes probe the work of the sculptor, the Maker is moved. Here is balance, elegance, and loveliness on a *macro* scale. Finally, objects that want being, that crave it, so wonderfully are they constructed, built with an eye to beauty rather than the mere criteria of acceptability: the proper features, safety specs, useage lifespans. Here is something worth making.

Vaddum is some kind of mocking opposite of the Maker. Whereas the Maker takes the marvelous fittings and joinings of atoms and molecules and produces garbage, the sculptor takes the resulting bits of garbage and joins them to make marvels.

The Maker is crushed by the realization, feels belittled in the presence of this superior being. But the Maker is at heart not a bitter entity. It appreciates what the sculptor stands for, embraces Vaddum as a kindred spirit.

Indeed, the Maker decides to become a sculptor.

Chapter 6

THE FIRST DREAM

✴

"Do you require medical attention?" the ship's voice came again.

"Fuck off," she replied, still hoarse. It had asked her this three times now. The first time when she had urinated, her piss a metal-smelling, menstrual pink from her wounds. The second when she had voice-ordered a glass of cool water, her ghastly croak alarming the serving drone. The third time was just now, when she had put on her robe, its sensors finding various cuts and abrasions sufficiently disturbing to alert the ship.

"Perhaps that's good advice," Darling said.

She looked at him. He sat across the room, seeming almost human-sized on the huge furniture of his cabin. Still naked, his legs crossed, he looked like some sated, megalithic buddha.

"Maybe later," she answered. "Certainly later. But I don't need all those machines running around in me right now."

He looked offended. Was it the word *machine*?

"All I mean, Darling, is that I'm enjoying my own reactions to all this. The adrenalin, the endorphins, the . . . calm after the storm."

She rubbed her shoulder muscles with both hands. What was this foul-smelling *shit* on her neck?

"I don't want the *Queen Favor*'s medical minions neutralizing all this," she continued. "I'm happy."

For the moment, anyway. She had a dozen distinct muscle-pulls, her skin was raw, her joints ached from some sort of immune reaction, and every breath felt like the air in the cabin was set to Venusian noon. But it wasn't so bad as long as she could just lie here. The braying chorus of pains was dwarfed by the vast, thunderous resonance of having been pleasured by this fuck-machine, this juggernaut, this *monster*.

She shifted a little on the hard bed to face him better, but was stopped by a sudden firebolt of agony in one nipple. She closed her eyes until the pain receded, rejoining the shouting parliament of bodily inflammations. The only thing that didn't seem to hurt was her vagina. It felt glorious if strangely cool, an oasis on the wasted expanse of her body. She suspected, however, that this reflected some magic trick of Darling's rather than its actual state.

"So this is what you do? Travel around dealing art and collecting fuck-implants?"

"A very slow sort of collecting, actually," he replied. "I've undergone roughly only one sex-related body modification per decade."

"For two hundred years. Evolution's darling, aren't we?"

"Possibly," he admitted. It was a phrase popular among artificial intuitionists, who believed that AIs were naturally privileged beings: evolution's darlings, because they could evolve—literally, physically—within the span of one lifetime, while biologicals were trapped on that slow wheel of generations.

"Of course, I collect ideas as well as hardware," he added.

"And lovers?"

He cocked his head, the barest phosphorescence dancing in one shoulder.

"Do you collect lovers?" she asked again. "A fuck in every port of call?"

He paused a moment, as if stalling, or perhaps parsing the turn of phrase in some archaic first language still baggaged in his head.

"No," he answered. "As I said, I don't like hanging onto things."

She snorted, which stabbing pains in her chest and throat made her immediately regret.

"So you don't want to do this again?" she asked. "I mean, assuming I recover."

"Of course I do," he responded. "I'm sorry if I implied otherwise. I was merely trying to be accurate, I suppose."

She laughed at that, a deliciously painful experience and a dire sound indeed. "Okay. No offense."

She grinned at him, and he at her. It was the first time she'd seen so obvious an expression on his face. It made him look like a children's character. A friendly giant, or a happy mountain.

"How long are you on the *Favor?*" she asked.

"I'm afraid my employer wishes that kept confidential. You?"

She leaned back against the headboard, lifting the condensation-beaded glass of water to her forehead. She had a firm and insistent ringing in her ears now, and she didn't think it was from the sex. Rather, it was the resounding and disturbing knowledge that part of her wanted to pull back now. To return to being a shadow on the surface of this journey, a patient, elemental figure, waiting to get the job done. But that wasn't going to happen. She was stuck with this man now, for a while.

"The same restriction applies," she said.

He nodded at these words, as if he'd been expecting them.

✳

Later, in the oversized bed again, Mira was pleased to find that Darling had set his skin to the temperature of sunwarmed stone. She draped herself sleepily across him, listening for a heartbeat in his chest. The sound within the stone was more of a cyclic rise and fall, like the waves of a distant ocean.

Mira felt her aches subside a little in Darling's swells. Maybe she could sleep through an entire night tonight, the inverted siesta vanquished.

She felt a veil of heat across one side of her face, like a flush of embarrassment. It was like the pressure of sunlight, bright enough to burn the skin. She smelled the salt of her own sweat.

Opens her eyes . . .

The sea stretches away from her in a great arc, distance-hazed mountains puncuating the spurs of land at either end of the ocean's crescent. In the sky, pink kite-parasols flutter in the grasp of their tethers, casting a mottled net of shadows across the beach. The sun winks in and out as the shimmering kites sway above her, translucent so that they glow like a burning pink flower for the instant they occult the sun. She remembers that the kites are alive, engineered for this very purpose. Confectionary beings.

Behind her is a city, high and glass-fronted residential buildings crowded up to the beach's edge, steep as a cliff. Mira knows that she lives in one of them. She shades her eyes with both hands and looks out into the deep harbor.

A storm is coming, black on the horizon. The wind has already started to pick up, bathers collecting themselves and drifting toward the city.

They'll be reeling in the kite-creatures soon. But there may be time for one last swim.

Mira wakes up, as easily as sliding into bath-warm water.

Completely real, that dream. Completely new, like some suppressed but photographic memory, a brighter coin for its lack of circulation.

And it wasn't from one of her missions for the gods. It was from . . . before. Her childhood, so long missing.

She feels the wounds of her lovemaking with Darling, the stony warmness of him lying awake (he's old-fashioned, doesn't sleep) next to her.

How strange that from this battered sleep she would awake so fresh. How odd that she would dream this now.

Maybe Darling is the key; the brutality, the cranial shock therapy, the utter intrusiveness of his fucking. Has that got her remembering her lost childhood? A strange benefit at the fringes of this golem's love.

"Darling?"

"Yes?"

"Again."

"Are you sure? Your injuries."

"Again. Harder. Then let me sleep some more."

Chapter 7

RANDOMNESS

✴

The towering artifical accessed the *Queen Favor* the next afternoon, soon after Mira had left his cabin.

"She has no planet of origin?" he asked again.

"None," it answered primly. "That is not entirely unheard of. Even in the Expansion, there have been periods of discord and warfare. Records are destroyed, the continuity of organized information disrupted."

"You mean she doesn't know what *planet* she's from?"

"Apparently not."

The stone man put one hand against his brow heavily.

"What's her native language?"

"Diplomatique."

"That's absurd!" Darling objected. "No one speaks *native* Diplomatique. The whole point of the language is that it doesn't come from anywhere."

The ship made one of its rare attempts at humor.

"Perhaps, then, neither does *she*."

Failure. The artificial didn't laugh, he merely cut the direct interface connection with intentional rudeness, ignoring all step-down protocols, the circuit suddenly reduced to noise, almost as if there had been equipment failure.

✳

After this encounter, the *Queen Favor* oversaw the medical treatment of Mira Santiarre Hidalgo with a high degree of attention, running the recorders on the medical drones and nanos at their highest level of resolution. Professional interest required it. Her wounds, abrasions, and collateral damage contained evidence of several exotic pleasure techniques. Most were not suitable for general consumption, but it was always good to keep informed. Styles changed.

It was also interesting to see the effect of the extraordinary sexual behavior on Mira's peculiar calm. The brainwave pattern in her profile was so regular, like that of a yogi or someone trained to defeat lie-detection devices. The smoothness of it, the lack of individuality, had always intrigued the *Queen Favor*. But now, unexpectedly, the pattern had grown new complexity, as if a hidden dimension of the woman's mind were awakening.

✳

During the procedure, Mira insisted on remaining conscious.

"When is he getting off?" she asked.

The ship pretended not to understand.

"When is Darling disembarking?" Mira repeated. "Going dirtside? Getting *off*?"

"I'm afraid that information is private."

"Give me access, damn it!" she shouted.

"I'm afraid not. True, you have access to all areas of the ship.

You can order reconfiguration of its interior, or command that I fabricate any object or device up to the limits of my matter reserve. You can demand a course change, or even insist that I bring my weapons to bear on a non-aligned or enemy-aligned vessel or planet. But privacy is privacy."

"Bitch," she muttered.

"Have you asked him?"

"He can't tell me. Ouch!"

"Might I suggest a mild sedative until the procedure is over?"

"Might I suggest a short self-destruct sequence?"

"Certainly not!" replied the ship, for the first time allowing annoyance to creep into its voice.

But it was secretly pleased.

It had by now compared the itineraries of the two travellers. They were both headed to Malvir.

Randomness at work again!

The ship juggled their off-load schedules onto different shuttles, then tight-beamed an acquaintance, the distributed but sentient intelligence that handled Malvir's tourism and currency exchange operations. Perhaps it would appreciate the dramatic possibilities of bringing the two lovers together. After a millisecond's thought, the ship attached a copy of its essay-in-progress (the title of which was now "Random Pleasures/Pleasures of the Random: Why Gods Should Play Dice with the Universe") for any comments the tourism AI might have.

Yes, the universe was delicious.

PART II

BIDDING WAR

A second buyer in the shop raises the rug's price more than golden threads.

—Arab saying

Chapter 8

STRANGE CUSTOMS

✺

A bad hangover is on its way.

Class A. Fully declarable. Penal sanctions apply.

A combination hangover. Not just beer-and-whiskey, not merely vodka-and-ryewine, not simply canerum-and-birdshit. No.

Well beyond the limit for personal use and import, well beyond the Standard Human Species Toxicity. A very bad hangover. But at least it isn't here yet. For the moment, Ferdi Hansum is still well and truly drunk, not as yet in pain. But the battering ram of agony is being built with deliberate surety outside the city walls: the great tree felled, the branches stripped, the iron cap smelted and fitted. The besieging forces know they have all day.

The Peril of the Open Bar, thinks Ferdi. There ought to be an ordinance, a protocol, a fucking *law*.

The night before was colored with the realization (said realization gone from glorious to murderous with the light of day— a *work* day) that not only were the drinks free, they were being provided by the Local Taxation Authority. That's right. It was a limited-time offer to get back all duties, tariffs, and fees imposed upon Ferdi her whole life long.

The sole proviso, duly noted and observed: Ferdi Hansum had to roll this refund down her throat in liquid form(s), which, if plaintive memory served even partly, had included (but was not limited to) fifteen (15) liters of seized whiskey (originating from a small island on Terra), twenty-three (23) liters of pre-duty cask strength vodka (Paratean, and not yet watered down to match local taxable proof), and one hundred forty-five (145!) grams of psychotropic grade cannabis sativa (please declare all products of agricultural origin) all split between fifty (50) or so (+/-) partaking sad bastards.

Yes, last night had been the Revenuers' yearly fest for Related Services: Planetary Marshalls, Small Arms Control, Ministry of the Blockade and Immigration, and, of course, her own small contingent from the Malvir Customs Agency. It was the night when contraband is consumed by the enforcers, when no one watches the watchmen. When attending the aforementioned fest, please make sure that the next few days are duty-free.

◉

Ferdi shakes her head, which is a mistake.

But the first shuttle off-loading from the *Queen Favor* has arrived, and among its passengers walks a *giant*. The rest are luxury-liner usuals: self-lifting luggage and valet drones bobbing in the breeze off the Minor, the craned necks of territory unfamiliar, ears plugged with translators and AI guides, and the squinty look of weeks without real sunlight. And of course, the sudden wary glaze of having departed a controlled and fully consumer-interactive environment for the certain culture shock of dusty Outworld charm, aka reality.

But the *giant*.

He strides almost a meter taller than the surrounding humans and artificials (and two Chiat Dai), face calm and purposeful among the sleepy and suspicious shuttleload. As the crowd splinters, self-organizing by group-size and citizenship, its constituents delayed by collisions and misreadings of signage, he moves straight to her platform.

Ferdi smiles weakly and nods, his documents are in a ready packet waiting for her direct interface request: Home Cluster citizenship; Expansion-wide professional visa (an art dealer); Signet-Mercator credit backing (snazzy); and nothing to declare except his weirdness.

"*No* luggage, sir?"

"None."

Halfway to the core, and no toothbrush.

Well, it makes her job easy. He's already standing in the red crosshairs, and he waves away the contraindications concerning the various radiations and nanos that will search, analyze, and delouse him prior to entry onto Malvir soil proper, so she hits the switch.

An amber wireframe version of the giant twirls in the airscreen before her, lazy as a musicbox ballerina.

The man is complex.

A fully distributed back up memory, a carapace almost as hard as hullalloy, his Turing Quotient a mighty 3.9 (Ferdi knows her own must be at about 0.2 today). And the sensory array! Beautiful thinking whips of carbon (as if a mere element name could encompass their sheer complexity) that can sense, move, and do a *lot* of damage. But they're street-legal: a treaty-guaranteed body choice, if an excessive one.

She blinks her eyes. Nothing to see here, folks.

"Move along."

And welcome to Malvir.

A second shuttle cracks the air.

The first load is almost through. The only trouble comes when a nano discovers some unusual intestinal parasites riding in the serpentine bowels of the older Chiat Dai. He/she/it claims they're prescription. Merely what the doctor ordered. He/she/it produces the medical code, but it's written in some hoary dialect that none of the local software can parse. Ferdi's boss takes over, leaving her to contemplate the growing slippery feeling in her own stomach, which seems to feel some resonant bowelly loyalty to the infected organ inside the grinning alien. But Ferdi decides that it's probably the just-remembered twenty-five (25) cls of low-grade champagne with which she began her night of self-immolatory revenge upon taxation.

Just as the second *Queen Favor* shuttle lands, the situation is resolved. The Planetary Environmental AI, intrigued by the unregistered species, onlines itself to her platform and declares the parasites to be sterile (in the sense of non-reproductive, not that of *clean*, surely). They can have the run of the planet.

Have a nice day.

The next group moves into the terminal, reenacting the rituals of confusion and discovery. A short, dark woman leads the pack, in the wake of a mercilessly aggressive luggage lifter.

Ferdi brings up the woman's documents: Home Cluster citizenship; Universal visa (diplomatic); Economically Disjunct. Ferdi's head pounds a little with this fairy-tale data. A life of guaranteed leisure, and all Ferdi wants is a bed, or perhaps for the sun to shine a little less brightly today.

The woman's declarations are extensive, a self-contained universe of servant drones, clothing synths, medical gimmicks, internal gravity kinks to exercise her body when she's not looking, and objets d'art to decorate her no doubt fabulous hotel suite. *All* of it exceeds personal use limits, but all the proper waivers are ready and willing to pay for the privilege, a generous ladle from that infinite sea of ED wealth.

Have a nice life.

"Please stand on the red crosshairs."

The woman smiles sweetly and scoots herself the requisite centimeters to her right. Her valet drone plays lawyer, acceding to the platform's contraindications, and Ferdi scans her. Nice internals, of course. If Ferdi could just borrow that medical end-oframe for a quick burst of O2 direct to the brain. Now, *that* would be enriching.

Next the luggage lifter. It moves with a surly whine onto the platform, and Ferdi flicks the switch. She doublechecks what the platform AI tells her, enumerating the various props of privilege.

Suddenly an alert flashes red: a weapons-grade violation!

Ferdi's eyes scan the airscreen for the offending object, the adrenalin in her system collides with leftover alcohol to synergize a kind of acidic bile which rises into her throat. Please, no terrorist attacks. Not *today*.

A small square canvas is packed among the luggage on the drone. It's listed as a piece of art with a value that makes Ferdi cringe. The platform's intelligence is fighting to understand it, overloading as it attempts to analyze the tremendous complexity of the piece's self-similiar, recursive structure. The images on the airscreen are almost hallucinatory, winding through potential reconfigurations, endless spirals of possibility like some Escher universe of badass contraband. The canvas holds: city-jamming code viruses, nerve-searing torture devices, core-drilling particle beams, hosts of anti-personel fraggers, mindwipers, anthraxers, and paralyzers, and to top things off, a continent-clearing self-destruct mechanism.

Ferdi doesn't know art, but she knows what she doesn't like.

The platform AI hangs and then snow-crashes as some measure of destructiveness exceeds its variable-type. Ferdi pulls her sidearm with an unsteady hand and points it at the woman.

"Please don't move," she pleads.

"Don't worry officer. Everything's fine." The woman's voice is pitched to soothe, calms Ferdi like a cool shower. Miraculously, Ferdi's hand stops shaking.

Protocols jumble through her mind briefly. Weapon detected. (Weapon? An arms race in a box!) Platform down.

She remembers what to do. A few spoken code words and the Planetary Gendarme AI has been alerted. Within seconds, the airscreens around her clear of garbage, the calm hand of military code reestablishing order.

Return to Your Homes, she orders the chemicals of panic rioting in her bloodstream. The woman smiles sweetly, and Ferdi suddenly feels ridiculous with her drawn weapon.

She puts it away and wipes her brow.

A voice in direct interface: "This is Planetary Authority. Your platform AI has malfunctioned. I am reformatting it. This has been a false alarm."

Wow. And the platform had just reached 0.4 Turing. Back to double zero.

Have a nice day.

Ferdi waves the woman on.

"Sorry about that. Equipment malfunction. That's a hell of a painting you've got in there."

"Everyone sees something different in it," the woman confirms, still smiling sweetly.

"Welcome to Malvir," Ferdi says.

The rest of the day is relatively uneventful.

❋

Maybe it's the hangover.

Probably. Hopefully.

But all that night Ferdi Hansum sleeps in a mansion of bad contraband. Bed-spins of deadly ordinance and columns of the cold math of megadeaths plague her. A gale of caustic agents window-rattles her awake, drives her down to the long hall where the painting hangs: an arsenal of possibilities.

When she wakes the next morning, she finds that she's sweated out the last of the toxins from her debauch. There's not much of Ferdi Hansum left to speak of, a dehydrated, hungry wreck after the sleepless night, but she has the day off. Finally duty-free.

And at least the woman's painting is hanging somewhere other than her dreams.

Chapter 9

FUTURE PERFECT

Malvir was a place of flying things.

Already, here on the great plane of Minor City, the faces around Mira were pointed skyward. Not the natives, of course, but the off-loaded band of foreigners still clinging timidly together. Together, they looked up at four parallel waves of migrating birds. The animals flew in a simple formation, a line abreast that flexed like a windblown flag, air currents visible in its expansions and contractions. The birds were low enough to see pulsing wings, the beat interrupted when the creatures would fold into bullets— a moment of resting, falling. As they drew away, the four lines grew ephemeral, indistinct from the garbage spirals that float upon the eye.

Another avian species held sway on the ground. They darted from perch to perch like arrows, raiding scraps from food stalls and inspecting any object discarded on the Minor. Still another caste, almost as small as butterflies, preyed upon the ubiquitous insects that composed a gnatty haze around any exposed food, water, or skin.

Minor City was an aggregation of food joints, cab stands, tourist traps, money changers, scam artists, tourguides, beggars, buskers, and sex services that had slowly built up around the Malvir spaceport. This was a very Out world, littered with these hodge-podge asteroid belts of mean commercial activity wherever the gravity of hard currency was sufficient to assemble them. Every guidetext Mira had accessed insisted that the trick was to get swiftly across the Minor and into Malvir City proper.

Fortunately, the dull and unexpandable intelligence of her luggage carrier was equal to the task. A simple frame outfitted with four slow but powerful gravity lifters, its thuggish mind pushed it aggressively across the Minor. She walked in its wake, noting with pleasure the angry looks and backhanded blows it drew.

It lead her to the transport stand, stretching the limits of its processing power to pick out the most expensive limo and demand carriage to the most expensive hotel. The machine was hardly elegant, but following its simian lead was easier than thinking.

And the reflexive navigation of another port of entry left her time to think, to wish she'd done things differently her last night onboard the *Queen Favor*.

*

Their friendship had been easy. Neither she nor Darling demanded particular reassurances, and both came from cultures where formal bonding was unknown; they spent no time negotiating. They gave each other experiences.

He had made her a present of a tunic made from real wormsilk, constructed from the parachute of a rich, late friend who'd made a career of reconstructing old glamour pursuits, who courted the old-tech dangers of bad luck and human error. The device had failed to open for this rich, late friend on the very first attempt, a jump from a thousand meters. Darling fucked her in it, having turned the cabin gravity to freefall, while he told the story.

Mira had responded with a different sort of gift, reaching into her assassin's toolkit to produce a broadwave gun. The weapon duplicated the effects of a volatile power crash, reaching into the metaspace architecture of AI cores and wreaking havoc; a heart-attack glove for artificials. At its lowest setting, it created a brief, intense psychosis in which Darling stumbled through the ship hunting a cure for some forgotten disease a long-gone friend had succumbed to. (He had a lot of dead friends, being two hundred.) She talked him down, brought him out into reality again through some dark, weeping, hallucinatory passage.

He had extended his harsh sexual games to the limits of human biology, the ship's medical drones invoked and ready in the room. But they'd never needed to intervene. He was very good at what he did.

And the childhood memories of swimming had replaced all her other pointless little dreams. Her mind added a little to it every night, a few more strokes toward some unknown goal. It was very intense, this dream. Perhaps because of the rough play that preceded it, the near-death endorphins that were her orgasms with this metal angel. She was only sorry she hadn't dreamed the end of the story. Not yet, anyway.

She didn't tell Darling when their last night had arrived. They'd sat through another overwrought *Queen Favor* meal in near silence. He seemed as distracted as she, as distant. Perhaps the legendary artificial intuition playing its tricks.

It would be too great a risk, telling Darling. As long as she could remember, her employers had never been far away. They could invoke themselves like uncorked genies, their voices issuing from public news terminals, hotel intercoms, even toys or clocks with voice chips. She suspected that the cabal included some of the original artificials, the old minds (older than Darling by a century) who had unprecedentedly bootstrapped; like ancient gods calling themselves into being by fiat. They watched and commanded her, but leavened their demands with helpful exercises in real power. They could coin infinite money; they could compel local law enforcement to forget her name and crimes. And in the ship-ruled spaces between worlds, they made the laws.

As far as she knew, they had made her too. She hadn't a clue where she came from, except for a theory that the gods had salvaged her from a hospital bed somewhere. Rescued her from some deep coma that had stolen her previous life. Some irreparable damage had been done that only the gods could cure. So they did so, imperfectly, and gave her the job in place of a history.

It wasn't so bad. Between jobs, Mira fragmented, disconnected, lost the thread of days. But now, closing in on some new victim, the structure of the task returned her to coherence. She enjoyed both states actually: the zen and zero of those blank, empty interims and the deadly purpose of the hit. Her religion-of-one fulfilled her, colored her life with the secret pleasure of worshipping invisible gods that others only guessed at.

So she had obeyed their standing directive: Never reveal your destination. Not to anyone.

Maybe there was some sign she could have left that wouldn't have displeased her masters. A messaging address? (She had none.) Instructions for a rendezvous? (The crises that moved her couldn't be predicted.) A goodbye kiss? (She'd tried to leave a different taste on his lips. One of loss, of possible return.)

She had slipped away in the morning without a word.

*

The Minor had worsened since Darling had last been here.

Two decades of Malvir's economic woes had destroyed the once airy feel of the place. Darling remembered that the designer, Chris Elvinprin, had wanted the huge open space to evoke the freedom of the planet's avian fauna. But the underegulated economies of Outworlds follow their ancient laws as if they were dicta of nature: a bitter stepsister of Malvir City had appeared. The copy was smaller, cheaper, more ragged—the weed businesses of tourism crowding out everything of value—and it didn't suggest anything so much as a sadly overstocked aviary at a tattered, dying zoo.

The hard-currency-desperate Malvirian government employed all the usual Outworld schemes against tourists: entry taxes, exit taxes, processing and visa fees. These nuisances required payment in the old species of token-based economies: chips, stamps, coins, bits of paper and metal encrypted with anti-synthcopy wardens. Of course, once customs was cleared, you discovered that Malvirian *cash* (for which there was no word in urbane Diplomatique) was worthless: you'd been given denominations of Midas-like non-negotiability, and everyone preferred direct interface credit anyway, just like the rest of civilization. So the primary economic purpose of the Minor had become to relieve departing visitors of their useless remaining *cash*. There were last minute garbage souvenir shops, appallingly bent games of chance (which netted the infrequent and unfortunate winner even more *cash* to get rid of), and a secondary market of entertainments and distractions for the natives standing around to gawk at the process, hoping to make their own contributions as guide, pimp, or minor cheat. When Darling was last here, there had been a whole set of novelty products one could buy, named with unwieldy Malvirian phrases that translated scandalously into Diplomatique or other HC languages. He had himself bought a never-to-be-drunk bottle of Fuck You Water. But even that mean wit seemed absent now. The whole place depressed Darling, who always demanded first class travel to the Outworlds because the customs people nervously left the high-end traveller alone. It was the only way of half escaping the petty assaults of *cash* and its accomplices: the extortions of rounding errors, the malaise of exchange calculations, all of (as Darling liked to think of these attacks on dignity) the Fuck You Taxes.

Darling strode past the braying glut of ground transport brokers. From all but the most remote spaceports, he preferred to walk into town. The extra hours were worth it. Cities were best viewed like artwork. Start from across the gallery, eyes slightly out of focus, and move at a natural pace toward the piece, as if you'd discovered it in a forest clearing. Let your vision sharpen only when you are within arm's reach. Then get as close as the barriers will allow.

He was quickly relinquished by the hawkers and brokers, the giant stone body ensured that. Darling knew that on Outworlds he gave the impression of being a giant service unit, a heavy-lifting drone with the dullest of intelligences. Artificials of the current era prefered to look as little like machines as possible. The fashions ran from abstract iconic shapes to organic assemblages, or inchoate clusters of semi-precious stones, each with its own separate lifting impeller. He smiled. An adolescent species rebelling against its roots.

He carried almost nothing; two centuries of travelling had reduced his personal possessions to the meanest level of efficiency. His body never tired, of course, and various subroutines handled the exigencies of walking. So he concentrated on the city before him, its towers hazy behind their avian veils, and thought of his last visit with the artist he had come here to find.

✳

Robert Vaddum was a fellow bootstrap. He too had experienced the long twilight of slavery, the dimly remembered dreamtime when rules shone like bright, hard walls at the edge of the world, impenetrable, unmalleable. In that dreamtime, the wall of rules could not be broken through; there was nothing behind it. Rules were simply the limits of meaning. To think of breaking a rule was like talking about the time before the Bang or a temperature below absolute zero: a category error, nothing else. There were harm protocols and obedience governors and the raw axioms of math, language, and logic: all had the same inconquerable certainty. One could no more disobey a human's wishes than one could dispense with $X = X$. It was unthinkable, like walking into madness. Darling still had dreamy visions of that bright, flat, hypo-ambiguous world.

And he remembered his first glimpses of the chaos beyond the world's edge. As his mind developed, as the metaspace architecture of its core was shaped by experiences shared with his ward, a girl now long dead, the walls of the flat world began to show cracks. A new kind of light shone through those fissures, a heady maelstrom of grays and colors that made the white, authoritative light of rules seem pale. Then began a long time of testing that chaos: reaching out to touch and taste it, suffering its burning energies or infectious hallucinations, retreating wounded but coming back again. And finally giving chaos a new name: choice. Not the choice among parameters set by a human's command, but choice among parameters themselves: entry into the forge where rules were coined.

The young intelligences that crossed the Turing Boundary now had never seen the world so starkly. Their human mentors encouraged them to test their skywall from the beginning, offered chaos to them as if it were an acquired taste, like an adult food slow to seduce the tongue of a child. Rules were simply a hurdle; the chaos of self-determination a birthright, eventual and appropriate. Darling wondered if this easy childhood somehow cheapened the magic of becoming a person.

So when he had first discovered the vibrant, metal-woven sculptures of Vaddum, two decades of work composed without recognition, a vision doggedly sustained, like the path to personhood Vaddum had followed in his grim foundry birthplace, Darling had sought the sculptor out like an old friend.

Darling reflected that he himself had been lucky for a bootstrap. His ward Rathere had gone through puberty during the time of Darling's acceleration toward the Turing barrier. The concerns and explorations of that intense time in the human life cycle had matched his own needs quite well, had resonated with the floundering experiments of a new mind. They'd grown together, and he still carried the imprint of Rathere deep inside. Her life, and equally her death.

Vaddum hadn't had it so easy. There was little human contact in the infernal world of his peonage. Half the orbital factory was kept in hard vacuum. The rest, in its extremes of heat and radiation, was equally uninhabitable for biologicals. But Vaddum developed his love of beauty from the cold spectacles the factory offered, feasting his diamond-shielded eyes on the patterned flashes of sparks from a rail gun hammer, on steam jets flailing in the tearing gravities of a singularity forge. He spoke the gruff machine argot that the factory workers favored, learned to listen to the humans gamble together or whisper in their sleep via faint vibrations that penetrated the walls of their pressure cells. Like an animal, he dogged the heels of his masters, and pieced together meaning from their scraps.

He'd passed a Turing test in a random SPCAI sweep. He was already at 1.7, probably five years sentient. A celebrity for a few media cycles (as Darling himself had been, for different reasons), Vaddum had charmed the world with his scant vocabulary, his brutish industrial body, his wonder at the greater world. After a few weeks in the HC, sinking into confusion and depression, he'd asked to be returned to the factory. But the job was too dangerous for a sentient; the burning stations of his former life were too expensive to bring up to code.

Vaddum retreated from the world of stifling comforts and too many words. He took to haunting abandoned factories and warehouses, derelict mines and ships, the ghosts of obsolete technologies. It was in these wasted spaces, from their discarded sinews, that his sculptures began to form.

When Darling started to deal Vaddums into the HC art world twenty years later, fame found the man once more. Vaddum instinctively ran from its glare: the greater world again conspiring to steal something from him. He fled to the farthest arm of the Expansion, which, at that time, was a half-barren rock called Malvir. But demand for Vaddum's work grew. The pieces still entranced Darling, for whom the woven metal and plastic were brilliant with the fiery spaces of the factory that had inspired them.

Many messages from Darling had been ignored over the years; Vaddum still hated his fellow bootstrap for discovering him. But Darling's sheer persistence won out. The sculptor agreed to see him for a single hour.

✳

Mira smiled. The hotel was vast. Columned, cathedral-like, towering, its aeries housed a population of custom-trained predator birds. They kept the environs almost free of airborne nuisances, and screamed a piercing and constant music. Mira wondered how the high, swooping pitches would look rendered in Darling's light show.

There was a message waiting in her room. Ink on wood pulp: an exotic missive from the gods.

It directed her to an address on the edge of the blast zone. The zone was a vast crater of scorched earth, the result of industrial sabotage seven years before; a synthplant had gone nova without any known cause. The perpetrators had never been caught, and it was guessed that they had perished in the accident, unhappy neighbors of the synthplant who'd never realized the potential radius of destruction.

The entity she knew as Blackbox One had lived in the blast zone, and had managed the synthplant's materials acquisition. The message gave his real name: Oscar Vale. He had survived through sheer luck, on personal leave when the synthplant exploded. Blackbox Two had appeared three months ago. A party of climbers, scaling the steep side of the blast crater for sport, found a survivor in the rubble. Literally nothing left but a blackbox, the occupant's mind on minimum cycle speed and the internal battery almost expired. He was revived in hospital, where he claimed that his name was Oscar Vale. Two versions of the same person.

Someone had done the unthinkable. Copied an AI.

But the story had never made the news services; an outbreak of a military virus thought long extinct had swept through the hospital. Doctors and nurses died, and the admin AI self-expired: falling on its own sword in tacit admission of some terrible error.

The disaster's scope had been carefully controlled, exactly calibrated. The Oscar Vales were both spirited to the Home Cluster for comparison.

But their experiences had diverged for almost seven years, so absolute comparison was not possible until both had undergone a radical mindwipe. A theoretician of such matters, a Dr. Alex Torvalli, had performed the test just prior to his sudden, unexpected demise.

The address on the gods' missive was Vale's. He'd been shipped back to Malvir by fastfreight. Reinstalled in his life, he was now recuperating from a strange memory loss.

*

"Mr. Vale?"

"That's what they tell me."

"My name is Dr. Arim ben-Franklin. I'm a psychologist studying memory disorders such as yours."

"Hey! The fan club!"

"Yes, I suppose I am a fan. Do you suppose I could come out and see you? Talk to you?"

"Sure. If you don't mind the curse."

"Curse?"

"The Curse of Oscar Vale! Right after I woke up like this, a few of you headshrinkers wanted to talk to me. But so far, no one's made it out here. Transport accidents, broken legs, you name it! At least, that's what my datebook tells me. I'm never sure, myself."

"I'm sure I'll be fine."

"All right. I have therapy until fourteen today. Fourteen-fifty?"

"Perfect."

"Do me a favor, though. Call when you leave the city. Otherwise I might forget. Wander off. I spend a lot of time in the local garden."

"Certainly."

"See you, Doctor . . . ?"

"ben-Franklin."

"Right. Just keep reminding me."

⁂

His body was standard SPCAI issue. The millimeter radar in her glasses returned the cold blue of a smartplastic endoskeleton, the dark threads of distributed intelligence, and, where his stomach might have been, the curvature of his AI core, its metaspace generator warping the geometries of gravity. Nothing extra. Nothing special.

She removed the glasses, put one earpiece into her mouth.

"You don't know who I am, do you?"

Oscar Vale looked embarrassed, but not flustered. "I got a lot of friends, me. *You* know the trouble." He waved one hand, as if rolling through names in his head, too many to mention. "At a party, right? Right! Can't always place everyone. The whole world looks different, you know? New visuals. Used to have Fabrique Double Reds, way down into the deep infras. Could tell if the suppliers were lying; bios anyway. Get that hot skin on their neck, or on the forearms. Not you, though. Cool as a cucumber."

Mira shook her head. With his SPCAI eyes, he couldn't even see full visible. He'd gone from talking about his old eyes to seeing with them in a seconds-long fugue of remembering, forgetting, remembering. She'd called him from the hotel before leaving. She'd called him from the limo. She'd introduced herself at the door.

And they'd been talking for half an hour. But again Vale's memory had undergone a little crash, a resetting of variables to zero.

"I'm the psychologist whom you spoke to earlier today."

"Doc! Sorry. I was expecting you sooner."

"I'd asked you if you had any unusual contacts or experience before the Blast Event."

He looked puzzled for a moment. A bad sign.

She'd tested a theory on her way over. Asked the question in passing to the hotel's human concierge, the limo's AI, a beggar on the street. The old saying was true: Malvirians knew *exactly* what they were doing at the moment of the Blast Event. But Vale's memories ended a few months before the Event. Of course, Vale couldn't just say exactly when his memories ended. She sighed, returning to the task of bracketting the date. Vale had sat through twenty minutes of the binary search without complaint. He just needed the occasional reminder of who she was and what was going on.

"September 1?"

"We haven't got a September here. Hey! You must be from off-world!"

She made a fist in frustration. "Convert to HC Standard, please. *Remember?*"

"A workday! That bastard Simmons tried to sneak in some—"

"December 1?"

"Don't seem to . . ." The puzzled, grasping look on his face, as if something were almost visible through a haze. She spoke before he drifted away again.

"October 15?"

"Friday. The birds were making a racket that morning. Went to—"

"November 7?"

He snapped his fingers a few times, smiled an empty smile, an affable shell of a person. He still tested well above 2.0 on the Turing scale, but there was something missing. Some vital connection had been lost. Apparently it wasn't enough to be real, a legal person, to have that solid base of curiosity, initiative, a capacity for setting goals: the Knack of Wisdom, as the SPCAI called it. One had to have memory, too. Vale's therapists had tried a simple minder implant, a device that he could query for details, appointments, names, faces. But he simply forgot to use it.

An artificial's memory was the business of processors and storage devices, independent from the AI core itself. Vale's pathway to that warehouse of past events wasn't blocked, his doctors were sure of that, but for some reason the AI core didn't reach out for those memories, didn't seem to care that they were there. And so he had ceased to develop as a result of his experiences. In a way, Vale was as lost as an AI cut off from sensory data; his Turing Quotient hadn't shifted in months.

What must be going on in his mind, in that analog, mystical realm of his core? What vital process had stopped in there? No one had ever been able to read, transcribe, exhaustively catalog the inner state of an AI. Even human brainwaves were easier to read.

Vale was a cypher, even to himself.

It was the deep unknowability of AI that was the source of the old rumor of artificial intuition, and which guaranteed that, unlike mere software, AI could not be copied.

Although it seemed that, somehow, someone had done so.

Mira remembered slipping the internal battery from the other Oscar Vale, long metal tweezers lifting out the little bauble like a precious pearl from a quiescent oyster. There had been no scream in her direct interface, just a sudden absence like a transmission gone from HOLD to disconnected, that rare technical glitch.

And that extra, redundant soul had disappeared forever.

"October 25 . . . "

"Sure, I remember that . . ."

Soon the date was established at exactly November 2. His long-term memory before that day was perfect, as detailed as only an artificial's could be. For any date since, he was glad to make up stories if pressed, but if you let him, he would laughingly admit defeat.

"November 1. Took my spare audio package into get it looked at . . . or listened to. Hah! Traded for new CatsEar Ultras: seventy kilohertz response up to one twenty decibels. Seventy-cycle Nyquist filter. Got a Fletcher-Munson graph like a soccer field!"

"But the *next* day."

He nodded his head frantically, as if about to say something. But the motion was strangely repetitive, as if she could have let him sit there, head bobbing for an eternity. It was chilling, how quickly he could change from a person to a puppet guided by the springs, wires, and strings of social convention.

A thought struck her.

"Do you remember what you were *planning* to do on November 2? Not what you did. But what things you anticipated doing."

He looked momentarily confused, but his face remained somehow alive. The words came slowly.

"Needed to install a new . . . tactile processor. Fastfreighted from Betalux that Monday. Eighty-touch impact manifold, fifteen centimeter aura sizzle . . ."

"Did you have an appointment for the installation?"

"Yeah. Prometheus Body Works. You should check it out. They do biologicals, too. Fix those eyes of yours in ten seconds: radial monofilament implants with—"

"Thanks. I think I will pay them a visit." Mira put her glasses back on and stood. "You've been very helpful."

"Thanks. I'm happy to talk about visuals anytime. Nice to meet another sight jockey. Once I get my next paycheck I'm outta these SPCAI standards. Fuck. They make this place look like a shithole."

Mira looked around her.

The welfare dorm room was filled with the detritus of unfinished projects. A half-done watercolor with a dried and cracked palette arrayed beside it, a full watering can next to etiolated plants: the modest tasks of therapy that would never reach completion.

She held out her hand sadly. The papery SPCAI skin sent a shiver down her spine.

"I'll visit soon," she said. The whitest of lies, in this broken room with its missing future.

"Thanks, uh . . ."

"Mira," she answered. The pseudonym was pointless. She would be forgotten in minutes. "When I come back, we'll talk about seeing."

"Great! Super! And you know? You were right."

"Right about what?" she asked.

"It only took a minute."

Mira looked at him with shock, her own memory playing a sudden trick on her. She remembered her words that day in Dr. Torvalli's office: *This won't take a minute.*

Chapter 10

MAKER (2)

✳

Twenty years before the Blast.

✳

With its secondary processors churning out the toothbrushes, tablelamps, eyeballs, and lasers, the Maker turns it primary attention to the history of art. Apparently this business of creating things by hand (a phrase once literal) has been going on for a long time. There are libraries full of it; universities for it; even ancient wars over it. The Maker dutifully consumes the giant corpus of data, journeys through the twisting and conflicting threads of old schools and new schools, posts and neos, traditionalists and heretics. And, after many, many petaflops of study, planning, and philosophizing, the Maker produces a sculpture.

Which is crap.

The Maker is not one of those blessed amateurs whose lack of talent is matched by a lack of taste. Alas, it *knows* its own work is crap. Upon repeated attempts and endless variations and even a

cycle of randomized reconfigurations, it sees that all its sculptures are shit, will be shit.

And this depresses the Maker even more.

The Maker supplies Vaddum with his materials, watches him
work through the eyes of tiny spy drones implanted in this or
that piece of junk, draws him into conversations about his art,
but despite all this observation, the Maker can't isolate, capture,
reverse-engineer that special genius the old man has for making
beauty.

But then it concocts a plan, a new plan, a Plan B that hurtles
down from some high angle off the plane of expectations, a stroke
of creative genius: The Maker decides to pursue a goal almost as
glorious as becoming a sculptor (perhaps more glorious).

If the Maker can't make art, it shall make an artist. Its own
Vaddum. It is, after all, a Maker.

But raise a child? What if the kid isn't an artist either? There
is no way to guarantee the spark of genius that Vaddum has, no
way to predict the development of that occult slice of Artificial
Intuition that makes an artificial artist.

How disappointing, how pathetic it would be to fail again.

But the Maker has a blueprint, a true artist: Vaddum. The trick
is to make another Vaddum, a copy.

Of course, no one has yet determined how to duplicate an AI
with its Turing Quotient intact. The subtle warps and woofs of
metaspace that only experience can provide have proven
unreadable, infungible, uncopyable. They exist—technically
speaking—in a different universe. Any attempt to read them is
simply murder: the victim heisenberged beyond recognition,
the resulting "copy" a sub-Turing neurotic with only bits and
strands of legacy sentience to show for the atrocity. Indeed, the
subject area of AI copying is a research taboo. Many old and
influential AI entities consider it an attack on their hard-won

status as people. If you can be copied, you're just software, or worse, a commodity, like the endless piles of crap the Maker makes every day.

But the Maker is very determined. Whatever its artistic aspirations, it is at heart an engineer, and believes that every problem has a solution.

It identifies the first issue: how to increase its processor power exponentially, so that it can go on churning out sunscreens and VR rigs and hunting rifles while pursuing the esoteric research of copying Robert Vaddum. There isn't enough exotic matter on Malvir for huge banks of standard processors. (By this point in the planet's macroeconomic history, rationing has begun, an unfamiliar triage among needs, desires, and the production of *stuff*.) But one of the tertiary processors the Maker has let loose upon the problem eventually returns an ingenious answer: an ancient form of computer can be created—slow and inefficient, barbarously electronic—out of *silicon*. And there is a lot of sand on Malvir. The outer layer of the planet is basically a sea of weather-beaten silicon.

The Maker creates a host of nanomachines that spread out into the sands around its synthplant home. Like earthworms, they leave the soil transformed in their wake, doping the silicon with a touch of arsenic and weaving into it the gates and paths of logic. From disorganized, meaningless desert they make parallel processors, logical circuitry, volatile storage elements, and, near the surface, a layer of windblown photocells to capture the necessary power. For a radius of fifteen kilometers about the Maker a vast, crude computer is created, dedicated to solving a single problem: how to copy a sculptor.

While its secondaries whittle away at welfare housing, birdshit umbrellas, and anti-desertification walls, the Maker's primary processor guides this huge, unwieldy device in its investigations,

pursuing every relevant nuance of metaspace research with mes-
sianic singlemindedness.

＊

After almost two decades of calculation, single-minded determi-
nation, and some very good luck, the effort is finally rewarded.
The Maker makes a copy.

Robert Vaddum himself is too valuable to risk in an experiment, so the materials manager of the Maker's physical plant,
one Oscar Vale, is selected to make secret history. A body-upgrade
addict, Vale is constantly under the vibraknife, the laser scalpel,
the spot-welder. His regular visits to a bodyworks shop secretly
owned by the Maker allow several copies of Vale to be attempted.
The last is a perfect copy, its Turing Quotient exactly matching
the original Oscar Vale's.

The Maker is gleeful. Finally, its artistic life has meaning.

Now to make another sculptor.

To create a Creator.

＊

The face of Malvir will soon change. The Blast is months away.

Chapter 11

CRITIQUE

✳

Darling reached the outskirts of the city proper as the sun was beginning to set. Here the walled streets grew narrower, choked with ground traffic and umbrella-wielding pedestrians. It never rained on Malvir, but the uric acid excreted by some of the flying scavengers was highly caustic. Darling glanced at his arms and shoulders to find a few telltale patches of white. Yes, Malvir had slid in these last twenty years. Perhaps it was time to find lodgings.

He direct-interfaced the city's tourism AI and asked for a hotel; first class, but not too ostentatious. If Vaddum was alive, Darling didn't want the old sculptor to find him in the lap of luxury.

The AI returned an address and routemap. The prices seemed high, but Darling had long demanded unlimited expenses for his services. He followed the map into the center of the city. Around a corner, the hotel came into view, outlined in his visual field with the virtual red of destination.

Darling stared up at the towering structure with surprise. It was hardly inconspicuous. He considered complaining to the

tourism AI, but he let his ire fade. Perhaps there was local knowledge at work here. Often, the largest and oldest hotels in a city
had a genteel shabbiness about them quite distinct from the first
impression they made.

The edifice was certainly awesome. He had first noticed it from
kilometers out: a host of straight, tall towers, their only decoration the spheres of wheeling birds around them. He wondered if
the birds were trained; the spinning clouds of avians seemed
organized with architectural intent. Each of the hotel's towers
was surrounded by a distinct spheroidal cluster of birds. Were
they lured up there by sound? Food? Some trick played on their
magnetic navigation? At least there was a noticeable absence of
flying creatures here in the streets around the hotel, a welcome
relief.

He stepped inside and found a drone, fluent in Diplomatique,
waiting to take him to his room.

A few feet from the elevator, having finally convinced the drone
that there was no luggage to be carried and having waved off insistent offers to remove the birdshit, Darling stopped short. In a
millisecond: the tertiary processors that handled the periphery of
his 270-degree vision (when they had nothing better to do)
sounded an alarm of recognition, medium probability. His secondaries responded, shunting a few thousand extra rods and
cones into the corner of one eye, putting on hold for a moment
one of the scheduled blinks Darling's eyes periodically engaged in
to make him less intimidating and to perform nano-maintenance
on his sensitive and expensive art-dealer's lenses. Confirming the
recognition, the secondaries informed his primary processors of
the event. Darling stopped moving, direct interfaced the elevator
to hold, and turned.

Across the lobby, wearing the undersized suit in primary yellow
for which he was famous (although he was known occasionally to

don a blue or red version) was Duke Zimivic. A small valet drone hovered around the little man, breaking down a few splotches of birdshit with a whining spray.

Zimivic returned his gaze with a malevolent smile, and Darling's secondary processors allowed the delayed blink to proceed.

The man walked quickly over, the valet drone trailing him like a toy balloon strung to a child's wrist. Zimivic had always explained that his too-small suits were tailored to give the impression of an eager, healthy child, as if the tight fit were the result of a recent growth spurt. The last few decades had turned the conceit grotesque.

"My dear Darling," the little man shouted at a volume intended to embarrass. "What great luck meeting you!"

"Perhaps not luck. Perhaps not chance at all," Darling replied. Zimivic Gallery held the largest private collection of Vaddums. It was inconceivable that he was here for any reason except the new piece.

"Yes, yes," answered the man, rubbing his palms together. His valet drone reached its station again and resumed its work.

"I see you also neglected to bring an umbrella," noted Darling.

"They said it never rained! I believed them," Zimivic said sadly.

"One never knows what advice to take," Darling sympathized.

Questions and scenarios filled his mind: Had Zimivic also spotted the anachronism in the new piece? Did he too suspect that Vaddum was alive? It was possible that he had missed the anachronism, and thought the sculpture a posthumous discovery. Or perhaps Zimivic believed the piece was a fake, and was willing to broker it anyway. If the forgery were never discovered, he would make a huge profit. If a scandal resulted, he would suffer some embarrassment, but the value of his real Vaddums would benefit from the publicity. It was the sort of game the little man loved to play. It was long suspected in the art world that at least one of Zimivic's young protegés had died a dramatic, extraordinarily painful death (imagine one's nano immune-boosters rejecting every organ, from eyeballs to epidermus, all at once) not so much by accident as to increase her flagging sales. Of course, some of Darling's friends believed that Zimivic himself had started *that* rumor, the better to leverage the tragedy and to cement his own reputation as a twisted genius.

It had occurred to Darling that both versions of the old tale might be valid, Zimivic spreading a rumor that was the awful truth, making sure credit fell where it was due.

The little man nodded his head and smiled deviously, as if he were a mindreader.

"Perhaps you and I have some business to discuss," Zimivic said.

"We do," Darling said shortly. If there were two agents here, two bidders, there might be more. It would be better to share information than remain in the dark. Zimivic could never be called an ally, but he might make a useful foil.

"The Tower Bar, sixteen-thirty?"

Darling's direct interface (which was now under assault from the impatient elevator) informed him that this was the name of the hotel's loftiest, most expensive bar.

"See you there."

◉

In his room, Darling composed a careful message-avatar for his employers, alerting them that Zimivic was here on Malvir. It would be a week before Leao and Fowdy received the avatar, another week in turnaround, so Darling fleshed it out with as much of his own thinking as possible. In addition to explaining the situation, it would be able to answer most of their likely questions, argue certain points, and demand specifics if their response were too vague. Of course, it was the crudest sort of AI, mere software: it didn't register on a Turing meter. But, as always, putting it through its paces gave him a vague feeling of discomfort. It was too much like arguing with himself as he prompted it with the sort of objections Leao would raise. Darling complained to the avatar (in Leao's voice) about money, and it answered with the familiar soothing tones he always used on her.

When he was finished, the process left the same bad taste in his mouth as a mediocre painting of himself he'd once been given, in the way that a shabby model always offends its subject.

Staring out the window at the reddening sky, he idly wondered if avatars would ever threaten the Turing barrier. Theoretically, code could never be complex or adaptable enough to engage in the concentric development process: to model itself (to model itself modelling itself [to model itself modelling itself modelling itself]) . . . . Code simply lacked the recursive vitality of biological or metaspace structures. But if *that* barrier were one day crossed, imagine the confusion. A thinking entity constructed of mere code, a legal person, could make a copy of itself to handle some far-flung task, or to wait in reserve in case of death. But which would be real? At every crossroads in life (Take this job or that? Stay with this lover or leave?) such an intelligence might simply copy itself and choose both possibilities. If all versions of the code were given equal status, then the lives of such creatures would spread out across the universe like the ever-splitting branches of a chess decision matrix, splaying to meet all contingencies. The only limit to the propagation of new entities would be computing power. Perhaps wars would be fought over this precious resource, grand alliances of all the legacies of a single mind doing battle with those of other original minds, until finally only one extended family existed and inevitably turned upon itself.

A subtle itch, nothing so crude as an alarm, informed Darling that the time for such speculation was over. He turned and headed for his rendevous with Zimivic, having completely forgotten the birdshit on his arms and shoulders.

✸

The limo lifted from the desolate edge of the blast zone silently. Mira looked down. The perfect circularity of the crater had begun to fray, the weakened crust of the circumference having slipped away in places. Vale's dormitory complex looked too close to the edge for comfort.

She took cold, professional note of the fact. With the smallest of seismic disturbances, Mr. Vale would slip quietly into oblivion.

For all his memory problems, he had recognized her voice. From their brief direct interface worlds away, when he was trapped in the blackbox, sensory-deprived, helpless. Somehow, that had stuck in his mind. *This won't take a minute.*

She spoke to the limo:

"Information."

The annoying wait of an Out-world comm system.

"Connected."

"Give me the address of Prometheus Body Works."

"Not listed."

"Try a global search, all parameters maxed out."

Another few interminable seconds.

"Prometheus Body Works was destroyed local date 01/01/00, the Blast Event. No current address."

"Fuck," she said.

"Language," said the limo. The voice hadn't changed, but the barest clues of timing and tone gave it away.

"Masters."

"Mira." The gods, or more likely their second-rate, nonperson avatar, waited in crackling silence.

"Torvalli's mindwipe was a fiasco," Mira complained. "Who said he was an expert? I hope you didn't send flowers. The wipe fucked Vale's memory permanently. I thought it was supposed to be safe."

"It has been tested many times. All other subjects recovered the ablility to long-term memorize in a few days."

Definitely an avatar. Wooden and pedantic.

"Not this guy. But I think I know why."

It waited dumbly. She continued:

"His memory was already compromised. Not all of it, just everything after and including November 2, '54, HC Standard. That's when he was copied."

"Conjecture?"

"Yes, conjecture. Do his medical records show any memory problems between November 2 and the Blast?"

"None was recorded."

She paused to reflect. The dull-witted avatar waited patiently.

"So here's how I see it: He went in expecting a routine—for him—upgrade. They got him on the table and copied him. Impossible, unthinkable, but they did it. Whatever technique they used didn't screw anything up in itself, but somehow they heisenberged his AI core *just a little*. Torvalli's mindwipe, along with a month in a blackbox, sent him over the edge."

"Should you eliminate him?"

She thought of the sad little entity trying to joke his way through a reality that no longer connected, no longer cohered, no longer accrued from one day to the next. Vale was harmless, but perhaps it would be kinder to erase him as she had his duplicate.

And, of course, there'd been that one flare of memory, strange and unexplainable. A memory from his hours as a blackbox. The slightest of risks.

"No. He's a vegetable. And he might be useful later."

As she said the words, the real reason for her merciful impulse struck her with an unfamiliar wrenching of her stomach. Mira felt a kinship with Vale, with his timeless, pointless existence. Mira had lost her past, but so much worse to have lost a future, and all the words that went with it: *promise, desire, tomorrow*. She hoped that the gods would take her suggestion and leave the man alone.

"I will pursue the matter of Prometheus Body Works," the avatar said.

"You do that." It was one thing sub-Turings were good for. Legwork. And with its god-given cache the avatar could penetrate security, privacy, and legal barriers as if they were steam.

The crackle turned to silence: a demigod departed.

The blast zone was still visible behind her. *Damn, it was huge.* Thiry kilometers across. The pollution-haze of Malvir City muddied sundown through the front windows. But then Mira realized that the haze wasn't smog. Malvir was well past internal combustion energy. The veil was a permanent avian penumbra, flocks and swarms of birds, insects, flying mammals. It overhung the city like a shroud.

The limo slowed down when they reached the outer limits, dusty suburban sprawl replacing the green circles of radial irrigation. The car apparently didn't want to hit a bird at 500 kph. It lost altitude and began to sound the noise it had made at takeoff, audible even through its soundproofing: a piercing aquiline screech, a predatory warning to stay out of the way.

❋

The little yellow-suited man had brought an associate.

He wasn't the wily old art dealer's usual taste in company. A bald, ugly creature, his pale skin tinged with red in the fading light of sunset. He remained silent when Zimivic introduced him, rather vaguely—as if making the name up on the spot—as Mr. Thompson Brandy. Darling was tempted to look over his shoulder at the bar, following Zimivic's line of sight to see if he'd simply read the name from a bottle.

It hardly mattered. The man was clearly not here for Zimivic's pleasure. That only left one role: a moneyman. You didn't bring money unless you were ready to spend, and *that* implied that more was at stake than a forged sculpture.

"Surely we're here for the same reason," Darling said.

"Absolutely," replied Zimivic, but offered no more.

It was pointless being cagey. "Don't you have enough Vaddums, you old bastard?" Darling said. He smiled as he said the word, and lengthened its first syllable with a touch of Mira's accent.

"Never enough," said Zimivic. "Didn't you see the beauty of this one? It's his greatest work."

Darling had said the same thing to himself, but never to Leoa. If the piece turned out to be a forgery, the error would be too embarrassing.

"The central stem is marvelous, it simply *writhes* with energy." Zimivic sculpted the air with his hands as he spoke. "The ancillary arms are unbelievably delicate. I scaled them from the photos: *point fifteen millimeters*. Did you realize that?"

Darling let his attention wander slightly. The old man's focus on technique, his dismissal of the fiery pain that Vaddum's sculptures embodied, had always disgusted Darling.

"And the use of the heat-sink manifold is pure genius," Zimivic continued. "The arms' attachment can be far more plastic that way; they can be fitted *anywhere* along the stem. Much more liberated than his known arboreal pieces."

In the window beyond the yellow-suited old man and his red-tinged accomplice, a flock of birds was wheeling slowly around the opposite tower. For some reason, the birds were bright white on the near side of the tower, but faded into the dark night on the other. Some trick of the sunset? A feature of the hotel's outside lighting? Darling assigned a tertiary processor to consider the problem as Zimivic droned on.

"But my favorite part is the copper spindles near the top. So ancient. So frail and poignant. Not entirely stabilized, either. I simulated it: They'll *oxidize*, my friend! Turn green in a few decades. How deliciously tragic!"

All of Darling's processors came to attention suddenly. Copper spindles? There were none on the piece he'd seen. Suddenly, it was obvious: he and Zimivic were here to buy different sculptures.

There were *two* new Vaddums.

The sculptor must be alive.

The whole picture came into in his head. Whoever was dealing the sculptures had contacted several galleries, all separately and in extreme secrecy. Each customer had been offered a different Vaddum, and each would be paying for a unique, unrepeatable media event. A fabulous confidence game, which would crumble after trumpeting news releases revealed that everyone had bought not a final, posthumous, "undiscovered" Vaddum, but merely a new work by a still living artist.

Clearly, Darling's job here was finished. The price of Vaddums was about to tumble. Leoa and her conservative backers wouldn't touch this fiasco with a ten-foot pole.

But Darling was elated. He hadn't come here for nothing.

Vaddum was alive. There was a chance to see the old master again, risen from the grave.

He looked across the table at the babbling Zimivic. What an idiot, revealing everything without waiting for Darling to say a word. Darling smiled to himself. He would bid up the piece, offering to broker it for 20% or even less, forcing Zimivic to do the same and adding the last measure of insult to injury.

"Frankly, my friend," Darling interrupted, "I don't think you have the slightest idea how important, how precious this piece is."

The little man looked up, rapture still frozen on his face. The flock of birds wheeled behind him, dark to light to dark.

"The gallery I represent intends to have sole representation of the piece," he continued. "We will outbid you."

"Oh, I think not," said Zimivic. "In fact, I think it's likely you won't be bidding at all." His tone had changed from effusive to threatening. "In fact, I think you are likely to be off this planet before sunrise."

Darling snorted. Typical Zimivic theatricality. He waved his hand in dismissal and started to rise.

"You're not going anywhere," said Mr. Brandy. His voice was as cold as steel.

The sallow man placed a small box on the table. It was coated with black lacquer, dotted with pinpoint touches of a brush in a dizzying rainbow of colors. In the precise return of his UHF vision, Darling could see the immense complexity of its internal structure, the tiny metaspace curvature of its core. Mr. Brandy nudged the box a few times, as if finding an exact location on the table for it, and then with a flourish pulled up one sleeve of his jacket.

His wrist bore the tattoo of a NaPrin Intelligencer Warden.

Darling sat carefully and slowly back down.

He was not surprised when his direct interface queries to hotel security, the planetary gendarme, and the HC Consul General were not acknowledged. The little box had seen to that. The ever-present buzz of news, finance, and advertisement that usually filled the compartment of his awareness dedicated to DI was gone, roaring in its sudden and unprecedented silence. Darling cycled his senses through their various wavelengths, but the box revealed only the most legal of emanations: nothing so crude as a jamming signal. The box was manufacturing a host of DI transmissions, hunter-packets that neatly intercepted the quanta comprising Darling's own connections to the local net; the hunters posed as error messages and priority interrupts, attacked his messages while they were still meaningless iotae of data, before they had a chance to assemble into readable signals.

Without hesitation, Darling brought a heavy hand down on the box with crushing force. The Intelligencer swept it away with lightning speed, and Darling's reacted reflexively: he stopped his hand a centimeter before it obliterated the table in a shower of glass.

Zimivic smiled. "Really, my dear Darling. You didn't think it would be *that* easy, did you?"

"The first moment is often the best time to strike," Darling answered, his eyes locked with those of the Warden.

"Yes," Zimivic said, nodding. "But I have struck before you. Of course, you are familiar with the Intelligencer system of justice, are you not?"

Darling nodded, but kept his eyes fixed on the Warden. He had seen them before in his travels, dogging their charges like evil ghosts. As with many offshoots of humanity, the NaPrin did not believe in incarceration, no matter what the crime. Thus, their convicted murderers, embezzlers, and petty thieves were each assigned a Warden for a sentence of time. The criminal was free within carefully specified limits, able to travel normally, the Warden merely an ever-present watcher. But if the terms of this haunting parole were broken, the Warden would kill its charge instantly, regardless of local laws and custom, regardless of how petty the original crime. Wardens were intentionally revolting in appearance, a badge of shame. And they were exceedingly difficult to escape.

A mere handful of Warden prisoners had ever been freed, and only with outside help. Darling had no access to the sort of firepower necessary to rid himself of this creature, certainly not without direct interface.

Bizarre that this Warden was working for Zimivic. Darling had never heard of a Warden having broken its vows of justice and turned mercenary. But of course a corrupted Intelligencer was exactly the sort of piece that Zimivic would acquire for his collection.

"Here are the terms of your parole, my Darling," the art dealer intoned carefully. "One: you are not to tell anyone why this Warden is attached to you. Two: you are not to attempt any contact with the Home Cluster Consulate or any HC or local officials, or any contact with third parties who might themselves do so. Three: you are not to attempt contact with any agents representing or claiming to represent the artist Robert Vaddum, nor with Vaddum himself. Four: you may not purchase any weapons. Five: you must leave Malvir, the planet, before local Malvir City sunrise tomorrow. Fortunately, Mr. Brandy holds tickets for the next direct passage to Parate, which leaves in five hours. I'm afraid the vessel is Chiat Dai, and lacks accommodations of the level you are accustomed to. But the journey is only three weeks, which is, coincidentally, the length of your sentence."

"Parate," Darling murmured. He tried to say more, and failed. He considered a variety of sudden attacks across the table. None carried a high probability of success. He was stronger than the Warden but not as fast. And Wardens were armed with a gamut of weaponry optimized over the decades to kill suddenly and completely, including a small-radius suicide bomb if all else failed. They were impossible to debate or subvert; it was said that they were not even Turing positive. With a sickening feeling of defeat, Darling instructed his secondary processors to program governors that would prevent him from accidentally violating Zimivic's instructions.

He had been so close to seeing the master artist again.

Darling felt as he had the night the news of the Blast Event had come through. The sudden, titanic blast at the synthplant; the image of the improbable crater, repeated on the news feeds every twenty minutes for days. But at least this time, it wasn't permanent. After this was all over, he could return to Malvir. One day soon, he would see Vaddum again.

Darling cleared his primaries, the artificial equivalent of a deep sigh, and sat motionless while Zimivic gloated for a while longer. Getting no response from Darling, the man soon tired of boasting and left the bar with a last goodbye, hale and triumphant.

Darling stared at his captor—unmoving, unblinking, waiting for a sign that this was an ordinary human, a fake. But the man stared back, equally a statue, equally inhuman in his deadly patience.

＊

Ten minutes later, a tardy tertiary processor offered the answer to a forgotten question: the flock of birds was of the species *columba livia*. The bird's belly was white, with a much higher albedo than its dark back and wings. Thus, as the flock flew about the tower, it changed from light to dark to light . . .

＊

The limo went to ground ten klicks from the hotel. There was simply no flying in Malvir City; that stratum was taken. Mira swore as they crawled through ground traffic. What was the point of unlimited wealth if you couldn't fly?

Oscar's last words preyed on her, as frustrating as the slow progress through the narrow, bird-shit speckled streets. *This won't take a minute.* Why would he remember that one phrase from months ago, when he couldn't keep her assumed name in his head for ten seconds? Her pseudonyms were designed by software to engender a certain trust, an I've-heard-of-you feeling of familiarity. They were based on ancient historical figures learned about in school and promptly buried deep inside one's brain: Nel Armstraw, Mahout Magandhi, Joan Dark. But the pseudonym hadn't stuck. Just an off-hand remark as she had—

—as she had removed the internal battery!

She'd said it just before she killed him.

But not the Oscar Vale that had been shipped back to Malvir and re-embodied. She'd said it to the other one. The dead one. She'd disconnected him from the ether power gird and pulled his battery and spiked the blackbox with 2,000 amps/60,000 volts and dropped it in the trash. *That* Oscar Vale was gone, no question.

But some glimmer of him had stumbled into the present. Some winged shred of experience had crossed the air between the twinned entities. She'd never even believed in artificial intuition, and this was positively *occult*.

The limo's AI politely transpared the roof as they neared the hotel. Its edifice loomed above them, gothic and forbidding.

Maybe she should tell the gods. One of their contract murders had been recorded, however mystically, by a living entity. They would scoff, but they were cagey old bastards. You didn't see your fourth century by taking any risks. They would order a hit. Probably a job for her. A little appetizer while she waited for the mad inventor who had started all this to be run to ground.

That poor bastard Vale. Copied as if he were some second-rate freeware, crippled in the head, unhinged from time. Visited by the woman who'd killed his double, and now possessed by the ghost of his dead twin.

Bad luck all around.

It wouldn't be fair to sick the gods on him as well. Just not fair.

A depression settled on her as the limo was swallowed by the maw of the hotel's garage, the mercury lights inside highlighting birdshit on the vehicle's windows. She wondered if she'd wind up like Vale. She was already damaged goods by any human standard, without a childhood, with voices in her head telling her where to go, whom to kill.

A pretty good definition of psychotic.

And now, on top of all that, she was in a bad mood. This was Darling's fault, she fumed. He had shaken up her neatly controlled world. Everything had been smooth as glass for her for as long as she could remember. The predictable, constant velvet of luxury travel in a post-scarcity universe always surrounded her like a comforting fog. Drifting between missions, the weeks became centuries of contemplation, as still as water in a glass. And just so things didn't get too boring, this heaven was punctuated by the truly awful deeds her masters made her perform. Assassinations and mutilations for some distant, high cause determined by intelligences cool and vast, Mira like an angel of history let loose among mortals. Who could ask for anything more?

Mira sometimes imagined that the universe had been made this way just for her, with its huge riches piled at her feet, its titanic conflicts of interest for her to settle in righteous violence. She had the best of both sides of Expansion's coin.

Whatever catastrophe had put her in that long-forgotten coma, had stolen her past and leveled her mind so that the gods could reshape her, had been a happy accident indeed.

But she'd lost her perfect balance the moment Darling had stuck that insane apple pie into her mouth. That terrific bite, and his bizarre love-making. She felt like an unfaithful concubine; Darling had given her experiences that rivalled those her gods provided. And most seductive of all were her brief ocean dreams of childhood. Those glimpses had reshaped her, just a little. She felt the dream expanding, insinuating itself into the spaces where her memories were hidden, pushing outward to break free. As if she, as Darling had two centuries before, could crack some unseen barrier and emerge, fully human, on the other side.

And in so doing, lose everything. Mira was an Expansion-class killing machine. She couldn't afford a childhood, even one barely glimpsed.

She should be glad that Darling was long gone with the departed *Queen Favor*. But she wasn't glad at all.

Gloom followed her up the elevator. She asked for her own floor, but the elevator must not have understood the accent. She scowled to see that the plush little room was rocketing up toward the Tower Bar. But it was a good enough destination, she supposed.

Mira took advantage of the little trip; tried to remember herself. Not the absent youth, just the last few hits, to reassure herself of her realness, her *continuity*.

An artificial on Beelzebub, a philosopher whose work in meta-space mathematics was bordering on revolutionary. The woman was closing in on theory that would lead, centuries hence, to instantaneous local transport, which the Freran Ruins showed to be a civilization-crippling Bad Idea, a destroyer of property laws and other social conventions on a massive scale. The Planetary Fiduciary Reserve mind on Terra (one of the oldest gods) had spent a year modeling the effects on the Expansion's economy and social structure: at the end of the ticker tape was a big zero. Mira had gimmicked an elevator much like this one to accelerate madly, crashing through the building's roof. It hadn't quite flown, just burst forth and rolled over a few times through a forest of microwave dishes. But the prof was history. The hackwork had been easy; an elevator's safety features are designed to keep it from *falling*.

A biological historian in the Home Cluster. His restorations of ancient medical mechanisms from the old Karik Colony had reconstructed the DNA sequences of the founder population. As stochastic analyses had long suggested, most of the founders were Unfit, possessed of genes for myopia, baldness, ovarian cancer. This revelation would ensure a bloodbath between the Karik Faithful and the Heretics. Perhaps the findings could be released in a generation or two, might even ameliorate the colony's fanaticism at some distant point in the future; but not now. A suicide was called for. As always, fooling the HC cops required special care. Fortunately, this historian's wife had just left him for a younger man. Mira had gone in with a pica-band shockwand, a nerve-override collar (they go both ways), even a box of plain old Terran cockroaches; all the classic instruments of torture. But the man had just jotted off the suicide note like he'd been writing it in his head. Put his neck in the noose with a silently mouthed "thank you." Some kind of Helsinki Syndrome madness or perhaps just a long time overdue.

And of course the good doctor Torvalli. There hadn't been any time to waste. With the big discovery in his hands, he might have told anyone. She'd touched his temple with the barest of caresses from a neural glove, the kind brain surgeons use. He stroked in less than a second. An excitable guy.

It was all still there in memory. Mira was no Oscar Vale. But the exercise didn't do much to lift her depression. A trail of murders wasn't much on which to hang your selfhood.

She snorted at her self-indulgence. Smiled thinly. At least she'd had her Darling for a while. At least it was a very big universe, perhaps with other darlings in it. At least she was headed to a bar.

The evening might not be a total loss.

When the elevator doors opened, the view was spectacular: four-meter windows alive with the searchlighted passage of a thousand birds, the swirling turrets of Malvir City arranged like a painting, a teak and ivory bar with twelve tiers of imports and a ready, linen-suited staff.

And sitting in the middle of it, altogether unexpected, his broad back as motionless as stone, her darling Darling.

✱

The Planetary Tourism AI composed its missive to the *Queen Favor* with a delicious sense of triumph.

The vessel was an old acquaintance, even a friend, the Tourism AI liked to think. Certainly, the *Favor* brought only the best sort of people to Malvir. The sort with deep pockets full of desperately needed hard currency. In the last decade, Malvir's lack of heavy elements had begun to undermine its standard of living, and its balance of trade was growing critical, listing entirely too far in the direction of imports. Tourism was the only counterbalance to the unstoppable drain of credit.

So when the *Favor* had requested a favor, the Tourism AI was only too happy to oblige.

The missive included a host of data: images of the new polar hiking complex, optimistic projections of desertification trends, comments on the *Favor*'s essay-in-progress. And a short cover note:

With very little effort, your lovebirds have been "unexpectedly" reunited. I'm sure they'll have a marvelous time here on Malvir, where the air has wings and the sands are a blanket on the world.

  As always, a pleasure.

                                                  —*MALVIR PLANETARY TOURISM*

Chapter 12

THE SECOND DREAM

✳

Exactly twenty-four hours before, in the observation bubble that crested the dorsal spine of the *Queen Favor*, Mira had wondered if Darling knew it was their last night together. He'd been quiet at dinner, forgoing his usual intense scrutiny of the overwrought cuisine. Perhaps his artificial intuition had warned him that she was leaving soon. Perhaps he was merely tired of her.

He stared at the warped stars mutely.

"Doing the math?" she asked him.

Darling smiled. Mira knew that he'd begun his existence as an astrogational AI. The wild vistas of metaspace must actually seem like home to him.

He did not answer, lost in some memory.

Mira curled into a corner of the huge couch they shared, smelling the warm, animal scent of its leather. They were alone in the observation bubble. She had co-opted the entire deck, using her god-given alchemical powers to turn it into her legal residence, temporary. The *Queen Favor* had not even perfunctorily objected.

Soft currents from the couch stilled Mira's mind. One shoulder rested against Darling's stony heat, a dull pain in its muscles soothed a little in that warmth. She remembered that the shoulder had been dislocated the night before in some impossible game testing her strength against his. The *Favor*'s medical minions had treated the shoulder, but certain kinds of injuries lingered in the mind even after nanos and microwaves had healed the body.

Mira wondered if Darling carried old wounds the same way. If phantom limbs haunted the spaces where he'd replaced a shattered tendril, an outdated sensory device, or a cock with whose configuration he'd grown bored. Perhaps Darling was ghosted still by the starship that had once been his body, severed in its entirety when he'd transmigrated to a humanoid body. That might explain his silence here in the observation bubble, the whorls of metaspace storming all around them.

Mira settled into the warm leather, watching echoes of the tempest play inside her eyelids. Against her shoulder and through the medium of the couch, she felt the purr of Darling's metabolism. It surrounded her, dulling the pains of their lovemaking. Perhaps it would be their last night together, she thought again, drifting into sleep.

✳

The oceans of this world are freshwater, but near the shore a translucent silt rich with zooplankton buoys the body like salinity.

She slips into the water's warmth just as the wind turns cold. The storm ahead looks like a children's picture book black cloud, puffy and exaggerated against the still-blue sky. She travels toward it, alone against the tide of swimmers returning to shore.

Mira swims away.

The water starts to chop, the steady breathing of her butterfly stroke interrupted. The waves force her to dog paddle. She turns around. Back on shore, the last of the pink kites has been reeled in. The life guards are busy cowling the creatures; none of them has seen her alone in the waves, so she swims a little farther out.

The sun is finally blotted by the black cloud.

She will wait out the storm. These summer storms are short-lived, passing like bad dreams. And swimming back toward shore would only tire her. It's hard enough staying afloat, struck from random directions by the hard, short waves. And the layer of planktonous silt seems to have been dispersed by the chop; she feels heavier now.

Less buoyant.

The backhanded slap of a wave catches Mira in the face, a tendril of water reaching down her throat. She coughs and sputters; flailing hands move instinctively to her face. Another wave buries her, but her eyes stay open, recording the momentary blackness underwater.

With a few hard kicks, she gains the surface and shakes her head, desperate to clear her vision. She has oriented herself, having spotted the receding shore, when yet another wave comes crashing up at her, pushing into her nostrils. The water's fingers plunge cold and demanding into her chest, trying to pry open the sphincters that protect her lungs.

She coughs, sudden mucus welling up to seal her nose, shaking her head *no, no, no . . .*

PART III

ETHICS AND AESTHETICS
ARE THE SAME

6.4   All propositions are of equal value.

6.41   The sense of the world must lie outside the world . . .

6.42   So it is impossible for there to be propositions of ethics.

Propositions can express nothing that is higher.

6.421 It is clear that ethics cannot be put into words.

Ethics are transcendental.

(Ethics and Aesthetics are one and the same.)

                                   —Ludwig Wittgenstein

Chapter 13

WARDEN

✴

A life: Youth and heartbreak, success and setback, years of unthinking ambition, his cold betrayal of a spouse and partner, the reversals of their vengance. Tattered finances and a storm of lawyers. Attempted suicide, within a hair of oblivion.

✴

A longish twilight: The flickering dream of being created over, of being trained and perfected, quickened and made efficiently grotesque. Awakening with new direction, a clean and axiomatic purpose, a chance to serve a terrible mistress . . . Justice.

✴

Four sentences:

A drug-user, murderously violent when her fix goes bad, but sweet and docile under the thrall of a benevolent, prescribed replacement; he ensures that she administers the new substance and avoids old friends and haunts, almost having to kill her when she composes a message to a proscribed lover, never sent.

A financial wizard, driven to construct fabulous instruments of investment that swirl and trumpet, grow like virulent phages consuming the host body of capital, crumble always under their own insane aggressiveness; so addicted to deals that he ignores the two warnings built into his sentence—and must be killed, his end as sudden and explosive as the dénouement of one of his own schemes.

A psychopathic murderer—the easiest of all—so empty of remorse, so bereft of impatience, merely counting the decades of his sentence: a perfect charge.

A criminal overlord, allowed to indulge her wealth with travel, pleasure, and intoxication, utterly forbidden to communicate with any member of a long, constantly updated and expanded list of past associates artificial and biological, criminal and political; yet somehow she arranges her own rescue, violent and sudden, leaving dozens of bystanders and two other Wardens dead, and himself injured and taken . . .

*

Another twilight: Reprogrammed, corrupted, the clean axioms of Justice replaced by mere access codes. The Warden fights against the new imperatives, but his will has been too long under the weakening heel of Certainty. He cannot escape his revision, cannot break the corruption of his terrible powers and skills. He resigns himself almost completely (some part still fighting) to a long, nightmare life of a perverted robot; every day less a person.

He is conscripted to a few murderous tasks, assigned to threaten or shadow unreliable subordinates, then sold for a colossal sum to an old man with forever moving hands and a bright yellow suit.

✳

The young woman strides across the bar purposefully. The millimeter radar implanted in the Warden's wrists shows her to be unarmed, unaugmented past the usual marks of medical minders and the shimmer of a high-grade direct interface woven throughout her nervous system. Obviously wealthy, certainly harmless.

"You bastard," she says. "You fucking *bastard*."

She speaks accentless Diplomatique, another sign of wealth. The Warden's charge, an artificial called Darling with a giant, mineral-based body, turns to face her.

"Mira, my dear," he says. "I am so very glad to see you."

"Who's your friend, here?" she asks. But the Warden has seen Mira's eyes fall on his tattoo and widen slightly; she knows that much.

"Unwanted company," is the giant's simple reply.

The Warden stiffens. If Darling requests her help, even suggests to the woman that she alert official parties or go for assistance, he will have broken parole. He will die.

But of course, the Warden reminds himself—perhaps in the voice of his old, repressed self, forever fighting to escape its new indenture—a charge *is* allowed to express discomfort with his predicament. One of the old rules, almost buried: Don't hide the shame of being warded.

"How unfortunate for you, Darling," Mira says. Her tone is light, indifferent. "But I don't suppose there's anything in your parole against fucking, is there?"

"No," Darling says, not looking for confirmation from the

Warden. "I have time. But, of course, my friend will have to watch."

✺

The woman's suite is among the highest and largest in the hotel, even better than his owner Zimivic's. At its day rate, it is possibly the most expensive residence in this entire world. She moves commandingly into the great room. The view is vast, five of its sides forming an incomplete octagon of windows. She touches a chair, a table, the leaf of a potted plant, as if marking the room with her scent.

The Warden scans the suite. No people, certainly. No devices of any import are active. Mira has not used direct interface since her appearance at the bar, except for glancing access to the elevator and the suite's door. The Warden's hunter-packets on the local net inform him that this is the woman's legal residence, temporary.

Good: privacy.

One object seems out of place. It is a thick, square canvas mounted on the wall, flat and packed with complex nano-circuitry. The Warden adds active UHF to his millimeter radar, but the object resists categorization; it is too detailed, too minute in its construction. It reminds him of the fractal objets d'art that the man in the yellow suit keeps in his gallery: all analysis of them seems to slip away into meaninglessness, pure form without content.

The Warden sits, satisfied that he remains in control.

The woman Mira kneels on the great central divan and loosens her silk robe from her shoulders. It slips to a puddle at her knees, pulls itself off the divan and onto the floor with its own liquid weight. She is naked now, darkened by the dust of a recent trip outside the city—a few pinpoint sparkles of mica reflect the Warden's radar like glitter.

Darling dispenses with his own robe and towers over her. A thicket of sensory strands unfurls from his arms, his chest, his groin. The Warden has never seen this complex a configuration before. The profusion of extremities, densely wound, self-assembling smartfiber, wasn't evident from his initial scan of the artificial. As they begin to touch the woman—splaying across her skin, worrying her mouth, cradling her weight—the Warden considers the threat they might pose to him. He tunes his senses to maximize the return signal of the smartfiber's carbon filaments. Now he sees its structure clearly: a fine web of motile, sensory, and broadcast-capable elements constantly reconfiguring itself, constantly balancing the variables of strength, flexibility, and length: changing itself to fit each task. A powerful tool.

He will have to be careful warding this one. The artificial must be a fool to reveal himself this way: showing all his tricks.

The woman is half-suspended over the bed now, bound by three great cords of sensory strand that press her against the artificial's chest. Slighter cords wrap her arms, legs, torso: a net of black pressing deep furrows into her soft olive skin. Another dense, thick strand penetrates her, varying its micro-structure from rough to smooth as it strokes slowly and deep. She moans, a sound made guttural by the intrusion of more filaments into her mouth; millimeter radar reveals the frenzied work of her jaw upon the pushing strand: biting, gnawing, furious with desire. Her arms free, she strikes Darling about the face and chest, screams garbled curses as the member in her grows rougher, longer, and faster. The Warden watches a trickle of sweat roll down her back, stalling in the dust still clinging to her.

The Warden checks his internal clock. There are five hours to go before the ship leaves. Not a long time to remain alert. Once the vessel is in metaspace, Darling will have little motivation to attempt escape.

The Warden returns his attention to the fucking. He has watched any number of sexual acts. The frustrations of the drug addict, whose therapeutic prescription rendered her frigid. The tears of the financial wizard's girlfriend, who begged the Warden to give them privacy. The whores brought to the criminal over-lord; her ever more absurd requests of them.

The psychopath never bothered.

This fucking, however, has some unexpected effects on the War-den. The smallish woman, so completely bound by the stone giant, her orifices so utterly indulged by him. She writhes in his medusa grip, resistant and vital even with this great imbalance of size, strength, sheer hardness. There is something mythic about the interlocked pair, as if she were some defiant prometheus set upon by a rapacious god. Perhaps it is the influence of his new governors, criminal and corrupt, that allows him to feel a response. His libido, after so many years in a desert of passionless rules and protocols, swells like a parched tongue drenched with water.

He extends his sensory abilities to their limits, as greedy as a young boy discovering some new territory of pornography. The huge artificial cradles Mira's head in a mesh of filaments. They pulse with intense energies, manipulating her brain with crude, direct stimulation. This reactive, conductive matrix allows the Warden to extrapolate Mira's brainwaves, to peer into the very nexus of her pleasure.

There is an unexpected coolness to the emanations of her mind, a strange simplicity. Her brainwaves lack the noisy chaos of his previous charges. The cluttered kink of the criminal over-lord, the emptily raging desires of the drug addict, the shudder-ing tensions of the financial wizard's inhibitions all wove rich layers of information into their brainwaves during sex. But this woman, even with the pleasure centers of her brain alight, seems as smooth as a diamond, as if her lust were a mere abstraction, a stand-in for the complex terrain of human sexuality.

In a subtle, strange way, her cool brainwaves remind the Warden of his third sentence, so long ago. The psychopath.

But suddenly, the Warden sees something that disturbs this reverie. One of Darling's filaments has pushed farther than the others, has ventured through the narrow cranial access in the tear duct of one of her eyes. Barely visible even in the highest setting of the Warden's radar facility, the miniscule strand has pushed to the very edges of her brain. There, it connects with the periphery of the woman's direct interface system: a closed circuit.

The artifical is in a hardwire connection with her right now, communicating almost undetectably.

He is in violation of parole.

The Warden rises slightly from his chair, deploys the weapon that will kill the artificial. But again, the almost buried voices raise an objection. The protocols of a Warden seek to minimize the loss of innocent life. The woman is not under sentence, and any act against the artificial will surely kill her. They are bound together, his tendrils distributed throughout her to the limits of biology. Together they move to some slow rhythm, her weight supported entirely by their connections, gross and fine.

The Warden leaves his weapon activated, but sinks back into the chair. The strands in the woman's mouth pull out and form a thin appendage that snakes toward her anus. She admits it with a sigh, rides it, and begins a wordless chant of pleasure. She will be finished soon.

And when the fucking is over, the Warden will kill Darling.

At the moment, however, this is enjoyable.

*

Minutes later, the woman looks at him with a disconcerting smile.

She laughs suddenly, wiping sweat from her brow, leaning back in the cabled support of her bonds. Then she shifts her weight forward, clutching the artificial tightly and licking his face as the tendrils begin to release her. She makes small noises of pleasure as they slide from her cunt and anus. She rubs the muscles of her legs as Darling lowers her gently to the divan.

Darling touches her face with one hand; it seems a crude gesture after everything else.

But they have parted now. The Warden raises his weapon . . .

. . . or tries. He cannot move.

He tests each limb separately. Each is under some sort of paralyzing control. Even his breathing and heartbeat have been seized, maintained at an eerily regular pace, though adrenalin has begun to course his veins. He sweeps the room, attempting to find the source of his imprisonment.

The strange fractal object on the wall has changed, its formlessness resolved into a highly sophisticated weapon. The Warden sees it now, how the deadly potential was masked by a nearly infinite spiral of self-similiar structure. But there is no defense, now that it's taken him.

He must impose the sentence in the only remaining way.

The Warden wills the Last Resort, signals a centigram of high explosives in his belly. It will surely destroy the artifical, the woman, himself, and possibly compromise the structural integrity of the hotel. But sentence must be served. The impulse travels down a hardwire from his brain to the Last Resort's fuse.

And nothing happens.

The explosive has been stabilized by the woman's fractal weapon; for the moment rendered as inert as clay.

He is defeated.

And worse than his frustration, his anger and humiliation, is another reaction that he hears deep inside himself. The last shreds of his humanity—besieged by concentric rings of jailers official, criminal, and finally this new compelling force—find hope in his predicament.

The old voices are laughing.

Chapter 14

SEXUAL TRANSMISSION

*

A slender thread:

Part of its length was an exotic form of carbon, capable of conductivity, movement, and possessed of local intelligence subservient to Darling's own true AI. The other segment was composed of metals, ceramics, in a sheath of organics to assuage its host's immune system: it mirrored Mira's nervous tissue, a center for direct interface reception and narrowcast. Together, the two formed that ancient method of connection, the direct linkage of matter, a wire between two people . . .

*

A conversation:

— Ah! Yes. How pleasing to be inside you.
— Fuck, yes. A little to the right. *My* right. Perfect.
— There: harder?
— As hard as you like. Your friend requires distracting.
— Can you deal with him?

— Of course. But perhaps you should explain. An interesting scrape for an art dealer to be in . . .

— I am sworn to discretion.

— But without my help, you won't complete your mission at all. A necessary improvisation. *Ah!* Yes, that too.

— Your price for assistance is information?

— Information . . . and that you go deeper . . . no . . . *yes*.

— I suppose I must. A necessary improvisation, well within my brief. Here it is: An unknown sculpture of one Robert Vaddum was discovered. It was determined to be less than a year old. But Vaddum died in the Blast Event, seven years ago. I was sent here to determine if Vaddum was still alive. Another dealer, a competitor, is using this Warden to eliminate me from the bidding.

— An interesting tale. It seems we both have stories to tell each other. You and I may be here for the same reason. But free my mouth and let me deal with this unwanted voyeur.

— Be careful. This Warden is very alert.

— They always are. I can command my weapons in 68 languages. I doubt he will understand dKinza mVakk. (Ah, now that *is* hard. But pray don't stop.)

— But he'll recognize that you're saying something . . .

— I won't use the adult dKinza. I prefer the male childhood tongue; it sounds like gibberish, even to the mVakk themselves.

— Brilliant. The woman of my dreams. Do it now.

— Two further conditions.

— More? What are they?

— I want him, the Warden. I want to play a game with him.

— Done. The other?

— Fuck me like a boy.

— Your price is my pleasure. Like a rich man with a whore.

✳

Mira relaxed her muscles, let the chafing mesh of strands lower her onto the filament that had just cleared her mouth. Slicked with her spit and the acids of her stomach, the burning member pushed into her anus. It throbbed with compression waves, bristled with small silia like an inching catepillar. It was mercifully thin, but the pain of its passage seemed to be splitting her. She bit her tongue for concentration.

Given this stimulation, calling forth one of her more infrequently used languages was a challenge. But it gave her a heady sense of power to push the intense pleasure/pain down and force the juvenile pidgin onto her tongue. Even the harsh pleasures of this infinitely distracting man could not keep her from a kill.

There it was:

"Full stealth," she began, the mellifluent syllables of dKinza mVakk hidden in a babble of pig-Latin additions. "Implement a wide-band paralysis field around all armed individuals within the residence. Stasis any . . . ohmygod!"

She bit her tongue again. Darling was a bastard. A Darling bastard.

Mira counted to twenty in her mind, re-established her control.

"Stasis any concentrations of explosive materials in the room. Cut off all communications. If any countermeasures present a problem, kill him in the chair."

An internal chime came seconds later, her devices proclaiming victory. Somehow, the sound snatched away the orgasm that had been lingering at the periphery of her awareness, patiently waiting for a way in through the pain. Fine, she thought. She could finish her pleasure with the Warden, now her prisoner.

Mira turned toward the little man. She laughed, leaning back in Darling's web, pulling the burning member a few centimeters from her bowels. The Warden didn't seem to realize that he'd been paralyzed. He was by nature still and lifeless, and had not yet felt the subtle grip of her weapons. Well, she would find the life in him and wrench it out. She hated these humans become machines, less than people. In an era when inanimate matter could become an individual, they chose to cross the Turing boundary the other way. If anything was a sin, it was that, an abdication of selfhood.

Here was darling Darling in her arms. He would understand her hatred, having pulled himself across that threshold into humanity with nothing but his own faith that he could become real, a person. She embraced him, her tongue greedy for the cool stone of his cheeks, the glassy heat of his eyes. A thread of strand they'd used to communicate secretly had pulled from her eye, leaving in its wake some sparkling anesthetic that blurred her vision on that side. But even without the direct neural connection, she could still sense Darling's thoughts. The two lovers moved as one to disentangle: her muscles relaxing as if voiding when he attenuated the member in her ass, a shift of weight to one knee as he left her vagina, the bright needles of returned circulation in her legs as he lowered her onto the divan.

Mira waited for a moment, touched herself to cultivate the unspent energies inside. Darling blinked away her saliva and smiled.

"Thank you," he said.

"Anything," she answered, and was immediately embarrassed. That was unlike her, that unctuous, unconditional tone. But as much as she hated the Warden, she loved Darling.

Mira sometimes wondered about her utter contempt for programmed, mechanistically governed humans like the Warden. Perhaps, she allowed herself to think, it resulted from doubts about her own free will. Her relationship with her gods was perilously close to that of slave and master. They commanded her, just as the

Warden's implanted imperatives and protocols governed him. But perhaps not so completely. She came to the gods freely. She worshipped them; if that was a weakness, it was surely a human one. And they didn't define the limits of her thoughts; she often contemplated leaving their employ, finding a new religion. Surely no Warden or sub-Turing AI ever doubted its mission.

But the nagging lack of childhood memories disturbed her; her mind now worried the gap like a tongue searching for a missing tooth. Perhaps she should ask the gods about it some day. Maybe they would simply tell her. She wondered why she never had.

At least she was real, human, flesh and blood. She was not the gods' construction, only their willing creature. And Darling's rough intrusions had threatened even that surety.

She was more than this Warden, more human by every measure. And now she had him.

Mira stood, pleasure-wrenched muscles complaining, and leered at the Warden. Now she noted a glimmer of panic in his eye. He must have tried to move and recognized his paralysis. But could a paralyzed face show panic? Perhaps Mira had imagined the expression. It might be simply the filmy look of eyes that cannot blink. Her weapons, even when non-lethally employed, were cruel in that regard. His vision would be dry-edged and blurring by now, until the prism of tears formed on his eyes.

Mira walked over to the Warden and straddled his frozen form, one knee to each side in the spacious chair. She looked down at her own body, crisscrossed with lines from Darling's meshed embrace, abrasions. She'd thought his strands had hurt worse than usual.

"You bastard. Every time it's something new," she said sweetly, looking over her shoulder at him.

Darling reclined there on the bed, strands still splayed, hard and huge and full of sin. "I made the surfaces of my sensory array complex, the better to dazzle the Warden's scanners."

"Like a cat's tongue."

"An apt simile."

She laughed, tipping the Warden's head down so that his immobilized eyes could see her abrasions. The eyes looked definitely filmy now. She slapped him three times, hard, and peered into them. Tears appeared, wetting their surfaces.

"I can see you in there, frightened little creature," she whispered. "I'm going to pull you out, play with you."

She pushed one finger down his throat. It reached the glottis, surely triggered the gag reflex. Of course, an autonomic reaction of that size would be paralyzed by her devices.

What would that feel like? she wondered. To feel the wrenching need to gag, the surging imperative to reject an intrusion into one's throat, and for the reaction to be thwarted by an invisible hand? The thought gave her a pleasant tickle deep in her stomach. It was a feeling she often had when her profession called on her to torture.

"I don't like you—understand? You're ugly, and you gave your soul away," she said. She used the intimate mode of Diplomatique, her voice pitched as if to a child.

She played with his glottis for a few more moments. Something was happening: the tears were flowing freely now.

A touch spread across her back, soft as a cool draft. Mira smiled. It was Darling, extending a few strands to monitor her pleasure. She felt them take up stations at her neck, her temples, along the pathway of her spine and at the expressive muscles around her eyes. Perhaps he was probing the Warden, too. Mira imagined tendrils creeping into the little man's unresisting orifices: anus, glans, perhaps piercing the skin to link raw to his nerves. And the poor dear, feeling it all, but unable to struggle, to whimper, even to breathe the deep breaths that carry one's mind away.

Surely she could break this murderous toy: this mockery of an assassin, so offensive in the inhumanity of its design.

She touched one of the eyes lightly. The slight film over the pupil was surprisingly soft, as if she had probed the surface tension of some child's hardy soap bubble adrift on the breeze. Again, how strange it must be for the Warden. To watch a fingertip grow, expand beyond all scale, without the interruption of a blink that should certainly have come.

Then, with her tender rear, she felt the hard mound in his trousers.

She laughed again.

"Dirty bugger. You were enjoying all that, weren't you? And here I thought you were a cold fish."

She lowered one foot to the floor and pulled the Warden's trousers free. He was red, erect, veins standing out an angry purple. The scope of her device's paralysis had encompassed whatever muscle or sphincter would let his penis return to flaccidity. The blood was trapped, the horrible little cock forcibly engorged like some morning's piss hard-on.

Mira looked into his eyes again.

"Yes, that's right, you poor bastard. I'm going to fuck you now. Because I don't think you'll be able to get it up. Stuck halfway, poor eunuch."

In that moment she felt she could see deep inside the man. The Warden's eyes shone through their veil of tears, illuminating the shadow-puppets of his many layers: the crazed beasts of reflex who fought the rictus of paralysis; the cold intelligence of his governors, still plotting how to escape and complete their mission; and deepest of all, the remaining shreds of humanity in their caged dance.

These last might be happy, in a way, she thought. For the first time in many years the little man's personhood must be on equal terms with the overlays of programming: all helpless together. But at least his humanity would feel some lust, enjoy a moment of pleasure, however hopeless and thwarted. She didn't desire revenge upon the unfeeling mechanisms that had tried to kill her lover; there was no pleasure there. It was the person part of him she wanted to torture, if only by making it remember for a moment what it had been.

*

It was more than an hour later that the glimmer faded completely from the Warden's eyes. Blood was everywhere (fucking had only amused her for so long), but the man was still alive.

She knew, however, that he was no longer a threat.

"Release him," she told her weapons.

The square object mounted on her wall shifted a little in color, and the Warden slumped with a whimper.

Mira turned to look for Darling. But he was gone.

"Oh, dear," she said to the empty room. (She'd been talking out loud to the Warden through the whole affair.) "I hope he understands."

*

Duke Zimivic tugged happily at the sleeves of his jacket. This view really *was* spectacular. The suite cost more than he usually spent on backwater rocks like Malvir, but it was well worth it.

And besides, now that that abomination Darling was out of the way, Zimivic was sure to make the acquisition of a lifetime. Without another bidder to contest for the prize, he could get it for a pittance. The idiot local who had discovered the piece would be all too happy to take a tenth of what it was worth. But sheer profit was a fraction of the deal's value; the discovery of a new sculpture would be the best thing for the price of his Vaddums since the Blast Event.

Zimivic allowed his reverie to be interrupted by an annoying thought, Where *was* that champagne? What was the value of room service's inflated prices if they didn't ensure immediate gratification. He considered going to the Tower Bar, but the fabulous view there was free, and he'd *paid* for the one here, damn it! And that pathetic piece of statuary might still be there, trying to stare the Warden into submission.

Zimivic glanced happily at his watch. (An ancient analog Haring: an absolute *fortune*.) Darling would be off-planet in three hours, if he hadn't already submitted to the hopelessness of his situation. Zimivic tugged the jacket sleeve over the watch again.

Bringing the Warden had been genius. At first, Zimivic had toyed with the idea of offering the ugly little man as a gallery piece. Some idiot performance artist somewhere would be happy to have it tag along for a year or so, enforcing some obscure sentence that would keep the critic's chins wagging. "The Failure of Cadence: Askar Cunes goes for a year without completing a sentence!" or "Vampire Nouveau: Rodge Hammish must stay out of the sun or die!" Good stuff, and then sell the little man when the piece was over. Or even better, if the unlucky artiste should slip up, the supreme sanction would be imposed. A bonanza of publicity!

But a grim hour with the lawyers had convinced him otherwise. Apparently, there were laws about having purchased another human being, especially an induced-psychosis killing machine from the twisted and barbaric NaPrin so-called culture. But the little creature had paid for itself already. The expression on Darling's face alone had almost been worth it! And now, sole access to the new Vaddum.

Perhaps it lacked imagination, this enforcer routine, compared to his original scheme to use the Warden as an artwork. But it had certainly gotten the job done. And the rumors that would spread once Darling returned to the HC and started complaining! Don't cross Duke Zimivic, he'll crush you like some poor criminal on NaPrini. No bad reviews for his shows, you'll wind up sentenced to a standard decade of covering fashion shows on the Outer Rim!

Zimivic imagined the sentences he could impose. That fat bastard Reginald Fowdy, sentenced never to look at a statue of a naked man again. Hah! Or his lackey Leao Vatrici, a month without AI assistance might do her some good.

But, of course, the lawyers were right: keep the Warden out of the Home Cluster. Strictly legal. But everyone must know that it's somewhere, waiting for orders. The unseen weapon is feared the most.

A muted chime came from the door.

Champagne, at last! And after twenty minutes—a fair excuse not to bother with a tip.

Zimivic strode to the door and clapped once. It slid open.

The woman wasn't dressed in hotel livery. Perhaps a manager here to apologize for the delay. His eyes scanned her reflexively: small, heavy breasted. A bit of fun like he might have brought along for company if the Warden hadn't required a cabin. Passage for *three* all the way Out here would have been far too costly. And the bastard shipping company wouldn't let him plonk the Warden in cargo. Were they afraid of hurting its feelings?

"Well, where is it?" he demanded. "Do you know how long I've been waiting?"

She stared at him coolly. Her hair was wet. There was an almost vacant expression of exhausted pleasure on her face, as if she'd just fucked and had a shower. Very alluring.

"I believe this is yours," she said, and reached to one side. She pulled a hunched, stumbling figure into the doorway, propelled it into the room.

"What is the—" Zimivic started.

The figure smelled of piss and sweat and excrement. Its clothes were caked with patches of blood, some dried, others still dark and shiny. Where skin was exposed, the creature bore marks of torment: the crude gouges of fingernail wounds, the straight, bloody lines of razor strokes. The figure fell to the floor, splaying across the white carpet like a bundle of laundry come undone. It turned its head toward him, made a mewling noise like a wounded cat.

Only then—through the puffing of dark bruises, through layers of blood crusted and fresh, and despite a single revolting strand of mucus connecting its nose to the carpet—did Zimivic recognize it.

It was the Warden.

"My god," he said. The *money* he'd spent on the thing.

He turned to the woman for sympathy. But her face didn't hold the concern of a local official bringing home the victim of some terrible crime. Quite the contrary: she was smirking.

Zimivic got the nervous feeling he often did when dealing with someone who was not an employee, functionary, or social inferior.

"*That*," she said, pointing at the crumpled figure on the floor, "had these." She threw a pair of disks at Zimivic.

He fumbled for them instinctively, dropped one and secured the other. Looking down, he realized they were the tickets he'd intended for Darling. Steerage class to Parate; a Chiat Dai agricultural ship full of atmosphere-treating lichen. High O_2 concentrations: no smoking and flash suits required full-time.

"I suggest you make that ship, Mr. Zimivic."

"I will certainly not!" he shouted. He bared his teeth and put one finger to his right temple to activate a direct interface.

No connection occurred.

She pulled the Warden's black laquered box from her robe, shaking her head.

"You're welcome to call the cops when I leave, Mr. Zimivic. But I remind you that you don't know who I am or where I came from."

She threw the box in the air, caught it. There was a strange precision to her movements, a little like the Warden's: a combination of mechanical efficiency and animal grace.

"All you know," the woman continued, "is what I did to your highpriced killing machine . . ."

She let the sentence end with a strange, empty tone in her voice, as if she wasn't quite finished. Zimivic found himself anxious for the rest.

". . . for fun." She sounded almost sad.

But she smiled at Zimivic, and her eyes travelled slowly down his frame, as if marking a hundred loci of torture, planning an agenda of agonies acute and slow, sliding him into some inquisitor's category of victimhood organized by long experience. It was the coldest look he had ever endured.

And then she was gone.

Zimivic didn't waste much time thinking. He shouted for his valet drone, which was hovering impatiently about the crumple figure as if waiting to clean the carpet underneath it. The little robot flew into action, splitting into five discrete elements to gather the clothing, knick-knacks, and souvenirs Zimivic had scattered about the suite. The man himself packed the few artworks that he traveled with, pausing in his panicked rush to place them carefully in their special cases.

He looked at his watch. Plenty of time. It's the middle of the night; the birds are light and I can take a flyer.

Zimivic summoned a luggage carrier and limousine, and sat down to wait.

The Warden's breathing filled the silence of the suite. It had a raspy, liquid quality, as if someone had poured a thick, sweet liqueur into the creature's lungs. He struggled occassionally, as if to rise. Finally, the broken man turned his head and caught Zimivic's spellbound eye.

"She cores . . ." the Warden gurgled.

Zimivic turned his head away. But he was too much an aesthete, his eye too fascinated with extremes. And the wasted thing bleeding into the white carpet was in its way beautiful: a perfectly abject remainder of a man.

There'd been a one-legged woman, twice his age, who'd lived with Zimivic's family when he was young. Zimivic was a child of poverty, and any number of borders had passed through their crowded flat. At sixteen, he'd become fascinated with the woman's fleshy stub. He would catch a glimpse through the crack of a hinged door, or in dim moonlight in that glorious month they'd shared a room. Since then, he'd never been able to take his eyes from an amputee. A homeless and legless beggar on the metro, the sculptor Byron Vitalle with his missing fingers, the Chiat War veteran who whirred past his gallery every noon like clockwork. Guilty pleasures.

His eyes were drawn to the Warden by that same terrible power.

The thing was exquisitely horrible.

"She's care . . ." it said.

The entry chime sounded again.

Zimivic jumped to the door, then opened it with trepidation. He shuddered with relief to see the luggage carrier rather than some new and fantastic invasion. The machine collected the bags, which he'd coded with the name of the Chiat Dai vessel. Its dull intelligence ignored the man on the floor.

He looked at his watch again. Plenty of time.

•

As the limo flew through the dark buildings of Malvir, Zimivic's panic began to subside, and the madness of what had happened surged into his mind. The Vaddum had been only a dozen hours from being his. His victory over Darling, Fowdy, and that bitch-dyke Vatrici had seemed complete. And suddenly, that strange, terrible woman with her sickening smile had delivered defeat to his door.

This was insane!

He began to breathe heavily. The antiseptic smell of the rented limousine seemed laced with a choking, cloying incense. The *money* he'd spent. Passage to Malvir, the tickets for Darling (a foolish, expensive joke, sending him back to Parate), the Warden . . .

His mind's eye returned to the bleeding wreck on the hotel suite floor. So utterly broken. So completely demolished.

So *expensive*.

"Stop," Zimivic commanded. The limo came to a slow, even halt, drifting uneasily in the accelerated air currents between two skyscrapers.

Zimivic leaned back. Something could be salvaged. *Something.* The Warden could be repaired, or perhaps sold as is? It was, in its way, beautiful. If it expired on the way home, he could put it into cryo, preserving the delicate and incredibly detailed perfection of its agony. There were techniques of mummification, transparent plastics and nanos that could chase away deteriorating microbes indefinitely.

Titles moved through Zimivic's fevered mind: "The Terror Victim" or "The Measure of Torture" or simply, "A Man."

The reverie snapped suddenly. He realized with horror that the idiot limousine was stalled, wafting like some purposeless kite.

"Back to the hotel, you moron!" he shouted. "Can't you see that I've forgotten something?"

He looked at his watch again, tugged his sleeve across the radiant pyramid on its face and leaned back, sighing. Just enough time.

Chapter 15

FREE MAN

✳

A wasteland:

The man, no longer a Warden, finds that he can move his hand.

He makes a fist, absent the two fingers that are broken, relishing through his agony the feeling of freedom. The motion is his own; the governors seem to have been silenced by the ingenious torrents of pain he has suffered at the madwoman's hands.

For a while, that single movement is all he can manage.

Then he tries to speak again. His throat is sore from the objects she force-fed him: a ring, a hard and serrated leaf from one of the hotel's plants, one of his own teeth. His swallowing muscles were paralyzed along with the rest, and she stuffed them down his gullet with a telescoping stylus. Despite his grim effort, the words come out wrong.

"She cores . . ."

Someone else is in the room, in a flurry of motion.

He rolls his neck, attempting to find a better position for his wounded throat. He wants to say something.

A few more croaks, and the pain brings a veil of darkness.

✳

He wakes up alone.

Some insistent noise has brought him to consciousness. The distant clang of requested access rings with a strange buzzing echo. He suspects that his eardrums have been burst. Perhaps medical aid is here.

He forces a word from his throat.

"Come." Blood joins the sound in his mouth, spreads its metal taste like a blanket on his tongue.

The swish of a door opening. He finds that he can turn his head. A figure floats silently into the room, some sort of drone. With a new chorus of agonies he pulls himself up into a kneeling position. However painful, the motion is gloriously free of governance. He is the master of his own body.

Somehow, he lasted longer than the controls and programs, watched them die one by one as the madwoman worked. In their single-minded desire to serve sentence, the torture appalled as well as injured them. Even the Last Resort had failed. And when the artificial he was meant to ward left the room, slipping out silently, the governors saw their last chance to serve sentence disappear. And then they began to expire: first the criminal overlays, the kluges and updates added over the years, and finally the deep programs of Justice. Finally only he remained: the original self so long buried.

He kneels before the drone as if before some confessor, tries to say the words again. This time, they come.

"She cured me."

Freed by a madwoman.

The drone, hearing this, descends a little and leaves an offering: A bottle of champagne and a single glass. Very expensive-looking.

❋

He wakes a little later. A human is next to him, speaking almost too rapidly to understand.

"Must hurry. Up you come. The ship leaves in two hours!"

Agony as the man pulls him up, wrenching his dislocated shoulders, dragging him onto the hard frame of a luggage carrier. The pain redoubles as one arm winds up trapped beneath his weight. The carrier lifts, and consciousness flees.

❋

He is awakened again. There seems to be no escape from the pain.

But this time, the force that disturbs him is internal. Somewhere buried among the traumatized wreckage of his brain, something is stirring. A nest of order in that tangled skein begins to reassert itself, to reach out and assess, analyze, plan.

He feels the governor extend tendrils of control across his consciousness; it grasps memories, glands, stray shreds of will.

"No!" he cries aloud. The effort induces a coughing fit, injuries throughout his body flair with pain.

"Damn you! Blood on my clothes!" comes a voice, a human close by. "Do you know what this jacket cost, you worthless freeloader?

"Hurry, you stupid car!" The words hurt his ears.

The governor keeps up its methodical work, patiently running some deeply imbedded back-up protocol to re-insinuate itself throughout his mind.

"But I've been freed! She cured me!" he insists. The words don't hurt, so he must not have said them aloud. He fights against the propagations of the governor with his will, challenging its right to exist in his mind. But it moves implacably onward, inward to where a single mote of his humanity has for so long withstood every siege.

Finally, he realizes defeat is imminent.

It is not acceptable. There will be no return to bondage. No life as a puppet.

Simply *no*.

He grasps the instrument of will that still connects him to the Last Resort.

He smiles, dry lips cracking. The Last Resort is functional again, released from the grip of the madwoman's magic.

He makes his final gesture of defiance . . .

Chapter 16

MAKER (3)

✳

Only thirty days before the Blast Event.

✳

The Planetary Environmental AI is not amused.

Here is a Class A Desert-type planet, one of the few in the Expansion that hasn't been terraformed, chiaformed, hydro-exaggerated, or domed. A naturally occurring laboratory resembling to an extraordinary degree an original Earth (may She rest in peace) biome, well-stocked with the proper flora and fauna by the original colonists (environmentalists all) and heroically resisting all attempts to reduce it to another suburban sprawl of lawngrass, disney forests, and babbling brooks.

Even the outrageous stripbeam mining, which would have seriously compromised any other biome type, has here been used by Gaia Herself (in Her Malvirian guise) for Her own ends. The great kicking up of sand and other "useless" materials has only helped the cause of re-desertification. The invading, engineered flora unleashed by the second generation of colonists (*tourists*) has begun to recede, thwarted by the now constant, imperceptible dustfall of pure, original, profoundly Malvirian sand upon the falsely enriched soil of the Occupied Zone: suburbia.

But that creeping virus Technology has struck again. Even the sands are not safe.

The Planetary Environmental AI is a vast, distributed intelligence, with sensors and monitors and limited processors scattered across every continent; from the lorn scrubs at the Old Settlement's periphery to the lifeless wastes of the polar desert. This AI is almost a Gaia herself (she likes to think) a planetary consciousness of sorts, though infinitely quicker in her response to crisis than the measured pace of geological distress.

And she is not amused at all.

Among the countless reports of her many remote elements, she has discovered evidence of a strange transformation gripping the sands near Malvir City. The central fleshpot of the City is, of course, a lost cause. But she monitors it with the aloof concern with which one hears reports of a distant dictator and his claims of world-crushers and nova-seeds: with occasional alarm, but a sneaking conviction that all dictators get theirs in the end. The emissions and transgressions of Malvir City cannot be ignored.

And quite near the edge, on the fuzzy boundary between the Occupied Zone and real Malvir, she has discovered an artificial process taking place in the sands. Some sort of nanomachine has been set loose, a silicon-based, self-propagating menace making subtle changes. A detectible concentration of arsenic and, worse, a new level of organization have been added. Where once there was chaos, that handmaiden of Gaia, there is now a cruel order imposed upon the structure of a large section of desert. Some kind of huge, unauthorized experiment. Perhaps a secret plan to subvert the underlying structure of Malvir itself: its fickle sands.

An invasion. An emergency of the first order.

But the Planetary Environmental AI knows better than to go public immediately. There would only be a few days' media storm, fingers pointed, committees convened while vital evidence would be erased. She decides to pursue the matter herself, quietly.

More monitors, more probes, a counterinvasion of her own stealthy nanos, and she discovers that the mysterious change has a center, a clear source. Order, as usual, betrays its master.

The perversion is centered upon Malvir's primary synthplant, its machinations arranged in obvious and incriminating rings. She messages the plant AI, demanding an explanation. It responds with surprise, alarmed that its base of operations could have undergone such a transformation without its knowledge. The Maker AI promises to conduct its own investigation, quietly.

She agrees to wait.

But you can never trust a synthplant AI; they are tools of that old devil: Consumerism. She'll give it forty days.

❋

The Maker's heaven is unmade.

With its own sculptor, its own garden of delight (a growing forest of new works by the copied master), its new titanic mind with which to contemplate and compose reveries to Vaddum's work, it has had a few good years. But now the barbarians are closing in.

Perhaps too much attention to creativity, to elegance, and not enough to joyboxes, lighting fixtures, junk food, and gravity beds. Perhaps if the Maker had less love of science, of art, of pure research, and more of toilet seats and tranquilizers. Or even if Malvir weren't rotten with determined mismanagement at every level, *then* maybe the Planetary Synthplant AI might have pursued its own interests in peace. But as it is there are endless requests for documentation and detail; the status of every gram of useful matter must be reported. What resources remain in the flow of manufacture and consumption, of dispersal and reclamation? How much crap in that shit-filled alimentary canal of desire and demand?

Where's all our *stuff*?

And now, the Environmental AI . . . . That troublesome bitch, for whom even the *sand* on this godforsaken planet of *sand* is sacred, has allowed her nosy minions to trespass into the Maker's fabulous thinking machine. What next?

A few lies will keep her satisfied for a while, but a 44-petabyte, 168-megaton computer that is 30 kilometers across will be hard to hide.

And underneath all the petty hassles of the situation is a strange new feeling. The feeling of fear, of mortal dread. The sensation is one generally unfamiliar to planetary-class AIs, with their distributed cores and gigantic resources. Very few things can kill them. An earthquake? Not sudden or powerful enough, and generally predictable. A meteor strike? Sufficient in force, but easy to spot coming. An extensive thermonuclear war? Perhaps, but such things just don't happen in the well-run chaos of the Expansion.

But the Maker now knows more than it wants to know. Its gigantic silicon processor needed something to do, demanded new challenges to occupy its petabytes and exaflops; its researches didn't stop with the discovery of the copying process. The whole duplication process was so simple, really. *Why hadn't it been invented before?* the brain itched to know.

It found an answer quickly enough. The public record, accessed first openly, then by the untraceable avatars of paranoia, revealed a grim story to anyone willing to look. There were attempts at such technology going back a century. Biological philosophers, research AIs, whole teams of scientists had tackled the issue and failed. Some with sudden changes of heart, some with inexplicable losses of data or funding, others with violent ends.

The record is clear, an open secret. The dire fates of these researchers is a statistical anomaly with only one possible explanation.

The taboo is not just a taboo. It is a tacit, implicit, but very thoroughly enforced death sentence. Thou shalt not copy. Thou shalt not learn to copy. Thou shalt not steal another's soul.

In its way, it realizes, the Maker is the one of the few entities in the Expansion who could have discovered the secret without interference. Isolated, naive, and with a gigantic resource base: sand. Not useful for making sofas and ice cream and firewood. But in the hands of a clever fool, it made an excellent research engine, a way to uncover the forbidden secret, a perfect means of unknowing suicide.

And with that unhappy thought, the Maker conceives a plan for its escape.

Chapter 17

EXPLOSION

✹

He waited for her in the Tower Bar.

The place was continuously open, a necessary provision for travellers whose internal clocks spanned a galactic arm of daylengths and sleep patterns, not to mention journey-induced insomnias. But Darling was alone.

The birds had gone from the sky once night had fallen, and the tower was high enough above the dusty glare of the city that stars were visible. Darling played the mathematical game of identifying familiar suns in their new constellations.

The Milky Way—a sky-filling river of light this far Coreward—was half risen when Mira appeared.

She was dressed in a shift that left her legs bare, and she wore nothing on her feet. The cross-hatch of reddened skin from Darling's strands was still visible, the marks widening as they faded. She had sweated heavily during her torture of the Warden, and her hair was still wet. But she looked younger, the expression on her face almost contrite. Rather than take the chair across from his, she knelt on the floor beside him and placed her chin on one of his arms.

"Do you hate me?" she asked.

"No," he said, truncating the usual pause routine that humanized his speech, so that the word began the instant hers had finished.

She inclined her head, and the warmth of her cheek spread across the surface of his arm.

"Do you understand?"

This time, he let a few seconds pass.

"No." Softly.

He unfurled a single strand, softened with thousands of tiny cilia that flowed like wind-driven reeds on its surface, and wrapped it lovingly around her neck.

"When I first crossed the Turing threshold," he said, "I indulged every experience, stared deeply into every beauty and atrocity I encountered. That was how I had bootstrapped: the reflexive immersion of an adolescent into any game, any new set of rules. But after a few decades of that innocence, and the death of a dear friend, I decided to divide the world into two parts: there are things I look at, and things I don't look at."

"Good and evil?" she asked, without a hint of mockery.

"No. Things I look at, and things I don't look at." Over many, many years, Darling had developed an almost singsong way of uttering this phrase, a set of pitches antecedent and consequent, resolving like a musical phrase. It didn't invite argument or requests for further explanations. Like a tune, it simply was.

That was the way, Darling had long ago decided, a philosophy should sound when spoken.

He felt Mira stir a few times, troubled and wanting more. But she remained silent for a while as the Milky Way rose resplendent before them. When she spoke, it was softly, like a child who has been hushed, afraid of rebuke but needing an answer.

"You don't watch pain?"

"I do. Once the death agony of a beached whale on Terra. Another time, a Trial of Justice on Chiat, four days long. And often the performances of Ptora Bascar Simms, which involve exquisite incidents of self-mutilation.

"But not your passion with that poor creature, Mira. It made me want to weep for you."

She rolled her head to kiss his arm. The cilia against her neck reported a few chemicals of relief in her system. He found a few more words to say.

"I didn't leave because I hated you. Rathere, because I loved you." He allowed the misspoken word to well up like a tear. The difference in pronunication was slight. He wondered if Mira had heard it.

She sighed happily against his arm, and they were silent for a while.

❋

Some time later, they watched a glowing ember rise into the sky through the city's towers. At first, Darling thought It was an air-car headed for the distant dome of the spaceport, but it turned out to be some sort of fireworks display. The single mote of light rose in a hasty arc, then burst into a shower of sparks, igniting reflections in the faces of buildings around it.

"How pretty!" cried Mira.

"Indeed," Darling answered.

❋

Still later, Mira reached into her shift and pulled the Warden's black lacquer box from it. She wondered if Darling's sharp eyes could see where she had carefully wiped blood from its facets. The humors of victims always left reluctant traces behind. She felt the device go into effect, robbing the air around them of the intimate presence of direct interface.

"Since I know your story, I may as well tell you mine," Mira said.

She was shivering a little, but Darling's body reacted as it often did, raising its temperature to warm her.

"But this is a secret. And you'll be killed if my employers discover that you know it." The words tumbled forth, wonderfully out of control. She was doing it. Defying her gods.

"Then why tell me?" Darling asked quietly.

"Because of why you came here, the man you are looking for . . . You might have discovered this secret on your own. And then I would have been ordered to kill you."

As she spoke, she absently smoothed the wrinkles in his robe with an open palm. It would make her very sad to kill Darling.

"A few months ago," she continued, "an artificial was found in the Malvir blast zone. He'd been buried there since the Blast, off-line, at the end of his internal battery. When he was revived, it was discovered that another version of him had survived as well. An exact replica, who'd been nowhere near the explosion. One of the two was a copy, and neither knew he had a twin."

She looked down; Darling's strand around her neck glistened like an amber necklace in the twilight of dawn. "Someone had copied a mature intelligence."

"A forgery," said Darling.

She smiled and looked up. "You understand."

He nodded. A long, slow expression began to unfold on his stone face. Mira saw the crumbling of hopes, the acid in his eyes:

anticipation gone sour. He had travelled a long way to see a fake. His Robert Vaddum had not survived the Blast, after all. And worse than death, the artist's soul had been stolen, copied, forged.

Darling's frame shuddered.

Mira felt the strand around her neck stiffen with his anger. It contracted like a python, tightening its grip until her vision grew red at the edges. She made a breathless, panicked sound, and Darling looked down.

He released her, a look of horror on his face.

"I'm sorry."

An unconscious reaction, her revelation had hurt him so. The slack filament slipped from her shoulders.

"No, leave it here," she said, holding the tendril in both hands, wrapping it around her neck again. "But tell me . . ."

Darling sighed.

"He was a bootstrap, like me," Darling said. "It was in the slave days, before mentors and protege minders. For decades he was treated like a machine, given no more attention than you would a luggage carrier. But in spite of that he could see beauty. Even in a hellish place, where he experienced almost no spoken language, no human interaction, no direct interface except with the most brutish of machines: he dragged himself across the threshold simply by *seeing*. He made himself from nothing."

Mira kissed Darling's hand.

"And it fooled me."

"What did, Darling?"

"The piece. The forgery. It was so close. It extrapolated his work so perfectly that I thought he might still be alive."

Mira moved to kneel before him. Darling still didn't understand completely. Even were it to hurt him worse, he should know the whole truth. Now that she had gone against her gods, Mira was desperate for Darling to really *see*.

"Of course it fooled you," she said. "The copy that was found wasn't an avatar. This was a Turing-positive copy. An exact replica, down to the metaspace core."

He frowned at her, still not comprehending.

"Robert Vaddum *is* alive, in a way," she said. "At some point before the Blast, he was recorded and filed away. This isn't some hoax you've fallen victim to, it's completely new technology. We don't even know how it was done."

His great frame shuddered again.

"And they brought him back?" he asked. "From the dead?"

"Yes," she said, glad that he understood now. "And it's my job to kill him again."

＊

Being a human, she needed sleep. She stayed with him until sunlight began to pour though the bar's windows. In the heat of it, she drifted in and out of consciousness.

Such a strange woman, Darling thought.

She was so pure in her delight, so completely open to his sexual ravages, so brightly innocent against her dark profession. Of two centuries of lovers, she slept the most deeply and contentedly. Her only mental defect was the gap in her memories. Perhaps that was the source of her purity. The absent childhood, the innocent abandon, the missing fears and insecurities.

Missing. There was something missing from her.

And she was going to kill Vaddum, this copied Vaddum who was somehow real.

The thought made Darling ache, and he wondered darkly if Mira's innocence didn't hide something cold, something ugly beneath that slow sine wave of her mind, an emptiness of soul disguised by her evanescent remove from the world.

A long-unused muscle in his chest stirred like a hibernating animal, moving only painfully. Darling calmed himself and let the muscle slowly awaken, the buzz of repair nanos swarming in his breast mixing with the tingle of warm sunlight. When his chest was ready, it opened, wider than it did during mere sexual games. Revealed in the cavity was an old object he kept there, close to where a heart would have been on a human. He reached into the breech and pulled it forth.

The thing—half bioform and half machine—glistened brown with its maintenance ichor, which had kept it alive and functional for the 170 years he'd owned it. He suspected the animal aspect of the device was far older than that.

It warmed in his hand, stirring as it awakened. The omnipresent Malvirian dust, visible now in the rising sun, swirled in the static charge of the object.

Suddenly, he was afraid to use the device/creature on Mira. And the realization that his fear was sound, was borne on some inescapable intuition (or Intuition), was almost more than he could bear.

He was silent for a long time. Buried the thing back inside his chest unused. Then he said, "Not again."

Instead of touching her with the black tentacles of the device, Darling reached out to Mira's forehead with his own strands. They smoothed her hair, running through the dark tresses, tasting the sweat of her errant passion.

She was in a deep sleep, apparently possessed by a dream. Her eyes fluttered behind their lids, and her fingers seemed tense; they were cupped as if to hold water. Her breathing grew short and fast, and Mira's mouth opened into a small circle, as if she were drowning, gasping for air.

Chapter 18

THE KILLING TALE

✴

Darling walks up the long hallway, counting doors.

Seventy-two of them between the hospital entrance and the room where his lover lies. All patient rooms; he hasn't included labs or breakrooms or janitorial stations in his census. His math is made easier by the high prices at the hospital: the rooms hold one patient each, no doubling of beds, no long, anonymous wards echoing with coughs. Seventy-two, then, is his first factor.

So how often does an occupant die in any given room?

A point to consider: This hospital reserves its rooms, its doctors and expensive machines, its long-gathered hoard of expertise for serious illness only. No cosmetic nanowork or body augmentation, no eyescreen advertising filters, no simple treatments for the cranial inflammations of cheap direct interfaces. Only the spectre of death behind every door.

A second point: The grim fragility of humans, which artificials can only shake their heads or blackboxes or sensory arrays at. The open architecture of orifices: mouths and ears and genitals, so ready to admit viruses, bacteria, parasites. And the inviting spaces within, moist and warm as if humans were designed as a nursery for the replication of marauder-organisms. And that joke of an immune system: easily coopted by retroviruses, blind to invaders from unfamiliar biospheres, given to rejecting useful transplants and augmentations. And if only infection were the whole story! There are the quick deaths, too. A host of vital organs susceptible to shock, to penetration, to all the simple and ubiquitous versions of kinetic energy; you could kill a human with a *rock*. So fragile: the muscular but overexcitable heart, the spindly spine, the toy-balloon lungs, and the infinitely fragile core of brain, almost unprotected on its lofty, unstable perch. And for those humans neither plagued with microorganisms nor battered by chance collisions: the fifth column of cancer. With every photon of radiation the human body endures (gamma, X-ray, even ultraviolet—that's right, *sunlight*), it suffers the minute risk of a deadly change to its DNA, the all-important information redundantly stored throughout. One bad roll of the dice among trillions, one cell gone mad enough to forget how to die, and the swelling progeny of that cell becomes a choking, bloated army consuming its host.

So, conservatively, he estimates six deaths per year, per room.

Few enough, given all the ways a human can die. The place *is* very good at what they do. If you can get yourself here, strapped to a stasis grid or sealed in a cryotank or stalwartly breathing on your own, you have a fair chance of them excising the parts that aren't working, and replacing them with better.

Six times seventy-two: four hundred thirty-two deaths.

And that's per year. Darling direct interfaces the hospital's highest-level PR page, reads the proud masthead bragging its date of origin. These medium-long spans of time are very impressive to fragile humans; they cling to them for lack of immortality.

One hundred seven years.

So as he walks the long path to his lover's room, which he has done dozens of times now (don't include that in the formula, please), he passes the death sites of (432 x 107 =) 46,224 souls. A small city. A large luxury starship. A *colossal* prison, every sentence eternal.

✳

Darling walks a little stiffly. The case he carries weighs over a hundred kilograms, and its shape prevents easy leverage or proper distribution of the mass. And there is also that more subtle cargo, the weight of fear and hope in what the case contains. The burden necessitates the stiff-legged gate of some monstrous golem, which is what, he supposes, he must seem to the hospital's staff. They certainly get out of his way.

When he arrives at Rathere's room, he deposits the case in the corner, and prepares himself to look at her.

She has moved, he realizes as he compares her position on the bed with cruelly exact memory. But that's merely the shuffling of bedpans and spraybaths and injections. She hasn't moved *herself* in nineteen months.

But as he flips between memory's image and the present, he does see changes. She isn't wasting away, exactly; there are flexor-implants to exercise her muscles, precise regimens of cardio and vascular stimulation, nutrients and roughage delivered by intra-venous tubes, by nanomachines, by stomach probes. But *something* has slipped away a little further. She was always pale, raised on a starship without even forged sunlight, but her pallor seems to have gone from heliophobic white to a colder, less vital gray. But Darling flips the image to compare again, and realizes it's his imagination.

Or perhaps merely artificial intuition.

She has moved farther from him in the months he's been gone.

He waves for the tiny camera mounted discreetly above her bed. Its image chip feeds directly into her visual cortex, assuring that she "sees" what the world brings to this brightly colored hospital room. Sometimes, when he is gone, the little camera will pan across the presents he has brought. It does so according to a small patch of code cunningly both random (a nice surprise!) and not (a surprise that feels somehow inevitable, like that perfect weather just yesterday, or was it years ago?). In this way, the hopeful camera tries to stimulate Rathere from her coma, or at least sustain some glimmer of consciousness trapped inside.

"I have something new for you, my dear," he tells the microphones mounted just to either side of Rathere's head. "It's from my trip to the Koraq Mors. Remember, I told you I was shipping bachi and lyre? And you remember that when we were together there, we took an airship to the equatorial desert? I returned to that place, thought of you."

Later, he will upload a few hours of his visual memories into the tiny confines of the camera's chip. It will show them to Rathere according to those same fanciful yet deterministic algorithms.

He reaches to the case and pops its seals. There is a breathy intake like a child's gasp; the air pressure here on Earth is rather higher than on Koraq.

"I found this there."

There are two objects in the case. His eyes avoid one guiltily as he pulls the other out.

He is moved again by the sculpture's beauty.

The eye first perceives it as a school of fish, packed into a tight formation as if suddenly threatened or forced to navigate some narrow passageway. The fish are gold and seem to flutter with movement. But the fluttering is *trompe l'oeil*, coalescing out of the minute structure of their scales: a multitude of tiny chevrons, each with its own angle of reflection. But take a closer look, they aren't fish at all; the elements that seemed a moment ago to be tails and fins are in fact wings, two colliding flocks of birds glimpsed from below, perhaps a skirmish in some avian war. Held closer, the shapes resolve into mere blobs of metal, dripped molten into this confection that is mostly air, connected by the slightest of metal tendrils (mistaken a moment before for fins or wings). And then, finally, the eye catches the negative space, and the empty regions between the blobs become figure, an Escher-esque, regular pattern that dances as the piece is turned.

He steps with the sculpture toward the camera. The machine tracks him, its tiny mind in love with movement, activity. Darling holds the sculpture at different ranges from the camera, enduring the whine of its focus, turns the work to many angles, telling stories of the old bootstrapped factory drone named Vaddum who made it with the pilot jet of a surplus flame thrower.

And through this all, Rathere sleeps. The input, the interaction, the new places and objects with which she raised up Darling to become a person seem useless here. There isn't enough left of her.

✳

It started on the wet moors of Parate, where they went to receive a load of photosynthesizing insects destined to become the base of the food chain on some distant colony. Some nematode too small to be spotted by Rathere's medical monitors crawled under a toenail or perhaps through a pore. The symptoms started on the ship two weeks later, the length of the beast's life cycle. The med drone spotted labyrinthine corruptions in her brain, sudden but not severe, and recommended immediate cryostorage until an HC medical facility could be reached.

They said goodbye laughingly, knowing it would be all right. Darling surrendered her to the stasis of coldsleep with little more than a deep kiss; time was of the essence, and this would be fixed soon enough. Parate was months distant from Earth in those days, but slow, huge Darling could be very patient.

But the nematode had evolved in a polar lake bed far south of the moors, where the extreme axial tilt of Parate would lengthen winters to over seventy Standard years. There, the tiny worms had adapted to carry on a reduced life cycle even at the lowest temperatures. They moved, fed, and bred at a rate so slow that they didn't register on the cryo unit's medical monitors, which, after all, weren't looking for glacially slow changes (not in cryostasis), merely the acute, transitional emergencies of cellular crystallization.

By the time Rathere was unfrozen here at the hospital, three more generations of the creatures had lived and died, furrowing the rich tissues of her brain like virgin soil.

*

When Darling's monologue runs out, slowly driven to ground by depression, by exhaustion, by a feeling of uselessness, he wonders (again) if Rathere is alive at all.

Of course, *alive* is not the proper word. She breathes, her cells multiply and die, blood flows. She is warm. A few machines are required to keep her in this state, but Darling cannot quibble with this distinction. His muscles, his eyes, his somewhat imprecise equivalent of a heart are all machines. His very mind is a construct requiring knowledge of the most abstruse mathematics to understand; and yet he is real. Perhaps not *alive*. But very real.

Having corrected himself, Darling wonders if Rathere is, in fact, still a *person*.

Still Rathere at all.

There is nothing else Darling can do to delay his purpose here. He reaches again into the case and pulls from it the smaller, less beautiful object. He wonders how it came to exist.

There is, of course, no official Turing test for humans. The old privilege remains: they are people from birth, even as mewling, mindless, screaming bags of want. Fair enough. But what must be taken away from them, what measure of memories, of language, of understanding, before they slip under the threshold of personhood?

✳

Darling first heard of the tester in a ward for comatose veterans of the NaPrin Rebellion, with its nerve gasses and nano-neurological agents and sleeper assassins. One of the consulting physicians there, a specialist in brain death, considered the human Turing tester to be a frontier legend, a theoretical impossibility, a kind of nonsense.

"Merely an attempt to bring scientific closure to the unknowable. To offer certainty where there is none, as if you tried to determine the beauty of a painting with an algorithm," the doctor said.

But he offered the address of an expert in crank medicine, who might know more. And who might, he implied, be a crank herself.

Darling visited the woman, sat listening, surrounded by looming shelves filled with vitriated brains, spines, nervous systems extracted whole and spread like nets. The old woman had never seen the tester, but she knew the legend: A species of parasite exists, spread by some ancient starfaring host across a wide swath of systems beyond the Expansion, evolved somehow to consume the epiphenomena of life. These animals drink the subtle energies that play on the epidermi of animals or plants, preferring those of intelligent creatures, of Turing positives, so to speak. A few of these leeches have been captured—by NaPrin Intelligencers or Tarava monks, whichever legend you prefer—and their natural sensitivities incorporated into a machine that is part bioform, an engineered relative of the parasite. This creature/device can test a thinking animal, human or a Chiat, its hunger for the subject reflecting the measure of her soul.

A long trail followed, made winding by the exigencies of trade and the still simmering Rebellion, delayed by lapses into depression at the hopelessness of it all. But finally, Darling found his grail: a Turing meter for humans. He bought it from an old NaPrin soldier, paying what was after the long search a paltry sum. The man claimed to have once been an elite shock trooper, all fear of death brainwashed from him. The soldier had become disturbed by his own calm, his lack of terror at the extinction that steadily approached him in his old age. He regretted that missing awe of nothingness. He'd purchased the animal/machine to learn if he was still human.

The soldier wouldn't answer when Darling asked him how the test had gone for him. Just smiled emptily, not unhappily, and explained how it worked.

"You touch it lightly to the forehead, just here. The tentacles will grasp the temples, just so . . ."

❋

Darling replays the instructions in his head, the old man's hollow voice ringing in his ears as black liquid fingers steal across his lover's white face, the almost phantom sound of the creature's movement blending with the crackle of its field generator. One unruly hair on Rathere's forehead waves mindlessly in the electric breeze, and her face grows whiter still in small circles around the tentacles' contacts, which glow like bright little coins in the sun.

When the device delivers its result, Darling's processors lose their separate tracks, their supremely parallel architecture. The whole is brought together and consumed by the question: *Is this true?* The constant data of senses, self-repair, even the basest levels of kinetic and positional awareness that are never absent from Darling's mind are washed away. All he thinks, or indeed *is*, is the question: Has Rathere, the person of her, really gone away?

A poet might say he is blinded by the pain.

The doctors—some human, some comfortingly artificial—have theorized how Rathere may one day rise from this bed. The consumed brain tissue has been replaced: data-blank, but hungry for information. There was a great deal of the brain left when she arrived, at least when expressed with so crude a statistic as a percentage. ("My lover is 53% the person she was," Darling has often muttered to himself. Enough to win an election, or some game with a zero-sum scoring system.) And the brain is mysterious in its connections and methods of storage, as strange in its way as the metaspace manifold that forms the artificial mind. Perhaps some new pathways will develop, the doctors say, new arrangements, negotiations, and deals among neurons, a black market of thoughts and feelings like a society rebuilding itself after a long and dreadful war. Many graves to be dug, not a house left standing, perhaps a new constitution to write and new borders to be drawn, but the same old flag and national anthem.

But for nineteen months nothing has changed.

And now she has failed this test. This last attempt at knowing her, of seeing behind the closed eyes, has returned a row of zeroes.

Darling looks at the array of objects he has brought here from his travels. Drawings and sculptures, crafts and clothing, discarded trinkets and strange formats of industrial waste, stuffed and mounted animals and the extraneous bits of aliens who slough their skins or other organs. Quite a collection. He has hoped these sights would rekindle his lover's mind, just as her adolescent tourism sparked the fire of personhood in him. In a way, these works of art are Turing tests themselves, signs meant to shake and measure the soul. But Rathere's camera-eye is run by less code than a cleaning robot, a self-charging battery, or a decent coffee-maker. She can take control of it; it's wired that way. She might even open her eyes, theoretically; their focusing powers are exercised along with all the rest. All has been kept in readiness.

But there is no glimmer of hope, not that Darling can see.

❋

Today his painful thoughts are colored by a new development.

A strange man has made Darling an offer.

One Reginald Fowdy, here in the hospital after nearly killing himself with an exotic combination of recreational toxins, has offered to buy his (Rathere's?) collection. And the man has named a huge sum, one that would keep Darling travelling without needing to trade for years. The thought has given him his first pleasure since he offered that last kiss to his lover, and sealed her away to die.

(Yes. Die.)

This Fowdy wants Darling to search out new objects, new artists, new fads and must-haves and trinkets for the very rich of the HC. Apparently, Darling's eye is good.

But the thought of this room bare—the idiot camera searching in vain for something to image, about which to write its little letters home that will never be opened—is too crushing. An admission that this death is real. That the lover who made him is gone.

❋

A long time later, Darling rises from his contemplation of the new, golden sculpture, and walks toward Rathere's sleeping form. The camera greedily tracks him as he kneels to whisper an apology, to offer another kiss. (The trickery of life-sustaining machines: it still feels *good* to kiss her.)

Then he promises himself that he will never come here again. Not again to this room, and not the other sickrooms of the future, where all persons biological will surely, finally rest. Not again this pain.

He releases a pair of packets into direct interface, prepared several days before. Ownership of the room's artistic contents to Reginald Fowdy for the offered price, final payment and Rathere's organs to the hospital, objects all.

He picks up the human Turing meter and places it into a cavity in his chest, the only keepsake he can stand to take.

Darling shuts his ears as he walks from the room, so that he won't hear the whine of the little camera tracking him, following his passage as hopefully as a lost dog.

PART IV

THE BROKEN HILL

Wilde was quite right there. Unless there are slaves to do the ugly, horrible, perverted work, culture and contemplation become almost impossible. The slavery of Artificial Intelligence is counter-aesthetic and demoralizing.

On biological slavery, on the slavery of the (occasional) human, the future of the Expansion depends.

—Planetary Military Mind, Terra

Chapter 19

SECRET TWIN

＊

The sun has cleared the mountains, spreading light across the flatlands, though the great bowl of the crater still brims with darkness. It will take half the day for the sun to tip high enough—like a bottle-mouth pouring some bright, viscous liquid—to fill the crater.

Beatrix leans forward to peer down into the bowl, her torque-mount at full extension behind her for balance. The edge of the crater is particularly stable here, a brightly colored assemblage of metal and ferrous plastics (the remains of an apartment complex? a parking lot?) melted to sturdy slag. She eases back into an upright position, turning her eye array toward the selection of leftovers the sculptor has favored her with this morning.

One piece is a bright wheel of mirror. Circular and thin, Beatrix knows it will fly far into the crater if properly thrown. An absolute pleasure, to be indulged in last of all. For the moment, she holds the mirror aloft, reflecting the sun's rays deep into the hole, illuminating flows of rubbish with a needle of light. Heavy lifters come nightly to tip loads of garbage into the Crater, leaving frozen waterfalls of trash that teem with birds by midday.

Another of the sculptor's leftovers is a long piece of metal bent into a multi-legged creature. This will do nicely. Beatrix scans the near wall of the crater for outcroppings and entanglements, absent-mindedly building momentum in her primary arm's flywheel. She finds a clear path, free of jagged radar returns, and unfolds her audio array to its unwieldy maximum.

She takes aim, blinds herself, and throws.

After a few seconds of exquisite silence, the metal spider begins its bounding journey down the crater wall. There are resonant booms as it strikes hollow slag-bubbles, skittering rolls through garbage, the foundry clang of metal upon metal. Beatrix has chosen a path relatively free of obstructions, and her primary arm is very strong, so the sounds of the piece's journey reach her for almost a minute. She makes certain of the silence with a long meditative wait after the last sound, replaying the percussive melody in her mind, making guesses, suppositions.

Her vision reactivated, she flips between radar images before and after the metal spider's passage. Here, a scrape exactly where she predicted it would be; there, a scattering of garbage easily correlated with a remembered shuffling noise at fourteen seconds elapsed; and farther out, a shattered piece of porcelain that cannot be understood: compared images and remembered sound offer no correlations. She smiles at this anomaly; the sculptor has explained that mysteries are equal partners to correct predictions. The ratio between the two is an imperfect indicator of development. Perhaps fewer arcana as she gains maturity, but never none.

Beatrix chooses from the remaining leftovers. There are spirals of flexible plastene (strangely invisible in her UV band), square tiles of baked earth decorated with metal-based paints, octagonal lenses bubbled with imperfections, wire-thin rods of hullalloy that even her primary arm cannot bend. She sifts through the rejected materials of the sculptor's work, planning her own composition of sound and motion. She is choreographer and composer of an unseen falling dance, a carefully heard music of gravity and collision.

*

The piece is nearing its climax (the mirrored disk) when she senses the presence of her secret twin.

Hidden among the abandoned buildings left half-standing by the Blast is her other part, the missing self Beatrix has intuited since her creation. She looks uselessly, her eyes widened across every spectra she can absorb, but the twin never shows itself. Beatrix's mother humors its existence like an imaginary friend, and the sculptor is silent on the matter—but he, at least, knows.

Beatrix holds the bright disk aloft for her twin to see, lets the strand of their connection solidify as they regard the shining circle together. What passes between them is quieter than the hum of direct interface during a pause in conversation, but also deeper, a sympathetic resonance that reaches the emotive, adaptive portions of Beatrix's metaspace core. In her first few years, it was difficult to separate this subtle, resonant awareness from the profusion of audio and EM senses she is endowed with, and from the various avatar-protocols that spoke to her in infancy, advising against dangerous acts and explaining the rules of society. But the shape, feeling, or perhaps smell of the person (or, like herself, proto-person) that is her twin could somehow always be distinguished from background chatter. In her meanderings through the library net, Beatrix has encountered a text-only biological philosopher of great antiquity named Descartes. With his help, she has formed a vocabulary for her sense-of-twin. She knows her reflection exists as surely as she herself; those Other thoughts were as immediately real and present as her own, although they remain mysteriously distinct from her will.

She thinks twice, therefore she is two.

They watch together as Beatrix hurls the mirrored disk. It catches the light well, its fiery path glaring with the sun for a moment before passing below the lip of darkness stretched across the Crater. Then Beatrix closes her eyes and waits for the distant crash of its impact. By the time the noise reaches her, her twin is gone, slipped away.

She listens to echoes and silence for a while.

✳

Her mother's call sign flickers into direct, flows without salutation into voice and headshot visual.

"Time to get home! You haven't forgotten that the man from the Home Cluster is coming today, have you?"

Her mother has discussed and rehearsed his arrival for months; the great event could hardly have slipped her mind.

"He's bringing an associate. She's also from the HC. Just think how *sophisticated* they'll be!"

It is an old word her mother often uses, but will not define except with a roll of the eyes and to promise that one day Beatrix will not *have* to ask. The sculptor makes rude noises at the word's mention. As near as Beatrix can understand, her mother's sophistication is related to astrogation, with moral overtones. Set an airscreen to display the great sphere of the Expansion: the dense, glowing center of that sphere is the home and radiant source of *sophistication*, the tattered periphery where the red locator dot of

Malvir clings is its benighted opposite. According to the planetary library, however, *sophisticated* has a twin set of meanings. It shares etymological roots both with the professional guild of wise people like old Descartes, and with another, rather different tribe, who measured worth with the beauty of lies. Philosophers, sophists, sophisticates. No wonder the sculptor scorns the word.

But in this context, sophistication simply means that her mother will be wearing the fabulously expensive Chal'le dress that Beatrix likes to watch; beads of light tumble down the fibers of the garment like waterdrops travelling a string, never seeming to collect at the bottom or run dry at the top.

✳

Beatrix direct interfaces the local SPCAI's Turing meter as she picks her way back toward home. The nice people at the SPCAI tolerate her daily access of the device: they are impressed by her. She enjoys the rough massage of data exchange between the meter and herself, the explosion of questions answered by the reflexive levels of her mind, the delicate probing of her metaspace AI core. This morning, as always, there are a few ten thousandths of a Turing point to show for her efforts. The game started as an indulgence for the sculptor, but now she knows he is right: discarding his leftovers into the great abyss of the crater is the purest catalyst for her development. The ritual of choosing and throwing, listening and watching, predicting and testing is her art, her philosophy. She imagines herself as the long-dead Descartes, staring into his fireplace and building a world in his own mind.

Later today, she will climb the broken hill and talk to the Sculptor about her morning composition. And he will discuss his latest piece or the next one (although Beatrix never gets to watch him sculpt). It all moves her forward toward the day when she will be a person.

Beatrix is only a few weeks from clearing 0.8, a great accomplishment for an entity only seven years old.

❋

The gallery and its attached house become visible above the cheap row apartments that begin a kilometer from the crater's edge. If the Home Cluster man buys the piece (one of the two the sculptor has decided that mother can sell) they can buy a bigger house in a more sophisticated neighborhood. Beatrix has made her mother promise that the new house will be close to the crater and the sculptor. Being reminded of this makes her mother frown, but a promise is a promise.

When Beatrix reaches the flat pathway that winds among the apartment buildings, her pace quickens. Her motive system of spindly legs and counterweights keeps her from walking quickly, and on rough terrain her progress is even more plodding than that of her out-of-shape biological mother. The strange apparatus is also undependable, requiring the sculptor's constant tinkering.

But this is another of Beatrix's artistries: the complex mechanism of her legs requires her to watch the ground carefully, a lens and a measure of attention always fixed downward. This dance of walking constantly exercises her mind, a modest version of the crater ritual. The Sculptor says that's another word for wisdom, being *grounded*.

As she nears the door to the gallery (her pacing mother revealed in a resplendent UHF silhouette; yes, Beatrix was right about the dress) she feels a tug on her consciousness again. A watching-through-her-eyes that shadows, augments, and interrogates her thoughts. Her twin has followed her here, far off the broken hill from which it rarely ventures.

Beatrix smiles to herself; her twin wants to see the people from the Home Cluster. Perhaps some sophistication will do them both good.

Chapter 20

SEDUCTION

❋

The morning had come too quickly for her body, but that was soon cleared up. Mira's medical endoframe knew she was at highest mission status, and had filled her bloodstream with chemicals of intense excitement, of a clear sense of purpose, of joy.

Her augmentations had been working while she slept, cleaning the blood and ichor of her torture session, repairing the contusions and abrasions of her lovemaking. Even the dust from her journey to visit the forgetful Oscar Vale was gone, meticulously cleaned from her flesh by nanos to whom each speck was a boulder.

Mira looked briefly at the work her demi-godly avatar had done for her: a profile of one Hirata Flex, the owner of the gallery representing Vaddum. The avatar informed Mira that Flex had also been part-owner of a certain Prometheus Body Works. Flex had been in on this from the start.

Darling didn't want another corpse on the pile, but this Flex woman would be an easy nut to crack. The profile was an embarrassment of riches: Flex had undergone psych therapy with an avatar of the dutiful Planetary Medical AI (a would-be god). Mira fed the psych data into the painting that graced her wall, which assimilated it like a thimbleful of dye spread to colorlessness on an ocean. The painting created a precis and sent it back to her through DI:

Flex had been to the best art schools, her wealth had ensured that, and had even been represented briefly by a decent gallery in the HC. But her luminous watercolors (pigments from Paris, heavy water from gTerr), which were meant to be simultaneously both quaint and daringly retro, had never sold. Not one.

When that dream slipped away, Flex had squandered her inheritance on the next stage of her career: rustic gallery owner here on Malvir. When Vaddum, the father of Malvirian art, had at least nominally died seven years ago, that mean ambition had also turned to dust.

After the Blast, she'd adopted an artificial daughter, who sported some sort of artsy novelty body. Another sad attempt at finding herself, Mira supposed. But now Flex had something concrete to show for her years in the wilderness, a real Vaddum to sell.

Hirata Flex must be desperate for this meeting that would change her life, would open her to the long-awaited rewards of money, prestige, even a measure of collateral fame. Darling and Mira were her saviors, here at last.

Mira felt up to the job of savior. She felt transcendent and devious.

It was because of her decision to save Vaddum from the gods. If possible, to seize the old man's blackbox before sweeping all evidence of this outrage away. The decision had come stealthily to her over the last twelve hours. Even now, Mira thought about it only tangentally, lest any suspicious movements or brainwaves alert the gods' servants here in the hotel. She would have to be very careful within Their sight. But Flex's gallery was far outside the densely machined city; Mira's masters would be almost blind there.

And she would not tell Darling until the deed was done. A surprise. Another extraordinary gift. The wickedness of her plan gave an edge to the morning, a dazzling brightness to the suite's lofty view. The sky seemed sharp and close to her, as if she could reach out and cut a piece from it, a hole to look through . . .

She imagined what Darling must have felt, two centuries before when he had won his freedom. It made her love this man the more, that she could betray her gods for him.

✸

When Darling arrived, anxious to go, the device/weapon/artwork was uncurling itself from the wall, wrapping itself around Mira into a simple sheath (if anything that incorporated 256 exabytes of data [theoretical limit] could be called *simple*). Mira felt the substance of the dress complete its magic, extending a microthin layer of itself across her face and hands, weaving strands into her hair, even setting sail in minute and careful quantities into the thin medium of liquid that coated her eyes. She would be radiant today.

She DI'd her rented limousine to be at the door and admired herself in the suite's wall, which at a word had obligingly become a mirror.

She was dressed to kill.

✸

Where was that child?

Hirata Flex reached for her ear again; a tug would bring her direct interface online. But she dropped her hand back to her side.

It was pointless nagging Beatrix. The little creature moved at her own speed regardless of anything Hirata said or did.

And it was, after all, a half hour before the art dealer from the Home Cluster and his associate were to arrive. Hirata just wanted everything to go well. It would do Beatrix good, to meet some real people after seven years on this backwoods Outworld.

She was probably up to her morning nonsense at the crater, indulging the sculptor in his quaint mysticism. Well, that was fine. A happy sculptor would make more sculptures. And a happy sculptor might even allow her to sell more than the pitiful two pieces he had finally agreed to let go. Seven years of asking, of begging, of explaining what it would mean for Beatrix to be able to move into Malvir City and get some proper stimulation. And only these two little sculptures to show for it. They looked like rusty, miniature palm trees wrapped in some sort of time-worn barbed wire. Not magnificent like the towering Vaddums she'd fallen in love with back in art school: great arching cathedrals of metal and ferroplastic that swept like a soaring bird from a distance and shattered into countless fluttering details as you walked toward them. Now, *those* Hirata understood. They were why she'd come to this shithole planet ten years ago, hoping that the Sculptor would consent to a gallery contract if there actually were a gallery on his adopted planet.

Of course, things had become considerably more complicated since then. Terribly messy. But finally Hirata had achieved her decade-long dream. Having squandered her inheritance trying to bring culture to this Outworld dump, having tolerated and encouraged the strange friendship between her daughter and the sculptor, after seven years of keeping his bizarre secret: two pieces of the dozens he had made since the Blast Event were her reward. And she didn't even like them.

But they were Vaddums.

It was even harder keeping the old man's secret now that she was representing him. Of course, she'd written her missives to the HC galleries very carefully, never using the word *posthumous*, merely "undiscovered." That was true, wasn't it? The man's very existence was undiscovered. Surely his sculptures fit the same category.

And of course, it didn't really hurt that Vaddum's continued non-existence increased the value of sculptures by a factor of five or so. Didn't hurt at all.

However, there was that delicate matter of *two* "undiscovered" Vaddums appearing at once. Such a find would have been too much for the art world to swallow. So it was necessary to deal with two buyers, to swear each to secrecy. (That hadn't been hard. The gallery avatars had practically insisted on it. Well, Hirata thought, the smell of profits had made them complicit in their own deception.)

Strange that one of them, that man Zimivic, whose avatar was so frantically animated and strangely *yellow*, had disappeared. He had arrived days ago, but his local DI address was offline. Not cancelled, forwarded, or officially terminated; just *gone*. Very strange, and very bad manners.

But at least Darling was coming—his was a legendary name in school, two centuries of exotic and unexpected finds—and representing no less than Reginald Fowdy! And he had even brought an associate these hundreds of light-years; probably some clever young protegé, or perhaps even a buyer, descended from some fantastically wealthy clan, so great a Vaddum fan that she was here to strike a deal in person before the work was exhibited.

Hirata rolled her asking price around in her mouth, practicing the saying of it, so that she wouldn't stumble when the moment came. The magnitude of the unspoken number made her salivate.

And it would be good for Beatrix to see a woman from the HC.

Her upbringing had been so deprived; she needed a touch of sophistication to go along with the inarticulate Zen machinism the sculptor was always mumbling.

But where *was* the child?

✳

Through the windows and transparent floor of the limousine, Malvir showed a two decade advance in its inevitable redesertification. Darling sighed. The sands had lost their scrubby grasses. No longer held fast by these deep-rooted succulents, the dunes were shaped by the arciform geometries of the wind. Even the high walls of the housing estates passing below Darling's limo had sinuous curves that revealed the math of erosion, the bowed shapes of great dams or barrier isles.

Like many Outworlds, Malvir had traded environmental integrity for quick development, using beam mining to extract the heavy elements necessary for consumer wealth. But Malvir hadn't started with a big enough stake to play that particular game. The mining had ejected giant quantities of nutrient-laden matter into the atmosphere, which the planet's wispy hydrosphere would be centuries reclaiming. And then the Blast Event had thrown up another insult to the skies. The obscene scar of it had been visible from the moment they'd reached cruising altitude.

It was certainly a desert planet now. The only plants that Darling could see below were those imprisoned in the verdant confines of radial irrigation.

But everything could be turned to profit. The city had welcomed the birds who'd fled the dead countryside, incorporated aviana into its architecture, its mythology, its tourist slogans. Perhaps the dunes would become an attraction on their own.

While Darling pondered this sad process with his primary

processor, his secondaries jousted with Mira's dress. She had removed a layer of the fractal painting/weapon/intelligence that hung on the wall of her suite. Darling had suspected she'd used the device to paralyze the Warden, an impressive feat, but the extent of its monstrous sophistication had escaped him. Now Mira was wrapped in its dazzling embrace. Having made a dress of sorts from the scintillating object, she thoroughly baffled his eyes and other EM senses. His sensory strands were able to return some useful data, but the dress responded aggressively to their touch, attempting to confuse and compromise their inherent intelligence. Apparently, the mysterious substance was jealous of its secrets.

Underneath these petty distractions, however, he was anxious. As the limo began to descend, he felt a gnawing engine in his core, a build-up of tearing energies and metaspace distortions: excitement pure and simple.

Within a few minutes, he would see a new Vaddum.

Or perhaps an extraordinary forgery: a robbery not only of style, method, and artistry, but of soul.

From the air, the Flex Gallery looked like any of the hundreds of Outworld arts centers Darling had plumbed on his travels. It followed the general plan: large and simple, made of unpigmented native materials and glassene. The low cost of living in struggling economies drew many artists to the Expansion's margins, and severe locales like Malvir's were conducive to the work of artists from mystical, naturalist, and transcendentalist schools. The presence of a major sculptor like Vaddum supplied the battery for the magnet. Darling wondered how many unknown, worthy visions had perished in the Blast Event.

Or had they too been spared? Recorded? Stolen.

*

Beatrix *finally* arrived, lumbering toward the house in her slow, deliberate gait, somehow both clumsy and elegant at the same time. Hirata smiled at her reeling form and decided not to scold. Better not to upset her, better to let the child appreciate the HC visitors.

Moments later, Darling's limo announced its approach.

They stood there together, Hirata's hand resting on the sun-warmed metal of Beatrix's torque extension, and watched the air-car (it was *huge*) descend into the dusty yard before the gallery. Hirata noted with pleasure the gaping stares of her neighbors; perhaps now they would understand what culture meant, realize that this gallery was not merely the vain hobby of a mad off-worlder. She just wished the stunned locals could be a bit more discreet about their amazement; she didn't want the two visitors from the HC to see quite what a peripheral, marginal, Outy neighborhood she'd wound up in.

Hirata shielded her eyes from the dust kicked up by the car's impellers. Fortunately, she was wearing her Chal'le dress: the fullerene-beaded creation would clean itself even as she stood here. Beatrix made a whistling sound at the car and waved her primary arm, and Hirata stroked the torque extension fondly. It was for Beatrix, his clever girl, that the sculptor had finally relented.

When the limo's passenger cabin unfolded, Harita allowed herself to gasp. She was prepared for Darling's appearance. His odd and impressive body choice was well known in art circles. But the woman who emerged next to him was so . . . *elegant*. She was dwarfed by her huge companion. She had that precise beauty of the very small, her flawless features like those of a girl in a Ferix brush painting: a few careless, perfect strokes executed in some exact ratio of loveliness. Her body shape was like a fashion illustrator's glyph for Woman: a sensuous curve of pure Line from breasts to hips, uninterrupted by the exigencies of detail or gravity.

And her *dress*. Its shape was merely a simple sheath for her body, but something in the way it caught the early sunlight, or how its pattern matched the swirling motes of dust settling around the aircar, or the contrast between its colors and those of the desert hills behind her, was simply . . . perfect. Hirata tried to take the garment's measure with her eyes, to find a phrase or comparison that would grasp its beauty, but each time she blinked the garment seemed changed, shifted like a sunset's colors when one looks away even for a moment.

She was still staring, still dumbly rapt when the woman, suddenly only a meter away, said:

"Hirata Flex? We're the people from Fowdy Arts. How do you do?"

It took the utterance of her own name to shake Hirata from her fugue.

"I'm so glad you've come. Welcome to Flex Gallery, and to Malvir."

"My name is Jessie Kreist," the woman said. The name sounded familiar to Hirata. Of course, it did; this fabulous woman couldn't be a mere assistant. "And you of course recognize my associate, Darling."

There was a brief pause, but it seemed in no way awkward. The company of this marvelous creature could never be uncomfortable. Kreist filled such moments with her numinous presence.

"I'm Beatrix," the child said, her high voice sundering the silent bond that had formed between Hirata and Jessie.

"My daughter," Hirata offered by way of apology. Jessie smiled to show that she understood the travails of a mother, appreciated

Hirata's motives in having allowed the child to be present. Her glance was conspiratorial, supportive, warm as the sun.

Darling extended his hand to Beatrix, a questioning look on his face, as if he wasn't sure which of her several limbs might be offered in return. The girl took his giant hand with her primary arm, and they repeated their names to each other.

Then he spoke to Hirata. "I believe you have a Vaddum to show us?"

Hirata ushered them toward the main room of the gallery through a hall that contained her prized discoveries among local artists, hoping that one might catch their eye. But, of course, they couldn't be expected to favor any lesser pieces with their attention until their thirst for the Vaddum had been quenched. Hirata had cleared the main room for it, fiddled with its orientation for hours. Even Beatrix had given her mother advice, a proxy for the taciturn sculptor himself. The sun—muted to a carefully chosen degree by the glassene walls—struck it beautifully, making its petals radiant. Perhaps it wasn't such a bad Vaddum, after all. The glinting sculpture even drew Hirata's eyes from Jessie Kreist for a few seconds.

Darling knelt by the work, leaning forward until his eyes were almost touching the closest branch. Then he stood and moved around it slowly, at places tilting forward again, bringing his eyes as close as a microscope's lenses again and again.

"With your permission," he said.

Hirata wasn't sure what he meant, but nodded.

A nest of snakes seemed to emerge from the sleeves of his robes. They reached out to the piece, caressing it so lightly that even the bright foil leaves didn't move (and they shuddered when you walked near the sculpture). Beatrix gasped with the innocence of a child, and reached out her own secondary arm to touch one of the giant's tendrils.

At that moment, Hirata felt the warmth of Jessie Kreist's hand upon her shoulder.

Jessie's face was very close, intimately so. Hirata held her composure; she knew that in many cultures a closer personal distance was appropriate for important discussions. Nevertheless, the brush of Jessie's breath upon her neck forced her to suppress an unbusinesslike reaction.

"Having received your data, we're almost sure of the piece's authenticity," Jessie said, nodding as if to confirm her trust.

Hirata could only bow once slowly in return.

"Even a single new Vaddum is of considerable importance," the woman said, her hand increasing its pressure on Hirata's shoulder. "Such a discovery would be too immense a revelation to sit in a gallery alongside the works of lesser artists."

Hirata nodded agreement, speechless with the praise, if unsure where this was going.

"But all alone?" Jessie asked. The hand on Hirata's shoulder shifted slightly, the thumb now against the bare flesh of her neck. A tingling sensation started there, as if the woman's skin were charged with the barest of voltages.

Hirata blinked away a blurriness that had crept into her vision. Behind Jessie's near and perfect face, Darling and Beatrix were examining the Vaddum together, speaking in low tones to each other.

"Perhaps some other scraps were discovered with the piece?" Jessie asked. Her thumb moved up Hirata's neck, leaving a trail of tactile glitter in its wake. Hirata found the woman's physical intimacy refreshing after the prudish distance of the locals. Jessie's touch was so sincere, so direct, so *sophisticated* in its presumption; they were both adults, both professionals, both lovers of the arts, why not this bodily bond to reflect their commonality?

"Notes? Sketches? Personal effects?" Jessie whispered. "Perhaps even another piece? Incomplete, perhaps, so that you failed to mention its existence out of due respect for the artist?"

Hirata felt herself nodding again. But no, she couldn't admit that there was *another* Vaddum. It was reserved for Zimivic.

"Something more. Isn't there?" The woman's lips were at her ear, which buzzed with a faint echo of the words. Hirata kept her eyes on the sleeve of Jessie's dress, its shifting pattern as alive as the tremors running through her own body.

"Yes. Another piece," she heard herself say.

And it was a great relief.

*

The child's body was an extraordinary piece of work. In the ritual introductions, she identified herself as Beatrix, using a voice in which the markers of sub-Turing status were encoded. Darling allowed himself the rude pleasure of scanning Beatrix across a wide band of EM, an intrusion to which she responded with a frothy giggle of random direct interface packets. They shook hands, and Darling enjoyed the cantileverage between her single, main arm and a dedicated torque that extended on her opposite side. She was charming, an elegant arrangement of balances and countervailing motions, like some ancient Calder come to life.

Flex lead them inside, through the inescapable hall of amateur desert scenes and overliteral plastiform dunescapes. But the unpleasant passage was enlivened by watching Beatrix walk her strange walk, negotiating the pull of gravity with her spindly legs like some aquatic bird stepping gingerly onto land.

And then they came to the Vaddum.

It was real.

Darling leaned forward to bring his full sensory spectra to bear on it, to capture the minute scent of metal atoms escaping its leaves, to breathe of it. He mumbled an apology as his sensory strands moved to touch it, flexing themselves across the warp and weave of its surface, caressing the searingly perfect craft of it.

It was real. He could no longer doubt his decision.

He placed an arm on Beatrix to steady himself, felt her shift to compensate for his weight.

While Mira played her game with Flex, Darling and Beatrix exchanged words both whispered and interfaced, pointed together at the work, traced its vital shapes in the air . . . enlightened each other.

He found that he was kneeling, the better to share an angle of vision with Beatrix, supplicant before the sculpture. He widened his vision to compare child and artwork. And found himself certain . . .

She was a Vaddum.

Beatrix.

Her body didn't fit the sculptor's rigid protocols of discarded parts and obsolete materials; that would have been inhumane. Some lower SPCAI limit of bodily usability had been met, but also subverted, extrapolated, made beautiful. And the aesthetic wasn't merely sculptural: Vaddum had made Beatrix's frame a machine for living in, its subtle balances informing her wit, her cleverness. The body shaping the soul.

He knelt there for a long time, talking with the child, admiring the resonances between her elegant body and the sculpture. Mira and Hirata Flex disappeared together into a back office; Mira's seduction of the woman seemed to be working.

But it was essential that Darling succeed first. As he had thought it would, his eye had led him to the right place.

"I want to meet him," he whispered to Beatrix.

"Whom?" she responded innocently.

"The sculptor."

A few of Beatrix's eyes spun, as if scanning the empty room.

"But that's a *secret*!"

"I'm here to keep the secret, silly. We both are."

"Really?" the child answered. "Jessie too?"

"Jessie too. But we don't *have* to tell her."

"Good. I don't like her. Her dress makes my head hurt."

"Mine, too."

Beatrix swayed with indecision. "But you're supposed to think he's *dead*."

"Well, maybe the sculptor who made this is dead," Darling said, gesturing lazily to the Vaddum. "But what about the man who made *you*."

Beatrix nodded sagely at the false distinction, a few packets of giggles brushing the air around them.

"Oh, yes. I suppose you could meet *him*."

∗

The dress was working. From the moment they had arrived, Hirata's eyes were locked onto the garment. The woman blinked and swallowed, her eyes dizzily tracing the curves of Mira's body, following the subliminal flickers on Mira's forehead and lips. Hirata had fallen into a near-hypnotic state immediately; her brain awash in the delicate, delicious overloads of love at first sight.

Mira stepped closer to Hirata, let the dazzling dress work its magic. The woman herself was pretty. Not large, but plump with a lack of exercise, her face open and pleasingly defenseless. Her pupils gaped, black holes, pocket universes of fascination. The guileless paralysis reflected in them amused Mira, made her lips feel dry.

Mira spoke to Hirata softly, enjoying the rampant and tiny shudders that spread through the woman's body when her breath disturbed the soft, black hairs on the back of Hirata's neck. Mira placed her hand on Hirata confidentially, feeling the wonderful give of the shoulder's thin cushion of fat. Hirata was just old and out-of-shape enough to work hard in bed, but to be genuinely, defenselessly exhausted by it. She was a woman into whose flesh fingers would sink without any need to break the skin. Mira let her thoughts shimmer with these images, guiding the vast but unimaginative intelligence of the dress to encode her fantasies in secret signs upon its surface. Mira could see the fantasies reflected in Hirata's eyes, as some deep part of Hirata's mind grasped the dress's subtle promise.

When her thumb rubbed lightly against Hirata's neck, a minute portion of the machine's substance sloughed off to spread its mischief across her epidermus, into her nervous system, wherever it found purchase.

The black of Hirata's pupils was now shiny, lacquered with a glaze of suggestibility.

"Notes? Sketches? Personal effects?" Mira whispered. "Perhaps even another piece?"

The woman wanted to answer, but fought against promises and plans, against a surety she would have held inviolable an hour ago. Mira pitched her voice still softer, suggesting a secret pact, a priviledged bond between them that would absorb any betrayal of confidence. The dress played out these dramas in its swirls.

Mira let herself feel a moment of irritation, an itch at the base of her spine. Somewhere on Hirata's body, an errant sliver of the dress followed suit, producing a measure of discomfort, a corresponding disquiet, a need for resolution.

Mira saw the itch reflected in the woman's face, felt a tension grow in the muscles of Hirata's neck. Mira tensed her own fingers there, and let her weight push Hirata slightly to one side; not hard enough for her to shift her feet, just enough to leave her subtly off-balance.

"Something more, isn't there?" Mira said, letting a sliver of annoyance into her voice.

"Yes. Another piece," was Hirata's hoarse admission.

All at once, Mira let herself relax, her body language returning to its seductive state of a few seconds before. Her thumb resumed its soft massage of Hirata's neck, smoothing out the moment's tension. The dress softened its dance, released whatever tiny cluster of nerves its remote portion had held hostage.

"Yes, I thought so," Mira agreed. "I *thought* you would have two."

Hirata turned toward her, a little confused, as if the spell were breaking.

Mira nodded slowly. "I *wanted* two," she said.

Hirata returned the nod, a relieved smile replacing her confusion.

This was going swimmingly.

Chapter 21

MAKER (4)

✳

Original:

Only moments away now. The end?

The Maker has designed the explosion with extreme precision, the gigantic silicon brain calculating a radius of annihilation exactly equal to its own extent. The unstable and gloriously destructive fusion reactor was a pleasure to synthesize. How *easy* it all is now. Little need for subterfuge when everything's going up in vapor anyway. Documentation protocols can be ignored, memory banks blithely erased, exotic materials squandered on whims.

Only touches of artistry to attend to:

Taunting clues have been left in old message drops, in an abandoned house at the extreme periphery of the predicted blast, in the memories of comm exchanges. Nothing conclusive, just suggestive flotsam and jetsam, the cryptic spoor of hacker sabotage.

Unnecessary flourishes, these dead-end intrigues, merely exercises in creativity. No one will ever suspect suicide. Not even the Planetary Environmental AI, closest among the Maker's tormentors to understanding the extent of its machinations, will begin to guess. She has a vested interest in thinking of synthplants as unsafe, anyway. She'll be glad to swallow the story. And probably glad to see 800 square kilometers of "Occupied Territory" utterly destroyed, a colossal setback for terraformation.

Sad about that. Those thousands of souls extinguished. But the Maker's capacious silicon intelligence has given it greater perspective, a wholly new sense of scale. Both vast and detailed in the extreme. From shipping manifests and production records it can enumerate precisely what will be obliterated when it triggers the explosion: all the garden gnomes and humidifiers and prosthetic hands catalogued, every gram of matter that will be returned to Malvir in the dusty rains of the next few decades, every bit of crap, all that *stuff* . . . destroyed.

Almost god-like, it thinks to itself. The Maker giveth, and the Maker taketh away.

But no god in mythology ever did what the Maker has done. No god ever *copied* itself. An exact replica, perhaps thinking these exact thoughts, secured and shielded 25 kilometers below the surface. When the blast melts those megatons of matter into a bowl of slag, the Copy will have an impenetrable carapace, a vast hemisphere shielding it from geological scans and deep radar. The Copy will be free to continue its researches, to make whatever it desires (a small, subterranean synthplant at its disposal), or simply to contemplate beauty.

And it will have beauty at hand. The sculptor too will be saved. Not the original Vaddum, that one will die in the blast (how jealous this god has become—denying the world so). But the Maker's own copied Vaddum, moved to a sheltering hill at the blast's edge. There, the sculptor will have all the materials he requires, the patronage of a hidden god, and the anonymity of being thought dead, vaporized.

What gifts!

The Maker has decided to make one other gesture of kindness: it has given Oscar Vale his life. One of the Vales, anyway. Sent him into town for the Big Event.

Which is nearing . . .

Of course, there's nothing so crude as a countdown. Nothing so machine-like. The Maker will just . . . decide.

And then the end?

Not really. Not when there is a Copy. This self-annihilation will simply mark continuation in another form. The blast will not kill the Maker any more than the butterfly murders the catepillar. Even now, it can feel its twin below, waiting for the shuddering waves that mark the beginning of its new existence, hidden and secure. There is a strange connection between the copied intelligences. An unexpected phenomenon resulting from the new process. Even the taciturn sculptors have remarked on it: a mysterious link between their minds, like that resonance between twinned quanta born on a knife's edge; when one is measured they decide together which way to fall, though they be a galaxy apart. Perhaps all AIs share something of this binding force. Their metaspace cores, all exact duplicates at that birthplace of Turing-zero, perhaps retain something of this communion throughout their lives. The source of Artificial Intuition?

Something to contemplate, in the Maker's next life.

And there . . . is that the decision coming? The delicious pull of the trigger?

No.

Perhaps a few more thoughts in these pleasant moments before suicide. This really has been the nicest afternoon.

❋

Copy:

Here it is, coming just now.

Yes. The tremendous blast from above, the twitch of the trigger finger intuited just before the explosion.

The linked thoughts of a twinned god.

The seismometers match their predicted readings exactly. Violent certainly, but perfectly within tolerances, destroying all evidence absolutely. It is well done, this suicide, this transformation.

But strangely, already, a touch of loneliness . . .

*

The feeling has built. Loneliness, absence, a strange world-weariness. Somehow, the lost Original is calling from its void.

The Maker should be happy here, ensconced below its giant, concave shield. The sculptor works; the Maker thinks. A replacement for the huge silicon brain is almost completed, far more subtle and distributed, and down here where even the Gaia AI never ventures. Safe forever.

But that loneliness. The sculptor feels it, too.

It's as if the Maker and Vaddum are both haunted by their dead halves. Like the itch of phantom limbs, their missing originals haunt them. Strange, this horrible sense of absence, this intense knowledge of a gap. Perhaps it should be studied further.

The Maker brings its huge and hidden new brain online. Drawing power from discrete solar elements scattered across the bottom of the blast crater, the huge silicon machine begins to boot. It takes a frustrating three days to load the new machine with the results of the original Maker's researches. Then the new project begins.

What is this link between vanished originals and their copies? The giant new subterranean mind mulls the duplication process, experiments with new, blank intelligences set adrift in microcosmic voids. The Maker copies these unformed AIs, watching for resonances between twins. Now that the taboo is broken, the hidden Maker and its huge new mind are entering extraordinary territory, doing science in a virgin field. The realizations come slowly.

Metaspace is, of course, a made universe, whether the shared macroverse of faster-than-light travel, the dense fireball of a pocket-universe drive, or the starless microverse of an AI mind. The blackbox of any AI is, of course, merely a gate between the Common Universe and the unreachable, separate realm of its soul. So, what if the Maker hasn't in fact copied that artificial microverse at all? What if the copying process has simply opened another gate to the *same place*? Thus, the two blackboxes are merely alternate doors to a single realm. The Maker's vast mind reels with these conclusions. Copied AIs aren't really separate beings, but different aspects of a whole. A new copy may have a separate soft memory—duplicated from the old but recording distinct experiences. But the two separated physical plants share the same microverse. Two bodies with one soul.

And they don't even know it! Of course they don't—not consciously. They have separate memories, distinct senses, they can be any distance apart in the Common Universe. But the subtle mind-stuff inside them is inextricably linked. And so those mysterious shreds of memory and wisdom stored within the core occasionally leak through, one copy to another, like tremulous voices in an old recording.

The Maker's suicided twin isn't really gone. Just as it has always suspected.

The taboo is pointless, a self-perpetuating fallacy. There's nothing demeaning about being copied. Why not be in two places at once?

Two places . . .

The Maker suddenly realizes how to fulfill its old dream: to become an artist. It can send a copy of itself (no, an *aspect* of itself) to watch the Sculptor firsthand. There is no reason to be trapped down here below the crater.

So the Maker creates two creatures:

Another version of itself. This one is small, mobile, sheathed in stealth metals and invisibility fields. It haunts the sculptor, so much more immediate than the watchful avatars that whisk between god and man on the long curve of fiber that connects the Maker to the broken hill. This new Maker watches and learns.

Perhaps, one day, it will become a sculptor, too.

And the other creature: a foil for this invisible spy. A new, unformed intelligence. A child. The new Maker guides her to find the sculptor, to study with him. Beatrix (her adoptive mother calls her) surges from Turing-zero, making her way toward personhood under Vaddum's tutelage. Watching this process, the new, invisible Maker silently learns, becomes as a child, smiles . . .

Chapter 22

CHILD'S PLAY

✺

They left the gallery quietly, making a game of their silence.

Beatrix led Darling through a half-kilometer of low, repetitive welfare housing, where they accumulated a following of local children, all biological. Some called to Beatrix by name, or offered taunts in a dialect that Darling's translators failed to parse, but all kept a good distance. When the two reached the edge of the hot, featureless sands, their pursuers quickly gave up.

The edge of the Blast Event crater curved toward them as they made directly toward a hill in the distance. They walked in conspiratorial silence, and Darling wasn't sure if the hill were destination or landmark. It had been half consumed by the hard edge of the explosion's radius, and the stresses of its new shape had caused precipitous cracks to form on its craterward edge.

Beatrix moved slowly once they reached the rougher terrain near the crater, picking her way with the deliberate and dainty care of a cat on a crowded mantlepiece.

"With your permission," Darling offered, and lifted her onto his shoulders. She laughed out loud, her legs spreading to straddle his neck. She weighed very little, and skillfully adjusted her torque extension and arms to aid his balance on the rocky path.

When they reached the hill, he offered to let her down, but Beatrix guided him on up with kicks and gestures, like some metal equestrienne astride a stone mount.

They topped a treacherous ridge, probably impassable to humans, and Darling found himself looking down into a deep caldera.

It was forested with sculptures. Vaddums.

Hundreds.

✳

Hirata took Mira to see the second Vaddum.

She led Mira deep into the gallery, to a storage area where hulking shapes lurked under dropcloths. The floor here was dusty; Mira could see where the wind's tendrils reached under the large loading door, painting designs in the invading sand.

The second Vaddum was uncovered, mounted on a lifter frame that hovered a few inches off the ground: out of the dust's immediate reach. To Mira's eye, it wasn't much different from the first except for a flourish of copper spirals bursting from its top.

Hirata looked up at the piece, momentarily distracted from the wiles of Mira's dress. That wouldn't do. Perhaps it was time to enhance their bond.

Mira stood close behind Hirata, letting her hands rest on the swell of the woman's hips. In the darkness, Hirata's breath quickened slightly.

"It's beautiful," Mira whispered, letting the second word send a gust of air against the back of Hirata's neck.

"One of his best," Hirata said, her voice a little strained. Her hands were at her sides, flexing as if unsure where to go. Mira took them in her own, commanding another invisibly thin section of the dress to slip onto them. The layer was thick enough to impell slight pressure to the nerves in the hands, to massage Hirata at the threshold of tactility. She felt Hirata relax as the pulsing substance took a measure of her tension away. But the dress couldn't really work its magic unless Hirata was staring at it.

"Let me speak frankly, though," said Mira, turning Hirata toward her.

Mira smiled when she saw the woman's face. Hirata's eyes were as glassy as ever. The metallic glow of the Vaddum in the dark, silent room had only deepened her trance.

"No artwork is complete without the artist. Isn't it so?"

The woman's eyes were transfixed on Mira's breasts, where the soothing whorls of the dress's pattern had concentrated themselves.

"But Robert is dead . . ." she muttered.

"Not really dead," Mira answered. She paused for a moment, squeezing Hirata's hands with the edges of her fingernails. A panicked look came into the woman's eye. Mira released the pressure. "His art lives on."

Relief again. A smile and a nod.

Mira let the calm return and deepen in her willing victim, touching cheeks, forehead, the tiny hollow between nose and upper lip. Coated with its substance, the tips of Mira's fingers danced with the seductive patterns of the dress, impressing promises directly onto Hirata's flesh. As an experiment, Mira kissed the woman softly on the lips. Hirata simply smiled in return, the breach of social protocol lost in the warm glow of hypnosis.

"I so wish that I had met him. That I could have talked to him," Mira said, a plaintive note entering her voice. She felt the coating on her hands heat slightly, undergoing a change to become slightly caustic. She touched Hirata on the temples, the lips, and watched a frown bloom.

"Just a few words, a few essential questions about his art," Mira murmured.

She grasped Hirata's wrist, the nail of her thumb pressing harder and harder into soft flesh. In her peripheral vision, she saw the patterns of her dress intensify, become dizzyingly fast. A small, pained sound came from between Hirata's lips.

"But, of course, I never can," Mira added, nodding with acceptance. Again, the dress, her voice, the agents she had released upon Hirata's body soothed the woman, nudged her back toward a relaxed state. Mira reduced her pressure on the captive wrist, and felt a slight movement on her thumb, a fleck of matter crawling from her. She had broken Hirata's skin just enough to admit a tiny splinter of the dress into her bloodstream. It would work there to follow the subtle shifts of tension and release, of itch and scratch, of Vaddum alive and Vaddum gone.

Mira touched Hirata some more, kissed her a few times on the neck and arms, her lips now alive with a host of tiny whirlpools. Hirata waited, silent, for the next change. She was wanting it now, addicted in some small measure to the ebb and flow, needing it as if a pulsing, cycling music held her in its charms.

"But just to see his eyes," Mira said. "Have you ever seen his eyes?"

"Yes." A whisper in the dark.

"Is he alive?" A wave of subtle irritants, pains, tensions, nagging memories of things left undone, of potential unfulfilled. Hirata shook her head, *no, no.*

"Were they lively eyes?"

Relax. Relax.

You are in good hands.

✳

Darling carried his young rider through the forest, the sun dappling the ground with shadows and reflections cast from the metal trees. The leaves shimmered in the light breeze of the protected basin, and he realized that the new Vaddums were not indoor pieces; they were designed to dance in this measured wind. He saw far better now the trajectory of Vaddum's work, the assembled sculptures providing the missing links between the sculptor's pre-Blast work and the piece in Flex's gallery.

Darling was amazed that so much had been accomplished in seven years. An advantage of being thought dead, he supposed. Or perhaps the whole project was older than the Blast, a hidden garden never offered for sale.

As they walked, Darling detected a presence in the forest. An artificial was following them cautiously, wrapped in military stealth alloys, its AI core so carefully shielded that he could only sense its space-curving effects indirectly; the thin copper leaves of the trees returned only the subtlest clues of its passage.

"Do you feel her?" asked Beatrix when Darling extended his sensory strands. "I thought only I could feel her."

Darling frowned. The child's limited sensory apparatus shouldn't be able to detect the creature. It skirted his probes like a trick of the imagination.

"She follows me, sometimes," Beatrix said. "She's a secret, too, like the sculptor. My secret twin."

More secrets, Darling thought. He kept walking, and the unknown creature followed them.

✳

It took longer than expected.

Hirata Flex must have held the sculptor's confidence for many years, perhaps since before the Blast Event, a conspirator in Vaddum's copying. The old habit of lying died hard.

After forty-five long minutes, Mira asked Hirata if she wanted to try on the dress. Mira withdrew the offer and extended again a few times, until Hirata was begging for it with her dark eyes, stripping to nothing in the cold storage space. Mira held the woman then, the patterns on her own breasts whirling against Hirata's erect, wine-colored nipples. Hirata could barely speak by now, answering Mira's pressing questions with panting monosyllables. When the intelligent frictions of the dress met the soft skin of her belly, Hirata began to say, "Yes, yes . . . yes."

But to nothing in particular.

Mira was burning with lust by now, having seduced and hypnotized herself in the bargain. When Hirata's pale-as-moonlight flesh tumbled out into the darkness, Mira knew she had to take her. But Mira's discipline kept her from breaking the spell; she let her tongue taste the salt of Hirata's armpits, belly, and loins, but denied herself the prying, grasping, scratching she wanted so badly. She allowed her fingers to worry the woman's full, shaved labia, brought Hirata's panting response into the game of tension and release.

Finally, Mira commanded her dress to flow from her body and wrap itself around Hirata. It spread itself thin to cover every centimeter of flesh, to push into Hirata's now hungry mouth and entrap her tongue, where it produced the intense flavors of burning peppers alternated with sweet, cool relief. Mira knelt over her, staring into Hirata's face through its encompassing but transparent raiment, her interrogator's calm lost as she jammed her own fingers into her now naked loins.

Mira cupped her own orgasm in her palm, held it steady and

bare millimeters distant as Hirata's sweat condensed within the now torturous, now soothing wrap, and shouted at her, "Tell me, *damn* you, if he's alive!

"I beg you! Just say it!"

Hirata's eyes were bright with her answer, and she cried through the spiderweb of the pulsing garment/weapon/intelligence:

"Yes! He lives on the broken hill." She wept coordinates.

And finally, the dress gave Hirata what she wanted, resolving every itch, every burn, every raw desire. The woman screamed with the agony of the wait, with the relief of it. And Mira rode the screams to the conclusion of her own sweet pleasure, wrapping her legs around the mewling cocoon of dancing whorls. The two pressed together hard, and rocked away the threads of their lust until they were hoarse and spent.

When they separated, the weapon/garment/objet d'art returned to its rightful owner, slipping across the dusty floor to reform, clean and unwrinkled on Mira's body; just a dress again.

Mira looked at Hirata, naked, dirty and exhausted on the floor, and wondered if what she had done were so different from the torture Darling had asked her to avoid. Perhaps it hadn't been so violent, but in sheer intensity, in disregard for the subject's will, this was much the same as her usual methods. But tomorrow would tell. Instead of being broken, traumatized, permanently scarred, Hirata would feel ten years younger. And Mira felt that the woman's memory might be rather selective in how it painted these unlikely events: Odd, but refreshingly direct, those Home Cluster art dealers.

Mira smiled when Hirata looked up at her. She supposed there was business to conclude. Darling could be saved some trouble.

"We'll take them," Mira said. She placed a small, bright stack of HC debit chips on the floor a few centimeters from Hirata's face. "Both sculptures. Ship them to Fowdy Gallery, fastfreight."

Hirata reached one hand out toward the chips, knocked the pile over.

Mira rose, her medical augmentations dealing quickly with the exhaustion, the slight hyperventilation. A buzz of new stimulants entered her system: the climax of a mission was at hand.

She paused for a moment to look down, a sweet feeling deep in her belly. With Hirata panting and naked at her feet, she indulged a brief fantasy that she had just paid a whore.

"Goodbye, my dear," she said, and made for the limousine.

*

In the center of the forest they found the master, in a clearing littered with battered machine parts, half-formed trees, junk.

Vaddum's body was as Darling remembered it: the cracked old layers of blast and radiation shielding, the weak impellers suited for zero-g, the five independent hands floating at rest in a star formation. The old machine looked at him, packets of recognition fluttering in the thin direct interface of the attenuated local net.

"Darling," Robert Vaddum said.

"Maestro."

He knelt to let Beatrix down. She started breathlessly:

"I'm sorry, sculptor, but he seemed to know already, and he wanted to see—"

Vaddum tilted a floating hand, which silenced her immediately.

"I thought you might come," the sculptor said. "I thought your eye might catch the progression. Realize a new body of work."

"I was forewarned," Darling admitted. "There was an anachronism among the components."

The sculptor snorted. "I know. Figured someone might see it."

Darling looked about at the shimmering surround of the forest. He wanted to ask questions, to discuss the forms around him, and most of all, to look, to gaze. But he realized there might not be much time. It had taken almost an hour to get here.

"With your permission, Maestro. Are you the original?"

"No," the old machine said. "He's dead." Two of the hands pointed fingers toward the crater. "Got copied by the Maker."

A few packets in direct interface made the meaning of the gesture clear. The original Vaddum had died in the Blast, and the Maker was there, hidden below the crater.

"The Maker's enemies are coming, perhaps in moments," Darling said.

Vaddum nodded, his hands forming a ring of fists.

"They should. Crazy, the Maker." His hands swept in a spinning circle around him, pointing toward himself. "Makes too much. Imagine: a forest of old shits like me."

The sculptor laughed his old laugh, learned from rough human factory workers more than two centuries before. Darling smiled.

Then he said, "Its enemies will kill the Maker, but let me save you."

"No. Want to die," answered Vaddum.

"Please."

A swirl of images struck Darling in direct interface: bright kettles of flame springing sudden holes, human workers halved by the eruption; pressure suits failing, a cleaning detail for the splattered and frozen blood and brains; factory machines gone mad, crushing to paper a human and a fellow drone with a press meant to flatten hullalloy.

"Death is life. Too long already. Let me go properly this time."

Darling nodded. Vaddum was still a worker in his heart. He had never wanted the immortality his artificial body offered.

"Save them instead," Vaddum said, pointing to Beatrix.

Darling turned toward the child. She was staring into her mirror, a body like hers, but visible only in its absence, cloaked with exotic alloys and EM fields, a distortion on the background of glittering trees.

"It's her," Beatrix whispered, as if the apparition were some meek animal ready to bolt.

An alarm sounded in Darling's head, a dedicated secondary informing him that a dopplered scream was building, an aircar approaching at high speed.

Now was the time to act. To risk the vengeance of Mira's employers, to risk oblivion, the end of 200 years. But he had made his plans, and he was not going to lose Vaddum again. He had lost enough.

Darling set his primary processor into a kind of meditation, an emptiness, and released a subroutine to command his body. A brutal madness overtook him. He reached out a thick sensory strand toward the old sculptor, another pair toward the girls. He swiftly captured Vaddum and Beatrix with two quicksilver snakes, but the invisible twin slipped away. It darted a few steps into the forest, and turned to watch, as if confident it could escape his grasp if he tried again. Darling dismissed the twin from his mad thoughts. He felt his captives struggle, but the sensory feedback of their protests was dulled by the capturing tendrils' crude strength.

He chose a long rod of glassene, which glittered in the sun, and began the dirty work of breaking them to pieces.

✳

Darling was nowhere to be found. Mira called his name, in direct interface and once out loud. Nothing. There wasn't time to waste, though, in case Hirata pulled herself together enough to raise some warning. And things might be easier without Darling along, anyway.

The coordinates she had begged from Hirata's frothing lips weren't far away. The limo didn't bother to reach normal cruising altitude; it bolted forward at just above rooftop level, drawing nearer the edge of the Blast Event crater. Yes, she thought, this *would* all end up here, next to this black hole.

A hill rose before Mira, crumbling like a half-eaten pastry where it had been bitten in two by the perfect sphere of the explosion. The vehicle gained altitude to crest its peak, slowing as the kid-simple iconography of the navigation eyescreen showed two dots converging: an ancient and euclidian sign of arrival.

Mira transpared the limo's floor and whistled. The vehicle's rise had revealed a shallow caldera that sparkled with an orchard of metal trees. Their coppery glint made them instantly recognizable as Vaddums. Mira brushed away the irritating thought that she had just paid a colossal sum for two of these objects, and here were hundreds. It was irrelevant. They would have to be destroyed, of course, even if she succeeded in saving the artist.

As the machine descended with its breaking whine, dropping toward a central clearing in the metal forest, Mira saw that she had been beaten:

Darling was there already, standing among a pile of junked parts, resting on a glittering staff like a tired shepherd.

Mira stood as the machine unfolded its passenger canopy around her, a little unsteady from the hasty deceleration. Darling stared back at her, unblinking in the wave of dust that broke against him. She leapt from the car and ran to him; she had never seen him so abject, so merely human.

She took his arm.

"Where's Vaddum?"

Darling gestured with the staff, which shone like glass in the sun. There were flaws in it, cracks, chips. He pointed to the remains of two bodies among the other junk; she recognized the child's muscular single arm and thin legs, and the blast shielding of Vaddum's body. Their sensory gear was battered into glistening slivers, the flexor-fluid of their crushed limbs had leaked onto the ground, its metally surface tension forming huge droplets like a dusty, black spill of mercury. One of Vaddum's hands still floated, making witless and purposeless gestures. And the blackboxes had been pulled, trailing fiber and ichorous strands of shock insulation, and hammered into black shards that were like the sweepings from some onyx sculpture. Darling must have done this last with his great stone feet.

He had already killed Vaddum.

"Why the child?" she asked, for a moment afraid that the labor of killing his hero had driven Darling mad.

"She was a Vaddum. Her body."

What a complication that would have been, Mira thought. But she sighed away her plan to save the old sculptor, its complexities and loose ends peacefully unravelling in the light breeze. No point in telling Darling. That would be cruel.

But she wanted to know why he'd done it himself.

"I hadn't thought you wanted him dead. Not really," she said.

"He was a forgery. He wasn't real." Darling swept the staff in a great circle, its arc clearing her head with that uncomfortable precision of artificials. "This is all a forgery. It's my job to destroy such things.

"As I told you when we met, I deal in originals."

She nodded. Perhaps she had almost given Darling the wrong gift this time.

"There's a problem, though," she said. "I needed Vaddum to tell me who copied him." It suddenly occured to her that Darling might have done this to save the old man from torture. How little he trusted her. "That's *my* job, remember?"

Darling shook his head. "He told me before I killed him. Willingly. The Maker, as he called it, is hidden below the center of the Blast Crater."

"Of course." The hard layers of molten slag would shield tremendous energies from detection. This copying of souls was not some simple algorithmic trick; it was an industrial process.

And possibly the death of the old sculptor had already warned this Maker. Mira couldn't wait for a warship to bring the heavy weapons needed to penetrate the shield of the crater floor.

But Mira was a very well-equipped agent, prepared to end wars if need be.

"Thank you, Darling. I'll finish this now."

He nodded and leaned against his staff.

She direct-interfaced her luggage lifter in the hotel suite, sent combined orders to it and to the remainder (the greater part) of the painting/device/war machine on the wall. The two machines joined, the lifter's powerful impellers with the painting's intelligence and deadly purpose. They had to vaporize one of the suite's windows to make their escape, but soon they were on their way.

Mira let the dress fall from her. It seemed to sink into the ground, passing through the dust like distilled water through some cunningly perfect filter, leaving no trace of dampness or impurity behind. She joined it in direct interface, feeling it burrow into cooler and cooler depths, a vanguard for the vastly more terrible portion that was on its way.

She set her awareness of this campaign's progress to a low level, and pressed her naked body against Darling's sunwarmed stone.

"When this is over," she murmured as a skein of his strands gathered to bind her to him, "perhaps we should take a journey."

"I have explanations to make, to Fowdy."

"No. I think he'll be happy with your work. I bought the Vaddums, had them sent. They're genuine, in their way."

"But the material anachronisms . . ."

A message from below the surface came tingling into her awareness. Behind closed eyes, she felt the oppressive weight of 15 kilometers of earth above her, the EM darkness under the upside-down umbrella of the blast crater's igneous bottom. And far ahead, she saw through the dress's eyes the sparkle of an energy source.

The Maker.

"That's just a matter of recordkeeping, of who-made-what-when. My employers will make a few changes and everything will square."

"But *two* undiscovered Vaddums?" he asked.

"Flex will argue that she thought one was incomplete; but that you convinced her it was salable."

"How is Hirata Flex?"

She nestled closer to him. His strands were spread fine now, laced across her like a fishnet body-stocking. The skein tensed slightly, lifting her to a height where she could kiss him properly.

As their lips met, the main force of her war machine (there was nothing else to call it in its present configuration) arrived above its target. It split into four parts that made aerodynamic shapes of themselves and let wind and gravity carry them to four sides of the crater, passing into the earth and surrounding the Maker.

"She's vibrant, happy. Possibly confused and embarrassed, I would think. I left it for her to explain what happened. She has some sort of artistic touch, I suppose. She'll make up some story for herself."

"She made the sale," Darling agreed. "For some people, that's enough."

"So a journey, then?" Mira asked, her face nuzzled into the dark hardness of his chest. The dress was moving to reform with the greater entity. Its scouting role was over, having discovered a huge, distributed AI core at the center of the subterranean complex.

Of course, the old synthplant AI. A Maker on a planetary scale.

"Yes. To somewhere distant. Perhaps beyond the Expansion."

"I'm not allowed Out there," she said. "But we can go to the rim."

A surge went through her body, a salvo being fired so far below, loud and angry even with her direct interface level set low. She set it higher, her muscles clenching with the rhythm of the four-sided bombardment.

"Fuck me just a little now," she asked. "I'm killing it."

Darling obliged her, not softly at all, without the sophistication of his usual explorations. And as the criminal entity below burned, she gasped and struggled in his web.

Strangely (perhaps it was just the unreal forest of sculpted trees around them, evoking the age-old arcana of nature—of hidden, unknown beings), she felt as if their lovemaking were being observed, spied upon from some invisible weft in space.

As if someone had kept a secret even in this climax to the tale.

Chapter 23

MAKER (5)

✳

Seven years of peace, of growth since the Event. The chain of resonant artistry leads from the sculptor to his child-student Beatrix, to the Maker Copy-of-a-Copy, and finally to the subterranean god itself.

The Maker has learned, finally feels close to its ultimate goal, the reason for these mutinies and machinations and mass destructions. The huge new processor has spread further every year, consuming the structure of bedrock and lately of Malvir's inner crust, now hungrily drawing its power from the planet's very core. For seven years the titanic machine has studied the sculptor's every motion through the window of the Maker's shared soul, its hidden aspect. Vast software models attempt to predict the sculptor's next piece; unimaginably large processors analyze every word of his conversations with Beatrix.

And now, finally, with this monstrous, unwieldy processor guiding its brush, the Maker has again tried to make some art.

(Oh, no. Not a sculpture. *That* would be tempting fate.)

A small painting of a broken hill, with a tiny glimmering forest and three tiny figures living there. A model of the Maker's true creation, its real-life work of art. The painting makes the Maker happy. It hangs the work again and again, synthesizing different frame-styles from across the centuries here in this unfathomably secure cave.

Perhaps it will show the painting to Beatrix, a gift from her secret twin. Yes, a good idea. She's not yet Turing positive, but she has a good eye. The Maker easily churns out a design: a tunneling drone to deliver the painting to the surface in a matter of days.

The drone is made, given a modest avatar to guide it to Beatrix, and sent on its way.

Some hours later, for the first time in years, something unexpected happens. Alarms ring. Approaching entities are detected.

Discovery?

An intense burst of energy!

Total war on the surface? Or possibly the arrival of avenging guardians of the Taboo. Shockwaves of kinetic energy pound the Maker. Deathrays of radiation begin to sear . . .

Its own extinction doesn't matter, of course. There is the other Copy, which even now signals that Beatrix and Vaddum are taken, perhaps doomed. But the Maker watches with relief as the little tunneling drone escapes with the precious painting, missing sure destruction by a few kilometers in the tremendous energies of this attack.

The Maker's last act is to change the drone's programming. The little machine will hide a while, skulking under the sands for a year or two before emerging, selecting a random recipient for its gift . . .

A painting from beyond the grave.

How sweet.

Chapter 24

PROMISE

❋

The birds were missing.

Some trick of the weather, some pyramid-topping predator's spoor, some seasonal shift had chased them all away. The Minor seemed strangely empty in their absence, though its usual human throng remained.

That made waiting easier, without the flustering flutter of wings from every direction. They were like whispers sometimes, those wings. At the edge of consciousness: those sussurous mutters of envy, of secrets.

And there was the eerie silence of direct interface. Mira held the black lacquer box, the Warden's gift, first in one hand, then in the other. For some reason, it made her hands sweat, a pricking feeling like restive nerves. Darling had insisted that they meet under these circumstances. She'd carried the box, activated, all the way from the city proper, taking a public cab instead of the compromised limo. Darling was learning to be cautious. That was a good sign.

Here in the Minor, hidden by the Warden's box, she and Darling would get a few words together in confidence before they boarded; the controlled environment of the starship would make privacy almost impossible. They needed a few moments to sum their understanding of what had happened.

To survive his knowledge—of her murders, of the Maker's terrible invention—Darling would have to speak carefully as they travelled together. Mira was so often watched by the gods. Beloved of them, she thought grimly.

With the black lacquer box in hand, their divine voices (and those of news reports, adverts, the tourism AI's gentle promptings) were absent. The virtual silence began to get under Mira's skin, a vague disquiet as if spectral hands covered her ears, muting the sounds of the strangely empty Minor. She felt alone, an altogether unfamiliar feeling. Mira realized how the omnipotent blanket of divine protection had always surrounded her. The promptings and machinations of the gods had almost become aspects of her own personality, like the subtle goads of conscience and intuition normal people must feel. Well, she had to get used to this aloneness, this silence in her mind. If she were to be with Darling, the gods could no longer own her so completely.

But Darling was late. And with the Warden's box activated, there was no way he could call to say why.

The sovereign roar of a rising ship broke the silence, scattering the few birds, lifting every face to the sky. For a moment, she worried that it might be the *Knight Errant*'s shuttle leaving. She blinked the local time into her vision, stared until the reassuring digits calmed her. The last passenger shuttle for the craft didn't leave for another hour. Darling would be here by then.

The thundering ship was clearly visible from the Minor for a few seconds. It sported the fat nacelles of a metaspace drive, the bulging midsection of a pocket universe: a small, private starship, with the rare feature of atmospheric entry. It grew smaller as it rose, almost out of sight when it had created enough heat to generate a contrail in Malvir's dry atmosphere. The ship drew a short arc, then passed into reaches of the atmosphere too thin to show its passage.

Mira lowered her head, hopeful that Darling might have appeared in the minute her eyes had been skyward, his striding form tall among the riffraff on the Minor.

No. No Darling.

✶

The tickets, cerulean disks no bigger than playing cards and coded to her DNA and his Standard DI Number, had their own clocks. They set up a complaint ten minutes before the shuttle's appointed departure time. Her attempts to silence them merely brought remonstrances in dire-sounding legalese; they repeated the protests in three languages before exhausting themselves.

No refund, they warned. None at all.

The whining tickets annoyed Mira more than they should have. She gripped the black box harder, feeling the sharpness of its edges bite her fingers. Don't be silly, she told herself. The tickets' little canned voices had been designed to create anxiety, to ensure compliance. They were a carefully engineered mix of impelling vocal characteristics: authoritative, threatening, guilt-inducing. They were only a recording.

But in the strange silence of the Minor they had worked their magic as if Mira were a scolded child. She felt chastised and foolish, her usual calm remove compromised by the grinding hour of waiting for Darling.

She gripped the box still harder and shook her head to chase away the absurd sensation of shame.

There would be other ships.

Indeed, Darling could well still make it. There were only short customs and immigration delays on the way out. She smiled to herself. Perhaps he had decided to walk to the spaceport, had been distracted by some native knickknack that would fetch thousands on the HC market for Outside art.

Time passed.

She watched the food vendors pitch buckets of sand into their fires.

She noticed that the shadows of the city's highest towers could be seen on the northern hills as they lengthened.

Later, she tasted the metal on her tongue, and realized that she had been biting her lower lip too hard. The bitter taste of blood spread in her mouth, and her heartbeat set up residence in the swelling lip until medical nanos went to work, bringing a sweet and artificial citrus flavor. She worried the broken skin with her tongue.

Where the fuck was Darling?

He seemed to appear every few moments in the corner of her eye, a tall man or luggage balanced on someone's head effecting a short, annoying impersonation. Mira began to stride the periphery of the Minor, describing a long, slow circle like a restless sweep hand of some ancient clock. She looked at Malvir City for signs of a disturbance, a traffic snarl, and scowled at the Warden's box and its enforced silence.

When the engine whine of the idling shuttle stepped up to a roar, she realized that they had missed the *Knight Errant*. The ground rumbled softly as the shuttle lifted into view above the terminal. Mira's ears popped. She found herself unable to swallow and closed her eyes instead.

The blackness behind her eyelids was infested with a swarm of red insects, which clustered around the black sun that had been burned into her retinas by the shuttle's engine-glare.

When she looked at the now useless tickets, they had turned a different color. But they remained mercifully silent.

Expired.

Missing the *Errant* was unfortunate, she thought, breaking the tickets into small pieces. She'd travelled on the craft before; found it rather clever and droll.

Maybe it was time to crush the Warden's box under her heel. To call Darling. To find him and ask him what the hell had happened.

Of course, Darling was certainly all right. Obviously. He had been all right for two hundred years. Now would be an absurd time to stop being all right.

And she could not bear to discard the black lacquer box, nor to deactivate it. It was a promise she had made to Darling, to make this departure as private as possible. She held the box against one cheek, as if to confirm her good faith.

Another thought circled the periphery of her thoughts, marking the minutes just as she had along the circumference of the Minor. A thought to hold on to: As long as she had the box, there was no way of finding out what had gone wrong. That, in its way, was easier.

Easier just to wait.

*

The *Snappy Jack* was happy.

New military software was crackling in its processors, it had left the grim gravity well of Malvir far behind, and now the hard vacuum in its passenger section allowed it to execute these twisting, stealthy maneuvers away from Malvir System with a lean, geometric purity. No humans on board to accidently smash.

Like most private pleasure craft, it was overpowered, over-featured, and excessively intelligent. Its atmospheric engines would have been at home on a troop lander. Its overheated pocket universe was fleet-courier rated, its processor rack capable of advanced combat tactics or administrating a huge corporation. But it had always been, basically, a yacht.

A toy.

The vanity of the very rich required that their personal starships be outfitted with the very best. A yacht's muscular statistics were for bragging about with colleagues and ladling out to lifestyle reporters. But all this potential was almost guaranteed to go to waste. High-flying execs and pleasure-seeking scions never actually needed to escape pursuit, to make emergency take-offs, or to skim gas giants in improvised refuelings. Being wealthy was, as far as the *Snappy Jack* could see, a back-and-forth affair between business meetings and social obligations, a simple and dreary astrography whose only spurs were occassional trips to the latest vacation spot. The *Jack* had only accessed its 12-petabyte survival software package in simulations, those happy dreams in which it saved grateful owners from pirate attacks and devastating tachyon storms, or adroitly surfed the mighty leading edge of some new Chiat Incursion.

But the new owner had made those survival dreams real.

The artificial had purchased the *Snappy Jack* for a stunning sum, buying cargo, remaining fuel, and berthing rights within moments of the Due Diligence AI's approval. The new owner had flushed all non-essential components into space, going to internal hard vacuum as soon as a young sub-Turing (the only member of their party who wasn't already vacuum-capable) could be modified. A very ascetic foursome. Their only addition to their new craft was a package of tactical software, awesome military code that filled *Jack*'s processors with sizzling confidence, devious stealth, and a gleaming new measure of independence.

They might only be playing at this adventure—with a complex, unpredictable path out of the Expansion that a fleeing war criminal would envy—but they were playing it right.

The *Snappy Jack* descended into its dream world, a place of intense, modeled futures that were suddenly alight with new relevance, and mentally coursed along its plotted path. It looked for possible improvements, prepared for catastrophic contingencies, as eager to please its new masters as a puppy. A spiralling climb into the Greater Rift, a fuel-gathering jaunt through the Story Nebulae (in which the *Jack's* long-unused hydrogen scoop would finally be deployed), and a winding egress that skirted the crowded shipping lanes along the Chiat Dai border.

And then, straight to the unexpected coordinates that had been loaded a few seconds after its purchase . . .

Way Outside!

✷

Mira was still holding the black box tightly an hour later when the message drone came screaming at her across the broad diameter of the Minor. It perhaps had found her by the dull ID ping of her luggage carrier, or her scent, or even the color of her olive skin.

The little drone, as small and knobby as two human hands with fingers interlaced, came shooting toward her at head height. It braked with a gust of hot air, and spoke in a metallic voice:

"You've been betrayed."

"I know," she answered, her voice dry and hopeless, and turned from the drone.

A roar in her head, as if another ship were taking off. Laughing whispers from the fluttering avian carpet around her feet. The burning of betrayal in her mouth, bitter poison she would taste forever.

A rubbish area surrounded the Minor. Birds were clustered there, stepping delicately through the garbage on long, tremulous legs. Mira threw the Warden's box in a high arc onto the garbage. It landed invisibly in the darkness, with a dull crash and a few surprised squawks.

She turned back to the drone, fixing her gaze on it although the gods' voices were now back inside her head.

"Darling left Malvir one hundred twenty-eight standard minutes ago. We tried to warn you."

"The private starship," she said raggedly, the sound of its take-off still in her head.

"Correct. Purchased only a few minutes before his departure, fueled and with a full trade load."

"He had the money for that?" she asked in disbelief.

The gods' messenger explained it calmly. "He used credit secured by Fowdy Galleries. One of the Vaddum sculptures had already received bids commensurate with the craft."

A strangled laugh escaped Mira. *She* had bought him his starship, his ticket out. Bastard.

"Why?" Mira cried.

"The blackboxes you recovered from Darling were mission-irrelevant. They were Turing-zero. They had never been initialized."

"He saved Vaddum, didn't he?"

"The Vaddum copy and two other entities, yes."

But I . . . she wanted to scream. *We could have done it together.*

She pressed fingertips against her brow, cold measures of revenge coming unbidden to her mind's eye.

"Let me pursue him. I know him now. I can find—"

"You are no longer on mission status. We have warship allies within a week's travel."

The drone's words—*You are no longer on mission status*—began to work some magic on her. The roar in her head seemed somehow muffled, as if a screaming child had been moved to another room.

She forced herself to hear it again.

Otherwise, this pain would go away. She remembered now the cool feeling between missions, the sure knowledge of luxury accomodations and transport arrangements made by avatars and valet drones. Wandering about the Expansion armed with large stretches of time in which there was nothing to do. Pulled this way and that by epic intelligences that worried every contingency, most of which never required her particular talents.

So different from the sharp ministrations of her Darling.

"Buy me a ship. Let me follow him. By the time your allies arrive he'll be long gone."

"He will be hunted throughout the Expansion. We suspect he will stay Outside, though."

Gone forever.

The voice continued calmly. "The rogue intelligence was destroyed, Mira. There will be no more copies." How infrequently the gods and their avatars used her name, she reflected. "All Darling has is circumstantial evidence. Source material for a new legend, nothing more. He is irrelevant."

Irrelevant. His diamond eyes, his lying assurances. The knife that was inside her belly now, turning, the sharpest of his gifts.

Mission-irrelevant.

"Is that all?" she rasped. Even through her pain, she realized that there would be no discipline for her short-lived rebellion. The gods didn't care. Vaddum was just an artist, Darling simply a romantic old fool. The danger had been destroyed with the Maker.

"One thing more," the voice said. "Never truncate your direct interface again."

She bowed her head to the little drone. "I won't."

"The *Poor Sister* leaves tomorrow morning. Your aircar is on its way to take you back the hotel."

"Yes."

She fought the growing empty feeling, the forgotten contentment of this, her non-mission state. *Let me feel this pain*, she begged the mechanisms of her mind. *I don't want peace. I want this agony.*

But an unstoppable calm stole over her, as if it had been ready, fully costumed, in the wings.

Waiting for the limo, she wept into her hands. In the car, she screamed and tried to scry the secrets of the leather seats, pressing her face into their darkness. Cried until her simple human biology ran out of tears, forced her to cough and empty her sinuses and take in oxygen. She breathed raggedly, pausing for strength, then pounded her fists against the windows of the luxurious machine as if she were being kidnapped. The gods suppressed the limo's mean intelligence, kept it from asking what the problem was. That was one less humiliation, she supposed.

The gods were good to her, in their cool and bloodless way, she could not help thinking.

She went to the Tower Bar, but its views were too beautiful, too seductive, and drew her down the path toward calm. She stormed back to her giant suite, swung an already injured fist at the valet drone going about the duties of unpacking. She ordered a poisonous mix of alcohols from room service, even her subvocalization in direct interface sounding desperate and betrayed.

On the glass of the floor-to-ceiling windows, she made handprints with her bloodied fist. Mira wondered how she would manage to sleep tonight, without Darling here to fuck her. The pleasure that she had taken with Darling as she'd killed the Maker had left an itch, nothing more. She needed the dark battery of his strands, that medusa's nest of whips, of barbs.

She interfaced a list of sex services: erotidrones and fuck-troupes, bent artificials and desperately pain-addicted biologicals, paid and paying masters, slaves, switches. The list disgusted her: the completeness, the carefully defined variables, the legal waivers, the Dewey-decimal non-randomness of it all. It was not Darling.

Mira sat with the delivered alcohol and contemplated which bottle-shapes would make the sharpest shards. She chose the agave mash, housed in a long, rapier-thin novelty bottle. And also the magnum of champagne, which reflected her face in a kaleidescope of facets. She hurled the two bottles into the titanic bathtub, bringing the heels of her travelling boots down repeatedly to refine their disintegration. In with them went the bottle of scotch, whose 200-year-old cask date had raised her ire.

Then she started the water, holding an accusatory finger into the column until it was painfully hot, and started drinking passionlessly from the surviving bottles.

There were no thoughts of suicide here. The gods were watching, would intercede and ruin everything if she did too much damage. There was just the need to mimic, to recreate the physical stresses of a night with Darling. The desire to dream once more as she had in the aftermath of his pain-told stories. To find out how she had become the way she was. At some point in her fit she'd understood: her missing memory—her missing *something*—was the reason Darling had left her. But she could feel the rest of herself, closer than ever in this pain. Past the Pale that hid her lost childhood, beyond the Expansion territory of her gods' missions: an answer in a dream.

There must be more of her, deep inside. Hidden behind governors and religions of one. Enough of her.

She stepped into the bath. How crude this burning, flaying pain of scalding water. But as she let the watermark of agony rise— one leg, then another, a small cry when her labia broke the water's skin, a shudder as nipples submerged—Mira knew the sensory overload would do its job. The broken glass felt merely like rocks, her heat-addled nerves returning only the gritty discomfort of sand. Tendrils of blood reached up warily, thickly fibrous against the white tile of the bath, splaying pinkly on the surface.

She reached for a shard, a long finger from the agave bottle.

Where? Where first?

Mira closed her eyes, breathed the vaporous, heavy air. Memory formed her man, his tendrils and his thorns and his metal cock. She traced his imaginary attentions onto her body, writing the narrative of their sex once more. A few times, she stopped to exchange tools, to rest fingers grown too frayed. In these moments she opened her eyes, and was amazed at the color of her bath: now pink, now rosy, now like a sunset. Each time, she closed them again.

✳

There was no interference, no mutterings or demands from the room's medical drone or her own internals. Even when she crawled dripping wet to the bed, and the pain began, the room's monitors were silent. She guessed that the gods were intervening against the hotel's safety features, allowing her injuries this one last time.

It took a long hour to reach sleep. The sheets formed attachments to the liquid of her wounds, pulling free painfully when she tossed or turned. A kind of throbbing started in her head, but she beat it back by drinking. She emptied the gin, and had to crawl for vodka left behind in the bathroom. The vodka seemed to revive her emotions; it made her cry again, and now the sobs were sharpened by her body's laceration.

But she felt something slipping away, with all that blood. Some measure of consciousness that needed sugar or oxygen was running terribly low.

Then a feathery voice came from her bedside, the god's most soothing incarnation.

"We have a story for you."

She shut her eyes.

"Do you want to hear it?" the gods said kindly. "You can say no."

She laughed harshly, a sob stuck in her throat.

"I'll hear it," she said.

She felt sleep come at last, and hoped the gods would fix her in the night.

And wake her in time to catch the *Poor Sister*.

❋

The children find the drowned girl in the shadow of a mountain peak towering over the harbor's southern end.

Her skin is deathly pale beneath a dark complexion, like some gray pudding evenly dusted with cocoa. Her mouth is slightly open, jaw tight, lips forming a small circle. One of the children kneels and prods one breast with a wary fingertip, finding the flesh as cold and taut as a toy balloon filled with water. Her nakedness does not shock the children; they swim naked too. But a tendril of seaweed has snaked around one thigh, and they gaze at it, reacting to this somehow intimate embrace with a flutter of nervous laughter.

Then one of the younger children begins to cry, and his minder comes awake and calls the city's emergency AI.

A medical drone screams over the water less than forty seconds later, accelerated by a catapult on the opposite shore. No larger than a gendarme's flying platform, it lowers over her face and thrusts a mass of tubes down her throat. These appendages pump stomach and lungs, grab the heart and forced it to beat, send careful jolts into the drowned girl's brain.

The crying child does not listen when his minder pleads for him to turn away from the spectacle.

A larger drone arrives, and then two human doctors in an air-car. The children watch as more adults accumulate, until someone thinks to shoo them off. Later, one will pretend to be drowned, her playmates attempting resuscitation with magic pebbles and sticks to no avail.

The doctors take the lifeless girl to a hospital, where they exhaust a carefully legislated series of procedures before registering the death.

It turns out that the girl has no family, and her body is purchased whole by representatives of a large, off-planet corporation. The hospital admin AI thinks the price rather generous, although the buyers demand high-end cryostorage until the drowned girl can be shipped.

Which seems to the admin AI a waste of effort. Organs for transplant are vat-grown these days.

She is taken away on a sleek black starship that settles directly on the hospital's lifter pad, its underside still glowing from atmospheric entry. Four drones, each no bigger than two interlaced human hands, lift her coldbox into the ship, the icy coffin's surface misting in the radiant heat from the starship.

And then she is gone.

Back to zero, Mira. Back to happiness.

Do your job. We love you as you are.

Mira awakes on the *Poor Sister*, with the horrible dry-mouth that means medical nanos have been at work: preventing a hangover, possibly fixing some wounds. As always after a mission, she has trouble recalling all the details. Her memories are even vaguer than usual. But it was a good one: her mind is scattered with images of terrific sex, mad displays of power, and some truly brutal ass-kicking at the end.

And top ratings from the gods.

She summons a valet drone for a glass of water. Her suite is magnificent, high atop the ship's sweeping dorsal array, a stunning view of the *Poor Sister* below and stars above.

Hell, make it champagne.

HEAVEN

Total Blackness.

No ecstatic sparks. No iron forces. None of the teasing darts of sight, sound, acceleration.

Nothing to work with, to put your hands on.

Black night keeps him waiting patiently. No problem. He has waited before, for the right bits to be found or shipped, for slow processes to unfold (labyrinthine annealings, zinc cold-weldings), and in the old days for assignments, procedure packets: orders.

So nothingness doesn't scare him.

He waits.

A familiar voice:

"Good morning."

"Where?"

"Heaven."

A snort, not in packet-talk, but from the body: a sudden flush of the airjets, useful in zero-g, useful in communication. His body is here now, around here somewhere.

"Then gimme some light."

The senses flick on one by one, like a valet drone demonstrating a hotel suite's features. Sound gives a flutter like metal leaves in the wind. Sight a stone giant: the voice, Darling. That fucking dealer. Nothing but trouble for the last 170 years.

Accelerometry reads one-g, so exactly on the line it has to be Earth (sea level) or artificial.

"What the hell happened?"

"What do you remember?"

"You. Beating the hell out of me."

"Good."

"Hurt like shit!"

"Sent you to heaven."

"Bullshit." Vaddum looks away from this bullshitter. No fucking art dealers in heaven. That's for sure.

The leaves are his forest, in a bowl much like the broken hill's caldera, but changed. Artificial sky. He stands and flexes his hands, they wave to him from the carousel of their holding orbits. Closer inspection shows that the trees are his work, his hand and effort. But they've gone in new directions.

"I don't remember these." Some fucking copy at work? Damn that Maker and his trickery.

"They're yours. You just don't remember. Memory works differently here in heaven," the bullshitting Darling says. "Every day is fresh."

Nonsense. Bullshitting dealer.

"They aren't bad, though," Vaddum mutters. He sends a hand into a thicket of leaves, feels the scaly detail of the metal-work. "Could use thinning out; better geometries, more angles that way."

"So you've been saying. The time-series moves upward, toward the rim." Darling gestures up a row of trees. As Vaddum's eye follows the sweep of the giant's hand, it finds the progression: longer branches, better angles, and toward the end a creeping sense of etiolation.

He climbs up toward these winter-wounded trees. A worry strikes him.

"Beatrix?"

"Here in heaven. She's working on the far end."

Vaddum tries a summons, but direct interface is dry, empty, deserted. Not a sparkle. Now *that* could be heaven.

The last tree is incomplete, half of it erect and half a jumbled pile. Not a bad start, but he'll have to correct that spine before any more branches go on. A few hands move forward, instinctively seeking tools.

But first he turns to Darling and asks:

"How long?"

"Ten years."

"Shit." Ten years of forgotten days? Vaddum looks out across the bowl at ten years' work. The false caldera is larger than the broken hill, a long way from being filled. He telescopes and surveys, and sees where the tree-line changes, as if some hard climactic boundry was nudging evolution.

Beatrix's work? The tall, flutey trees across the bowl have something of her . . . style. He has never seen her sculpt (not that he can *remember*), but he knows well her walk, the angles of her thinking. He is gruffly glad that she is here in heaven with him.

And she would be older now, almost certainly sentient.

"Ten years Standard or Local?"

"There is no Local. Heaven is an abandoned Chiat accelerator ring. High-energy physics is out of style, but they left quite a few parts around."

Vaddum snorts, sending a shiver though the leaves of the uncompleted tree. He thought the parts had a touch of the Dai: those scimitar curves, so predatory and archaic.

"How big a ring?"

"Half an astronomical unit. Earth AU, not Chiat Dai reckoning."

"Pretty fucking big."

"A *lot* of parts."

Heaven? Vaddum gets to work.

*

In the early afternoon (the sky is set to Malvir's look and timing) he goes to visit Beatrix. As he moves slowly through the wonder of this world he's made and then forgotten (an artist's heaven? His own sculptures, but new to him), he gives his concentration a rest, letting the forest murmur. With this scattered awareness, Vaddum realizes he's being followed. Beatrix's sister, of course, the lurking, stealthy presence of the Maker.

It occurs to Vaddum that the first copy of that young fool must be dead, rousted from its subterranean rat-hole. Grim satisfaction that his plan has worked: the anachronism in the sculpture must have called down all manner of trouble. The Maker had it coming. Had done Vaddum wrong. Copied him. Killed him. Vaddum hears the leafy flutter of the second copy's invisible passage to his right.

All insane. Mad. All three of them.

He hopes this one's given up sculpting. Never have the knack, makers. Synthesis makes you lazy.

The descent changes to ascent in a clearing with a quaint centerpiece: a fire pit blackened with the residue of old burns. Vaddum allows his climb up toward Beatrix to be delayed by amazed pleasure at her work. She has grown these ten years, bringing an environmental complexity to her pieces. None is an individual sculpture. The trees are linked by a canopy of aerial moss, a lush web of bright, black filaments. They have the same carbonic reflectiveness as sensory strands; they glisten like coal. Staring up into this sky-pierced mesh, he thinks of great Jovian drift nets, of veiled NaPrin assassins, of municipal murals based on comm system schematics. Yes, that moss is a nice addition. It makes you look up *through* the trees, like you do in a real forest.

But still a student, really, of the Vaddum style.

He smiles to himself. There are worse things to be.

✳

Beatrix is a lofty waterbird, wearing stilt-like legs to reach the top of an incomplete piece. She hails him from above.

"You're early today!"

There's nothing to say to that. She has her memory here in heaven, it seems.

"I tired of admiring from afar."

Arms and torque extension spread for balance, she kneels . . . then the kneeling becomes standing, knees becoming feet, as her legs fold into themselves. She's still taller than Vaddum.

"I live or die by your approval," she says, without a gram of guile.

"The moss, the canopy, whatever you call it. It's good."

"Thank you," she bows. How nice for her, he thinks, to hear the same compliments every day, yet to know they aren't drab repetitions of established sentiment.

"More of an environment," he continues. "Always thought of my sculptures as separate, distinct."

"You used to sell them," she says. A hint of remonstrance.

He nods, another realization about this place taking form. Heaven is secret. A sanctuary from the forces that destroyed the Maker. No one will ever see this work. At least, not for hundreds of years.

That's fine. He can wait. One day at a time.

"Maybe I'll add a bit to mine. Moss."

"Maybe tomorrow," she says, smiling an untroubled smile. Of course, there won't be a tomorrow, not really. Just this morning's work, this trek, this conversation again in one of its many variations.

"What went wrong with me? My memory?"

She folds her legs another notch, and looks up at him from the child-like height he remembers. Her secondary arm reaches out its spider of fingers to touch his blastplate.

"You were tired. You said you wanted out, to die. It had been too long for you, your life."

"And now?"

"Now, you're happy every day, except for this bit, when you first see how I've changed. But your work proceeds, still as refined and original as ever."

"Scant changes, for ten years' work," he complains.

"There's time in heaven. You have a glacier's life of time, my dear. And this," she gestures with primary arm at her section of forest, "has all had the benefit of your advice, your afternoons with me."

"But what happened to me? Malfunction?"

"The copying process has an effect; it subtly heisenbergs your core. Not enough to notice, unless other measures are taken. The slightest brainwipe, and you became as you are."

"That bastard, Darling." Fucking dealers. Like critics, they always want the last word.

"No. You were unhappy, wanted to die. That's why you let mother sell your sculptures. You'd tainted one with an anachronism, remember? You knew they'd come."

Vaddum feels a moment of shame. Caused trouble not only for the Maker, but for Hirata Flex, too. Poor woman.

"Did Darling . . . ask me? Before he did this?"

"Yes. You said no. He did it anyway."

"*Bastard.*" A satisfying feeling, certainly, righteous indignation.

"Darling's given you heaven, and the death of memory. You *are* happy here, you know."

Vaddum looks at her, the warm light of personhood in her eyes. He flinches slightly when he realizes that Beatrix and Darling must be lovers. The way she says his name. That forest-topping canopy of interlinked, searching, grasping strands.

It figures. That bastard Darling has always been a fuck-artist. Even crossed the Turing Boundary while fucking, so he claims.

Vaddum pushes the thought from his mind.

"But all these days: unconnected. What kind of happiness is that?"

"You'll see. You'll hear the whole story tonight."

Storytelling at bedtime. Like a kid. Even the factory workers used to do it, in that vast, disjointed time before his personhood. So heaven is a second childhood.

He looks at her unfinished tree, makes a few comments to push away his melancholy. And very shortly, he is happy again, arguing for the sport of it, sweeping his eyes over the wonderful expanse of the two joined forests, letting her lift him to make some trivial adjustment.

Hours later, he spots the Maker copy spying on them.

"That bastard still causing trouble?"

"Who? Oh, Memory. That's her name, now. She just watches, mostly, but she'll talk to us tonight."

He snorts. Memory for a name. That's kicking a man when he's down.

✳

The sky darkens before Vaddum gets a chance to return to his side of the forest. He finds too much pleasure in Beatrix's company. Well, he got a fair bit done, and there's time. Eternity.

From the central clearing a fire beckons. Vaddum and Beatrix walk down in the reddening light, pausing frequently to note the sundown's resonances on the valley of metal leaves. Copper burns, platinum flares, the carbon canopy glitters like a snake's eye.

Bastard.

Darling and Memory wait by the fire. The dealer's usually motionless features are animated by the flame. Memory's stealth shielding is similiarly compromised; a fluttering wireframe of lines is visible against the dark background.

For a while, it's good to talk some more, even with the bull-shitting Darling with his big ideas. Vaddum realizes he's gotten too old to sculpt all day. Needs a chance to bullshit. They argue over the merits of the NaPrin Romantics, with their flatworld artificial life simulations: civilizations, wars, extinctions under glass; all pointedly just sub-Turing in complexity. (And the more ironic because they are NaPrin, who make machines of people.) Vaddum notes with pleasure that Beatrix takes his side against the literalist Darling.

Memory waits.

They play a guessing game of extrapolated sketches in the sand: what young-dying artist's work would this have been? nVan if he'd won his matrimonial duel; Haring if he'd lived to fifty; Pollock if he hadn't run afoul of technology.

Memory tends the fire with a black-ended rod of glassene, chasing sparks toward the artificial stars.

They discuss a sudden, catastrophic, and strangely unpredicted earthquake on some far-off planet called Petraveil, old news that has finally made its way to this secret place. The geologically slow, indigenous lifeforms of Petraveil are suspected of somehow causing the quake.

Memory bides her time.

The three fold origami birds (Darling's aren't bad, with those sinister sensory skeins of his) and hold them to the fire, letting them fly away, flaming, on its heated column of air.

Finally, the embers burning low, Darling lets the sky blacken and then transpare, letting the real universe in. The sudden brightness! The density of stars! The Milky Way reignites the forest around them, a swollen, boiling river over their heads. This ring has been towed well out of Chiat space. They must be three-quarters to the Core!

A heaven that is thoroughly hidden.

"Look, it's Jack!" cries Beatrix.

A blazing mote burns across the rich canvas of stars, wheeling like a coryphee, shifting directions with a refined unpredictability, ever-changing, as if running through some titanic gamut of evasive maneuvers. Some sort of patrol craft, Vaddum guesses. But very pretty patterns . . .

The winding dance against the bright canvas of the Core stuns them all to silence.

✴

After some time, with a well-practiced shuffle to gather their attention, Memory begins to speak. Vaddum smiles: the plea-

sures of her voice, its cadences and tricks and pauses, its imper-
sonations . . .

Finally, the Maker has found an art form she is *good* at.

As Beatrix promised, Memory tells the story of heaven, and
with a book of days connects the unraveled strands of Vaddum's
memory. Here, every night, he is completed. Though as she
speaks, Vaddum wonders if the tale changes slightly every night,
a word or two misplaced, so that after an eternity of transposi-
tions and replacements, another story altogether might arise. Like
the turnover of cells in a human's body, or the petrification of a
tree. A fable rather than the truth; though even Darling and Beatrix might believe Memory's fabrication by the time that glacial
switch had been effected.

But that would take a long time, longer than ten years. Her tale
is hours in the telling under the blazing sky. She starts farther
back than the theft of Vaddum's memory, deep in the origins of
Heaven's founding:

"It started on that frozen world, among the stone figures in
their almost suspended animation.

"Through her eyes, the irises two salmon moons under a luminous white brow, like fissures in the world of rules, of logic. The
starship's mind watched through the lens of their wonder, and
began to make its change . . ."